Alexandra Brown

The Great
Village
Show

HARPER

Harper
An imprint of HarperCollins*Publishers* Ltd
The News Building
1 London Bridge Street
London SE1 9GF

www.harpercollins.co.uk

A Paperback Original 2015
1

Set in Birka by Palimpsest Book Production Limited, Falkirk, Stirlingshire
Printed and bound in Great Britain by Clays Ltd, St Ives plc

MIX
Paper from
responsible sources
FSC
www.fsc.org **FSC C007454**

ACKNOWLEDGEMENTS

Dear Reader

This is the second book in my new Tindledale series and I really hope it puts a smile on your face and warmth in your heart. My first thanks goes, as always, to all of you, my darling friends and readers, who chat to me on Facebook and Twitter, or who send me messages and emails: you're all so inspiring and your kindness and cheerleading spur me on through it all. Writing books can get lonely sometimes, but having you all is like a family, and this means the world to me. Thank you so very much xxx

Special thanks and gratitude to my agent, Tim Bates, for always having my back and telling me what's normal. Many thanks and appreciation, as always, to my wonderful editor and friend, Kate Bradley, for being so kind and funny and for getting me through the tricky times. Of course, none of the other stuff would happen without my dream team at HarperCollins, especially Kimberley Young, Katie Moss, Jaime Frost, Martha Ashby, Claire Palmer and Charlotte Brabbin, with their wonderful enthusiasm, energy and expertise. Penny Isaac for her copy editing skills.

Thanks to Lisa Cutts for the police stuff and to Samantha Bowles for talking to me about bee keeping and for giving me a jar of her delicious Burwash Honey.

Thanks always to my dear friends Caroline Smailes and Lisa Hilton, your kindness and continued support is what also keeps me going ☺ xxx

My darling QT, and husband Paul, aka Cheeks, for taking yourselves off for coffee and cake so that I could write – I couldn't do any of this without you both, thank you and lots of love xoxoxoxo

Now, sit back, slip off your shoes, slap on the suncream and pour yourself a large glass of Pimm's. Luck and love to you, and wishing you all a wonderful summer,

Alex xxx

For Mavis Holdsworth Mercer
26 November 1928 – 15 January 2015
My Doncaster nanny, a lady who was always very
kind to me xxx

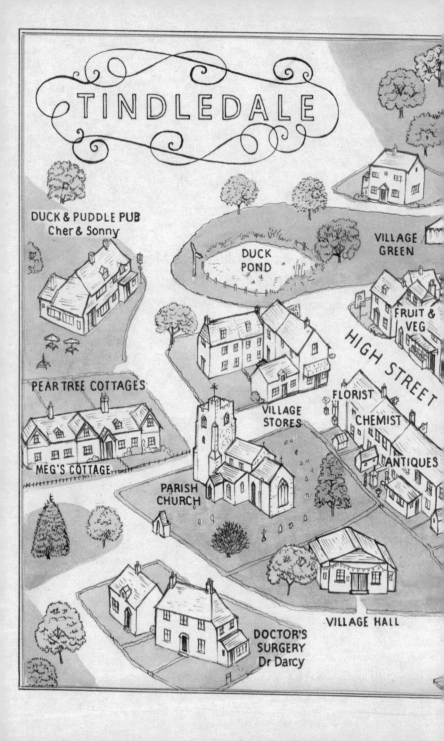

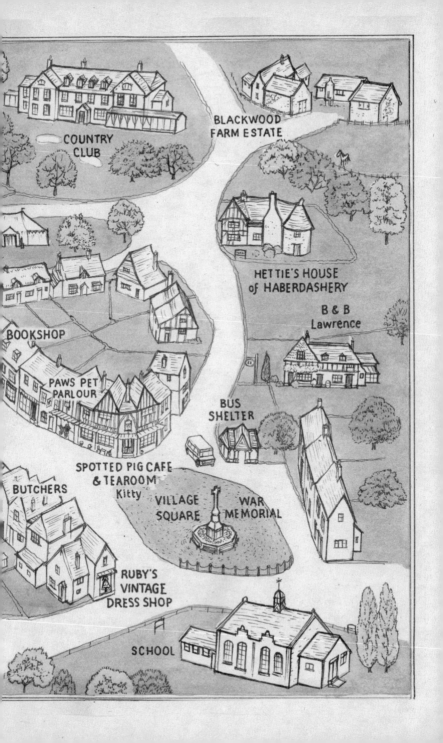

'Love is to the heart what the summer is to the farmer's year – it brings to harvest all the loveliest flowers of the soul.'

–Anonymous

Prologue

Jessie Cavendish hadn't been sure about uprooting from their elegant Chelsea mews house and relocating to the quaint, but quite muddy, little village of Tindledale. Having grown up in a rural, close-knit, welly-wearing community, she knew first hand how incestuous they could be and how isolated they could make one feel. Yet, as she hiked on up to the highest point overlooking the valley, landmarked by the biggest oak tree she had ever seen, pausing to catch her breath as she slipped off her cardy and tied it neatly around her waist, she realised that the more she saw of this idyllic part of the world, the more she rather liked it.

Tindledale was surrounded by lush, undulating green hills dotted with lambs and an abundance of pretty wild flowers, pink apple orchards and strawberry fields. At its heart lay an adorably cobbled High Street, flanked either side with black timber-framed, white-wattle-walled shops with mullioned windows – it really was a special place. And Jessie wasn't the naïve person she had been back then, when Sebastian had enticed her away to the bright lights of London, to the city where all the women lived fabulously glamorous lives in their pretty ballerina pumps, or so she had thought. But Jessie had grown to realise over the years that it was often far easier to 'get onboard', as Sebastian was fond of saying, whenever one of his big, life-changing plans was mooted. Plus, the children would be so much happier in the village school, with its postage-stamp-sized playground and quaint clock tower on the roof – no more navigating the super-shiny 4x4 (Sebastian had insisted she drive the triplets in the oversized, but extra-safe tank, but she hated it, much preferring her clapped-out, old and *very small* Mini) through the narrow, congested streets of London on the nursery school run.

Moving here would mean just a short trundle through the village where the triplets' new friends were bound to live, and perhaps Jessie would meet and make some friends of her own too! Yes, far nicer than having the children cloistered away inside some archaic boarding school, as Sebastian had been planning for far too soon after their sixth birthdays, having registered the children's names before they were even born – so at least she had managed to hold out for something in return, *this time*, for distancing herself from her old life, her family, her friends, her support network . . . But then Jessie was under no illusion that this was precisely *why* Sebastian was so keen for them to move 'down from London' to the countryside. She'd make the best of it, as she always had, and maybe living in Tindledale would help them relax, Sebastian especially. That would be bound to have an enormously positive impact on them all.

Jessie closed her eyes and tilted her face up towards the rejuvenating rays of the early summer sun, letting the warm breeze cool her flushed cheeks as she wrapped her arms around herself and then ran a hand over her perfectly taut abdomen. She allowed herself a moment of contemplation, before her mind drifted back to more trivial thoughts – would she manage to find a yoga class to replace the one she loved in London? Tindledale village hall, perhaps! The estate agent had mentioned the thriving community and all that it had to offer: Brownies, Scouts, an amateur dramatics group; even a knitting club in the local haberdashery shop – and she had been meaning to learn to knit for ages now. And something about a summer show being a big part of village life – Jessie made a mental note to find out exactly what this entailed, as it certainly sounded more exciting than the flower-arranging sessions with the Women's Institute that Sebastian had said would suit her. And then something else occurred to Jessie, something that made her heart sing, something that she hadn't thought about for such a long time. Bees!

Jessie had loved keeping bees as a child. And chickens. Her dad had taught her how. And, for a while, she had even written about country life for a variety of farming magazines, before her own life had somehow turned into looking after the children and the home instead, so Sebastian could concentrate on his career. Well, maybe this was a chance to change things around and rekindle her passion for bees and chickens . . . goats and gardening too! The possibilities were endless. So Jessie made her decision. She would do what Sebastian wanted – what she wanted too, she was sure of it now – and move here, to the village of Tindledale.

So with her mind made up, and a sudden urgency to hike back to the car and drive straight to the estate agent's office to sign all the paperwork for the new house, Jessie took a deep breath and allowed herself one last thought of 'what if?' before shaking her head and exhaling hard, knowing there really was no other solution. This was how it had to be. And besides, a fresh start away from London and the distraction there was probably for the best . . .

One

As if on autopilot, I flick on the kettle and select two mugs – one with *Best Mum Ever* on for me, the other with a swirly letter J for Jack. I spoon coffee granules into each of them and then I remember. Jack isn't here any more! I let out a long breath, before twirling my wavy fair hair up into a messy bun, securing it with a red bobble band from a wonky clay dish Jack made for me in nursery all those years ago – it's been proudly displayed on the windowsill ever since – before storing his cup back in the kitchen cabinet. Jack has only been gone a week, but I have to say that it's felt like the longest seven days of my life. Although not quite as bad as when he first went away, back in September – that was really difficult. For a while, it was as if a chunk of my heart was actually missing, which might sound completely melodramatic, but it's true; it was like a physical pain, a knot of emptiness wedged just below my breastbone that I just couldn't seem to shift. You see, Jack and I kind of grew up together – I wasn't much older than Jack is now, when he was born. I know it's only university and he'll be back again in a few months for the summer holidays, but still . . . I guess it's taking me some time to adjust to my now empty nest.

But I am so proud of him, I really am, and that should make this transitional phase of my life a whole lot easier to cope with. It's just that I'm so used to keeping it all together for Jack and me – now it's only for me, it feels very strange indeed. I inhale sharply and drop a sugar lump into my cup, before giving it a good stir, taking care not to clatter the spoon excessively against the side of the mug – Jack hates the sound of it, especially after a late night of gaming with his mates up in his attic bedroom, and even though he isn't here I find it comforting to remember our familiar family quirks and oddities. I smile fondly at the memory of me bellowing up the stairs for him to turn the volume down or at least put on the expensive Bose head-phones that he saved up so long for – working weekends collecting glasses and helping out in the Duck & Puddle pub in the village.

Dunking a digestive biscuit into my coffee, I allow

myself a small moment of satisfaction on thinking how well Jack has turned out; even pride, perhaps, as I remember how tough it was too at times – everyone knows that being a single parent is certainly no sauntering stroll in the park. There were many occasions where another adult, someone else to rant to when Jack had ripped his new school trousers after only a day's wear, would have been very welcome indeed. And someone to share the highs with, like when he was Joseph in the school nativity play and delivered his lines so promptly and perfectly as I watched on with happy tears in my eyes. And then more tears when his place at Leeds University was confirmed, studying architectural engineering, which is no surprise, as Jack has always loved building things. I blame Lego! But no, everything isn't AWESOME! Well, I guess it is for Jack – a whole new life, an exciting adventure; but why does he have to do it so far away from home? Our lovely little village. Tindledale, the place where he was born, right here in our cosy, tile-hung, two-bedroom cottage, to be exact, on the Laura Ashley rug in front of the log burner in the lounge.

I had called an ambulance, but by the time it had hacked along all the country lanes from Market Briar, the nearest big town, Jack's scrunched-up bloody face was peering up at me, and my dear friend, Lawrence, who runs the local B&B and is a retired thespian (strolling home on that balmy summer night after a Tindledale Players rehearsal) heard my sweary screams through the open window (and I really am not a swearer, but the pain was excruciating, to be fair) and dashed in the back door to placate my mother, who was hollering out of the hands-free home phone, perched up on the mantelpiece, for me to 'Pant hard, Megan. PANT HARD!' And adding, 'I knew I should have booked an earlier flight', in between chain-smoking her way through a packet of Lucky Strike, followed by lots of sympathy sighs and intermittent ear-splitting shrieks from her duplex apartment in Tenerife. And Mum has never forgiven me for making her miss the birth of her only grandchild, allegedly . . . although I have no recollection of actually telling her the wrong due date, but for years she was adamant that I had. 'Why else would I have written it on my wall calendar, a total of nineteen days after the actual event?' she had said in an extra-exasperated voice.

Anyway, having Jack is the best thing that has ever happened to me, and I adore children, which is very handy given that I'm a teacher – acting head teacher, to be precise – at the Tindledale village school, the same school that I went to, and Jack also. And Mum and I can laugh about it all now, even if it is long distance. Jack and I have had some glorious holidays over the years, staying with her, just a few kilometres from a lovely, secluded sandy beach, and of course she comes to see us whenever she can, but it's not the same as having family here all the time. Thank God for friends! Talking of which, Sybs, short for Sybil, cycles past the window before popping her head through the open half of the stable door.

'Hi Meg, not intruding am I?' She grins, carefully leaning her bicycle next to mine against the honeysuckle-clad fence. Sybs used to be a housing officer in London before giving it all up and settling in Tindledale last year.

'Of course not, come on in and have a coffee with me,' I say, thrilled to see her. I go to scoop up Blue so he doesn't escape when I open the bottom half of the stable door – he's my super-soft, caramel-coloured, palomino house rabbit, who used to live outside in a hutch until Jack found his poor female friend, Belle, dead one morning, having been savaged by a fox in the night. So Blue lives inside now to keep him safe, and can usually be found basking in the heat from the log burner in winter, or, like today, when it's so warm and sunny, he likes sprawling prone across the cool, quarry-tiled kitchen floor. I plop him back down, and after a quick twitch of his tail, he scampers off to his bowl to munch on some carrot sticks that I sliced up earlier for him.

'Ahh, better not,' Sybs says. 'I don't want to ruin your lovely home. Another time, perhaps, I'm just on my way up to the High Street to see if Taylor can squeeze this filthy mutt in for a much-needed appointment at the pet parlour.' She glances at the basket on the front of the bike where Basil, her black Scottie dog, is sitting inside, caked in mud, before shaking her head. Her red curls bounce around abundantly.

'Oops, what happened to him?' I ask, laughing when Basil lets out a disgruntled growl and then hunkers down as if in disgrace. 'And what is that horrendous pong?' I quickly place my hand over my nose before leaning in closer to the honeysuckle, hoping to catch a whiff of its glorious scent to take away Basil's noxious one.

'Err, this little rascal decided to leg it across Pete's newly ploughed field after spotting a brace of pheasants on the horizon, and then found a pile of fresh fox poo in the hedgerow and thought it would be a brilliant idea to roll around in it. And he's ruined my new

Converse – I bought them especially to wear in this warm dry weather – but then I had to chase after him.' She waggles her left foot up in the air to show me the once lovely lilac trainers with polka-dot ribbons that are now a mottled mud colour. 'His recall skills certainly need working on!'

'Hmm, no wonder he's skulking.'

'Indeed. And so he should. Next time I won't bother going after him; he can fend for himself in the Tindledale woods for all I care. I'd like to see how he'd cope having to forage around for wild mushrooms, berries and the odd dead mouse to live on.' Sybs lets out a long huff of air, pretending to be cross, but all of us villagers know just how much she adores Basil, even if he is the cheekiest dog in Tindledale, and probably all of the surrounding villages too.

'Awww, but he still looks so cute,' I say, giving Basil a tickle under the chin, deftly avoiding the tarry mess on the side of his neck.

'Oh, don't be fooled by those "butter-wouldn't-melt" eyes; he's a little devil dog sometimes, and so greedy too – you know, he snaffled a whole pizza from the kitchen counter last week. I turned my back for a moment and it was gone. Still frozen. I had only just taken it out of the freezer.'

'Wow! That's impressive, but tell me – how did he reach a paw up to the kitchen counter to swipe the pizza?' I ask, intrigued.

'Oh, you won't believe the stunts he can perform,' Sybs says, exasperated. 'He only hopped up on the footstool that I use to reach into the back of my cupboards – Ben spotted him performing the same trick only the day before.' Sybs shakes her head again. 'The footstool has since been removed, I hasten to add.'

I smile. 'I bet he regretted it soon after. I imagine his stomach was arctic.' Basil does another feeble groan by way of agreement.

'Yes, and he slept for hours afterwards, comatose from the cheese and carb overload, no doubt.'

'So, talking of injuries and ailments, how is Dr Ben, that gorgeous boyfriend of yours?'

'Ahh, Ben is as lovely as ever. And as busy as ever! It's funny, though – since we started living together, we seem to see less of each other than ever before,' she sighs. 'There's no time off for a village GP – you know how it is. He can't even go into the Duck & Puddle for a pint after surgery hours without being fawned over by his patients, all wanting to buy him a thank-you drink for sorting out their illness, or ask his advice on a whole range of medical issues.' Sybs laughs and shrugs. 'But I wouldn't have it any other way,' she beams.

'Well, it's lovely seeing you so happy.'

'Thanks Meg. And I truly am very happy – it's wonderful how things work out in life sometimes,' she says in a dreamy, faraway voice.

'Sure is. And you know what, it's always been that way, with the village GP being mobbed whenever he sets foot outside the surgery,' I grin, resting my elbows on the top of the stable door. 'As a child, I remember Dr Ben's uncle, Dr Donnelly, getting the exact same treatment from the villagers, pardon the pun.' We both laugh.

'Sooo, how's Hettie getting on after her fall last week?' I ask, pulling off my cardy and pushing up the sleeves of my navy striped Breton top – the sun is really warm today. Not that I'm complaining, I love this weather, but jeans with long wellies and too many layers really isn't suitable, but then there was a definite nip in the air this morning when I took my tea and toasted crumpets down to the end of the garden, to sit on the old tree stump beside the magnolia bush and draw in the breathtaking, lemony-vanilla-scented view across the stream that runs down the side of my cottage.

'You heard about it then?' Sybs sighs. Hettie used to run the House of Haberdashery down the lane on the outskirts of the village, before it became too much for her, so Sybil manages it now, while Hettie takes a back seat in her oast house next door. But Hettie is eighty-something, so I reckon she's earned a bit of a rest.

'Of course,' I wink, and then quickly add, 'you know how it is around *these here parts*,' in a silly voice, exaggerating my country burr. Sybs giggles.

'Hmm, I certainly do! News sure does travel fast, and everyone knows your business . . . before you even do yourself, sometimes.'

'Yep. Good or bad, that's the Tindledale way I'm afraid.' I shake my head.

'And I rather like it,' she nods firmly.

'You do?' I lift my eyebrows in surprise. 'It used to drive me nuts when I was growing up, as a teenager especially; it was really stifling at times. And even now, I sometimes hear stuff about my pupils' parents that I really wished I hadn't.' I pull a face, thinking about the time when I overheard Amelia Fisher's mother in the playground, gossiping to her mate about the new family, the Cavendishes, who bought the big farmhouse over on the outskirts of the Blackwood Farm Estate – how Mr Cavendish is a 'right dish' and sooooo charming, but how much of a shame it is that he's hardly ever around – maybe that's why his wife seems so sad, because they sure as hell wouldn't be if they were married to him. Good looks, lots of money – clearly every woman's dream, apparently! And Mrs Cavendish has little to complain about when she clearly has it all – perfect, tall, slim body; shiny hair with expensive highlights, and a recently refurbished home 'like something out of *Hello!* magazine it is, with its acre of land', and 'what does she do all day?' It had taken all my willpower to walk away and not to threaten to put them in detention or something, as I imagine Mrs Cavendish is probably a bit lonely in that big house all on her own while her husband works away – I do wonder sometimes if detention wouldn't be more effective for the parents instead of the children in my school.

'But better that than nobody caring, or looking out for each other,' Sybs says.

'That's true,' I agree, thinking of my next-door neighbours, Gabe and Vicky, in the middle, and then Pam, Dr Ben's receptionist, on the other end of our little row of three Pear Tree Cottages. They are more like friends than just people I live next to, as are so many of the people in the village.

'And if Hettie had lived alone in a bigger community, she could well have gone unnoticed for days after her fall.'

'I imagine so,' I nod. 'So what happened then? Is Hettie OK?'

'Yes, she's fine. It turns out the fall wasn't anywhere near as bad as we all feared, but Ben did have to give her a telling off . . .' Sybs' forehead creases.

'Oh?' I frown too.

'You know how fiercely independent Hettie is,' Sybs continues, and I nod in agreement, remembering all the times I've tried to help her and she's politely refused. 'Yes, apparently she was standing on a chair, in her slippers, trying to reach her favourite blanket from the top shelf of the airing cupboard, when she toppled over and fell down on to her left hip. Luckily, her hall carpet cushioned the fall and she suffered some minor bruising and not a fractured pelvis.' Sybs shakes her head.

'Oh dear, but thankfully it wasn't far worse. I can't imagine her coping at all if she had to lie around in a hospital bed for any length of time.' We both smile and shake our heads.

'Absolutely not, Hettie would hate that. Anyway, I'll let her know that you were asking after her.'

'Thanks, Sybs. I'll pop down and see her soon. I take it she won't be running her cross-stitch class this week?' I glance over at my first attempt hanging on the wall by the window – a simple 'Home Sweet Home' sampler in a gorgeous cherry-red thread with a dainty, creamy-coloured blossom flower detailing. Soon after Jack went, I realised that all my evenings were my own again – there was no more need for the Mum-taxi service, taking him to hockey practice, rugby, swimming and such-like in Market Briar. I really fancied trying some-thing new and different, so I signed up to Hettie's 'Cross-stitch for Beginners' course. It's totally informal; about eight of us meet up every Wednesday evening. After a good thirty minutes or so of catching up (gossiping) and devouring packets of custard creams and Jammie Dodger biscuits, and whatever delicious cake Kitty has brought with her (she runs the Spotted Pig café and tearoom on the corner of the High Street), Hettie shows us how to cross-stitch as beautifully as she does.

'Don't be daft!' Sybs nudges me gently. 'Why on earth would you think a bruised hip would stop Hettie from soldiering on?' We both laugh.

'Hmmm, I've actually no idea why I thought such a thing,' I say, enjoying our banter. 'I should have known Hettie wouldn't let us down.'

'Absolutely not. And you should have seen the look she gave me when I suggested that of course you would all understand if she wanted to give this week's class a miss.'

'Ha! I can imagine. You are one brave woman, Sybil Bloom,' I chuckle.

'A foolish one more like,' she pulls a face. 'Anyway, I'd better get going and sort out this stinking dog before the whole of Tindledale whiffs of fox poo.'

'Sure,' I laugh. 'Well, thanks for popping by.' I give Sybs a hug.

'Oh, I almost forgot – can I give you these?' She opens the top of her beautiful fuchsia hand-knitted bag – it has rose-print fabric lining – and pulls out a wad of leaflets. 'It might not be your thing, but I wondered if you wouldn't mind putting one inside each of your children's book bags? For the parents. Well, children and dogs too – or ferret in Molly's case,' she sighs, and an image of Molly, the butcher's wife, walking her pet ferret around the village on a lead, pops into my head. 'Yes, the more the merrier. Ben reckons we really need everyone to get involved if we're to stand a chance of winning.' Sybs grins and I grin back, feeling brighter than I have all week. I like Sybil; she's always cheerful and eager to help out if she can.

'Sure,' I say, taking them from her and glancing at the leaflet on top of the pile.

Tindledale Needs You!
Come along to the Duck & Puddle pub on Friday
29 May at 6 p.m. to find out how you can get involved
in this year's GREAT VILLAGE SHOW. All welcome
(dogs on leads please).

'Ooh, so the parish council got over its embarrassment, then, and decided to have another go?' I say, trying not to sound too amused.

'What do you mean?' Sybs asks with a curious look on her face.

'Well, last time, it, um . . . didn't go quite to plan.' I arch an eyebrow, unsure of how much I should tell her. I imagine some members of the parish council would prefer that the revered village GP and his girlfriend weren't aware of how badly behaved some of them were last time Tindledale put on a show.

'Last time?'

'Yes, it was in the summer before you arrived, which I guess is why you don't know what happened.'

'Oh dear, this sounds ominous – what?' She frowns. 'Ben thought it might be a good idea, you know, to boost community spirit and really put Tindledale on the map. Apparently the ten best village shows in the whole country get listed in one of the national newspapers, with a full colour feature in their Sunday supplement magazine.'

'Hmm, Dr Ben is right, it is a good idea, and it certainly does boost community spirit, but last time two of the parish councillors took *spirit –*' I pause for added emphasis – 'to a whole new level and had to resign. There was a falling out over a giant marrow!'

'Ooops!' Sybs makes big eyes.

'Indeed. And we were doing so well, having been pre-selected by the National Village Show Committee to have a celebrity to help with the judging of local produce – food, preserves, cakes, bakes, eggs, vegetables, gardens in bloom . . . that kind of stuff, which is always a bit of a kudos thing. Stoneley Parish Council were most put out when they had to put up with the plain old ordinary judges. *Sooo*, Alan Titchmarsh turned up, fresh from his telly gardening programme, and the two Tindledale councillors started bickering and accusing each other of cheating – something about having bought the marrow from the new Lidl that had just opened up in Market Briar, instead of cultivating it on their allotment as per the rules. It was shocking, but hilarious too – one of them completely lost it and ended up grabbing Alan's clipboard and smashing it over and over and over into the offending marrow, at which point Marigold – you know, the wife of Lord Lucan?' Sybs nods in acknowledgement, aware I'm referring, not to the famously untraceable nanny-murderer, but to Lord Lucan Fuller-Hamilton from Blackwood House on the Blackwood Farm Estate. 'Well, she had to step in with a roll of kitchen towel so Alan could wipe the marrow pulp from his face.'

'Oh no, that's awful,' Sybs says, trying not to laugh.

'And that's not all. The day before the show, the village green was defiled. Mud everywhere. It was such a mess. A runaway tractor was to blame – one of the farm boys lost control as he came over the brow of the hill and ended up doing twenty zigzag laps with the plough mode in full throttle, across the immaculately mani-cured lawn. Carnage, it was, and with absolutely no time to re-turf the green before the judges arrived.'

'Blimey. Well, let's hope it isn't a disaster this time around.'

'Yep, fingers crossed.'

'Why don't you come along to the meeting?' Sybs suggests, slipping the strap of her bag over her head, cross-body style, before getting back on to her bicycle. 'Sounds as if we might need a teacher, someone in a position of authority, to bring some order to the event – especially if last time's disastrous chain of events are anything to go by. What if the villagers start behaving like a bunch of children, bickering and bitching over the provenance of their allotment produce?' Sybs lets out a long whistle, while I ponder on her suggestion.

'Now, there's an idea. I might just do that,' I nod purposefully, thinking it could be just the thing to kick-start my life. Jack isn't the only one who can look to new horizons. I'm still young, so who knows what the future might hold?

Two

Monday afternoon, and I've just arrived home from a very long and difficult day at school when I spot Lawrence leaning against the frame of my sunshine yellow front door. Tall and fifty-something, he's the most debonair man in the village, and his head is mere inches away from the hanging basket that's in desperate need of attention – the rainbow mix of mini-petunias have really come on, so much so that they are now cascading almost down to the top of the wooden welly storage box. I make a mental note to sort them out later on. I find it therapeutic, and just what I need right now.

'Hungry?' He waggles a pink paper carrier bag from Kitty's tearoom high in the air, before giving me a huge hug. Dressed in a smart tweed suit, complete with waistcoat and open-necked checked flannel shirt, he looks every inch the perfect country gent – very Ian

McKellen, albeit with cropped short hair and classic aviator-style sunglasses, which he takes off and slips inside his breast pocket, swapping them for his usual black-framed indoor glasses. 'I thought we might enjoy afternoon tea together?' he adds thoughtfully, stepping aside so I can balance my bike against the brick side wall and unlock the door.

'Ahh, I'd love to. Thank you, Lawrence, what a great idea.' I rummage in my handbag for the bunch of keys.

'I do try,' he says modestly, with the vague hint of an American accent. 'Here, let me help you with that.' He takes my enormous cloth school bag, bulging with various paraphernalia – exercise books to be marked, laptop, empty lunch box, book, magazine, make-up, my current cross-stitch project to do in the staffroom if I have a minute to spare, staff folders (their quarterly reviews are due soon) and, lastly but most ominously, the A4 envelope that was handed to me as the team of school inspectors left after their impromptu visit this morning.

'Thanks,' I say, grateful to offload the massive weight from my left shoulder.

After pushing my key into the front door, I take the bag from Lawrence and heave it into the space on the floor under the coat stand. I purposefully tuck the brown envelope under my arm and walk down the narrow hall and through into the kitchen. Lawrence follows.

'Summer is definitely here, thankfully. It's practically tropical out there,' he exaggerates, putting the paper carrier bag on the scrubbed pine table before slipping off his jacket. He rolls up his sleeves and, after placing the envelope next to the bag, I lean forward to give him a hug.

'Thanks for popping in,' I grin, taking a step back. 'And perfect timing. It's been,' I pause for the right words, 'an interesting day.' I open the top half of the back door to let the glorious, honeysuckle-scented sun cascade in.

'Sounds intriguing!' Lawrence lifts his eyebrows.

'Yes, I'll tell you about it . . . Here, I'll make us some drinks,' I say, going to pull open the fridge door. 'How are you Lawrence? Have you had a good day?' I ask him distractedly as I rummage about trying to find the ingredients. I was actually OK for the rest of the day after this morning's meeting, but then I didn't have time to let my feelings spiral. I had three children each requiring an hour of additional reading and numeracy practice and, as far as I'm concerned, the children's basic learning needs come before the school inspectors', quite frankly, very spurious ones! I let out a big puff of air, determined not to get het up about it again as I did when cycling home from school. At one point, I was so distracted that I very nearly sped straight into Pete, the cattle farmer, on his tractor as I took a bend in the lane too sharply – luckily his tractor was stationary; he'd stopped to enjoy a roll-up as he listened to the weather forecast bulletin on his beaten-up old radio that he keeps on the seat beside him in the cabin.

'Yes, thanks,' Lawrence says, obviously waiting to hear more about my day.

'Fancy a glass of something chilled and fizzy instead of tea?' I turn to Lawrence with a 'dare you' grin. 'Go on.'

'Oh, naughty Ms Singer, drinking in the afternoon . . . but such a good idea!' He grins back. 'Come on, let's eat cake and you can tell me all about it.'

'And drink fizzy elderflower champagne . . .! Hmm, well, it's wine really, but champagne sounds a bit more glamorous,' I say, swinging the bottle from the fridge to show him.

'My dear, I wasn't aware you had perfected another batch,' Lawrence says in his usual stately, old-style gentlemanly way. It's very comforting.

'Sure have. Six bottles chilling nicely in the fridge.

Would you like some to take back to the B&B for your guests?' I ask.

'Only if you let me pay for it this time. I insist,' he says, politely, 'and it's only fair, given the love and care you put into making it. And I know you give bottles of it away to some of the villagers, which is very generous, *buuuuut* . . . I'd just feel happier . . .' He shakes his head.

'Oh don't be daft, Lawrence. Making wines and cordials is a hobby, something Jack and I have done together for years – it makes good use of all the wild berries, fruits and flowers in and around Tindledale, plus the surplus veg from my patch at the bottom of the garden. You know that. And there's plenty . . . look,' I tell him, pointing to the four wooden crates stacked up just inside the pantry door next to the steps leading down to the cellar, where my little home brewery is housed. 'Help yourself. Please. Take as much as you like – there's plenty more where that came from, my garden is overrun with elderflower this year. Must be the early summer weather,' I say, plonking four unopened bottles from the fridge on to the counter for him.

'OK, lovely, thanks Meg.' Lawrence knows better than to quibble with me – we've been friends for such a long time and I can be very 'scary teacher', as he calls it, when I need to be . . . which I do try not to be unless absolutely necessary.

'You're welcome.' I find two glass tumblers and pour us each a generous measure of bubbles before popping a couple of ice cubes and cucumber slices in too. After adding a lime-green plastic giraffe stirrer, I hand one of the glasses to Lawrence.

'What do you reckon?'

'Mm-mmm, delicious. Thank you,' Lawrence says tactfully, before taking a quick sip. 'And I think this could actually top that truly scrumptious sloe and blackberry gin you made last summer.' He swirls the liquid around his mouth, as if examining its vintage, like a proper wine connoisseur. I smile as Lawrence swallows and gives the drink a good stir in anticipation of having some more. 'Cheers,' he smiles, and then looks at me steadily. 'So, are you going to tell me what's wrong? You're not still fretting about Jack, are you?'

'No, no,' I demur. 'Really not. I mean it's hard – I love it when he comes home for a holiday, and I do miss him, but of course his life needs to move on. It's a great chance for him.'

Lawrence smiles kindly. 'Absolutely. He deserves it after all the work he put in to get his A-level grades. And he talked about nothing else for months – years even. And how marvellous to be that certain of your future, of what you want to do, of what you want to be! It really is something to be admired.'

I nod, thinking properly about what Lawrence has just said. 'That's true. What an amazing feeling that must be. Hmm, I'm not sure I've ever really felt like that,' I say.

'But you're a wonderful teacher, or so I've heard . . .' Lawrence smiles wryly, then puts down his glass and looks seriously at me. 'So maybe you found your métier anyway, just by chance.'

'It's true, I do love being a teacher, but I sort of just drifted into it. It fitted in nicely with all Jack's school holidays . . . Mrs Pocket, the old head teacher – it was actually her idea.'

'Oh yes, I know Mrs Pocket – prominent on the parish council and does all that genealogy stuff. Firm but foreboding, in a sensible-shoes-and-plaid-skirt, Miss-Jean-Brodie kind of way.' Lawrence pulls a face.

'Ha! I shall tell her you said that,' I joke. 'But seriously, she was an amazing mentor, very inspirational. Anyway, she encouraged me to train properly as a teacher, fitting it in around Jack, and that's what happened.'

'So you see, you got your chance to shine, and now it's Jack's time.'

I nod in agreement, and glance at the brown envelope on the table.

'Shall it read it myself, or do you want to tell me?' Lawrence asks softly as he takes the envelope from me and opens the flap.

'Oh Lawrence, I might as well just tell you, but please don't breathe a word,' I say, anxiously. 'I don't want the villagers – especially the children – to worry.'

'I absolutely promise,' Lawrence says earnestly.

'OK. Well, put bluntly, it looks as though the village school might have to close!' I turn away, unable to hold eye contact. Saying the words out loud seems to make it sound so much more inevitable.

'Hang on a minute,' Lawrence eventually says, weighing each word carefully, 'but can they do that? Just close a school? What about the children's education? Surely there are laws – don't children have a legal right to an education in this country?'

'Absolutely!'

'So how come then?' Lawrence lifts his eyebrows. 'I mean, it's a bit out of the blue, isn't it?'

'Sure is. A team of inspectors turned up today and are going to be assessing the viability of the school over the coming months . . . working out the cost of everything we do and use,' I tell him.

'I see.' Lawrence's calm tones are incredibly reassuring. 'So what does that mean in real terms?'

'It means, because our pupil numbers are dwindling, the council wants to see if it's worth keeping the school open.'

'But of course it is.' His eyebrows rise. 'It's at the centre of everything. And didn't most of the people here in Tindledale go to the school?'

'Yes,' I sigh, 'but realistically it comes down to money at the end of the day. If the school . . .' And it really does feel like *my* school, and I'm sure all the other villagers feel the same way – the school belongs to each and all of us together, Lawrence is right; we love the school, it's just been a part of Tindledale life for ever and ever – since the mists of time, and I'm not even exaggerating. '. . . isn't deemed affordable any more, then they'll close us down.'

'But surely it's not just about money – what about all the extra stuff you do? The special needs support? Just last week you were telling me how well that little boy recently diagnosed with ADHD was doing.' Lawrence now seems as shocked as I did when I first heard the news. 'It's about a whole *community*.'

'I know, and you know, but from the point of view

of the council, unless I can find a way to attract more children to the school, then it'll be closed down.'

'That's too bad . . .' Lawrence lets out a long whistle.

'Well, it is a massive problem: there are only four children in this year's Reception class and the nursery numbers are dropping too, so next September's intake could be even less. We have capacity for sixty children in total, but there are currently only forty-nine, so unless we can find an additional eleven children, it's cheaper for the council to pay for the school bus to collect my pupils and take them to the big school in Market Briar,' I explain, having already gleaned this gem of information from the woman I spoke to on the phone at the council. I called right after I had inhaled my ham and homemade plum chutney sandwich at lunchtime, and before I went to spend the other twenty minutes of my lunch break helping Archie Armstrong with his speech therapy exercises because his mum, another single parent, is profoundly deaf so can't really do it herself. So, firstly, I enquired as to why the council felt it necessary to send in a team, without warning, followed by a formal letter, and not just pick up the phone to chat about it first, and secondly to ask what this means in real terms, to which I was told, and quite tersely I have to say, that unless the pupil numbers pick up, the school will most likely close at the end of the next academic year, with a decision made by the end of this year's summer holiday period. So we'll know in September.

'Hmm, well, from a purely selfish perspective, I need the village children close by for the Christmas pantomime rehearsals – how else am I going to find twenty singing children to perform "Ten Little Elves" for the grand finale? And be available to rehearse during the school day?' Lawrence shakes his head as we sit quietly, each of us pondering, searching for a solution.

'Well, you won't. And I can hardly see the head teacher at the big school in Market Briar agreeing to let you use the school hall for rehearsals because the village hall's heating has packed up again,' I puff, and it's a very good point, one I must remember to bring up at the village show meeting, as last time the judges commented on how it was extremely chilly in the village hall – and that was in summer time, so they 'dreaded to think how arctic it might be in winter'. We don't want to get marked down again for making the same mistake – perhaps we could get some plug-in radiators or something, if the parish council can be persuaded to part with some funding.

'So what are we going to do then?' Lawrence looks concerned.

'Well, short of asking if any of the villagers plan on adopting lots of school-age children in the next few months, I have no idea! But one thing I do know, Lawrence,' I pause to take a breath, 'is that I'm not going to stand by and let the inspectors close down my school. Certainly not!' I say, getting into my stride.

'Good! That's the spirit,' Lawrence rallies. 'We need to attract new blood to the village – young families, young couples to have lots of babies – yes, and how about Sybs and Dr Ben? I wonder if they've talked about having a family yet. A BIG one.'

'Hmm. Funnily enough, Sybs didn't mention it when I saw her yesterday,' I joke.

'Then you must ask her right away!' Lawrence turns to face me with a very serious look on his face. 'There's no time to waste. And she's a twin! And they say that twins run in families, so if she and Dr Ben get cracking now, you could have two more pupils lined up for the nursery in nine months' time. Surely if we can show the demand is there, babies that will be five and ready to start school in the blink of an eye, then the council will have to change its mind.' His voice trails off.

'But I can't do that!' I say, horrified. 'We are friends,

but not that close – can you imagine? "*Oh Sybs, I was just wondering if you and Ben were getting it on, frequently, as in making babies any time soon, because I'm now touting for business!*" I could do a poster perhaps – *WANTED!* Children to fill my school. What on earth would she think?' I shake my head.

'Oh, I'm sure she wouldn't mind. Sybs isn't one to take offence,' Lawrence says gently, and I soften, knowing that he's just trying to help. I quickly reconsider – maybe he has a point, and what other options do I have right now? It could be my best chance.

'Hmm, maybe I should go a step further and open up Tindledale's very first fertility clinic, just to be on the safe side.' I laugh.

'Good idea,' Lawrence says, not missing a beat.

'Or perhaps you could ask Sybs – you're closer to her than I am,' I smile.

'Yes, I might just do that!'

'But, joking aside, Lawrence, we do need to come up with some serious ideas to boost business for you and to make sure the school stays open,' I say, pointing an index finger in the air, as if marshalling a rescue package for a major conglomerate.

'What about coffee mornings? Parent and toddler groups where you can show off the school and its facilities to prospective parents? Do you do stuff like that already?' Lawrence asks.

'Um, no, not really. But I know St Cuthbert's does,' I say enthusiastically, my mind going into an overdrive full of taster sessions and newsletters, spring festivals and teddy bears' picnics in the Tindledale woods. That would be fairly easy to organise too . . . Hmm, I'm going to get on to that right away. 'And how about a crafting circle? Children love making things – I could ask Hettie or Sybs to show the older children how to knit, crochet, quilt and cross-stitch – broaden the curriculum, because it's not all just about numeracy and literacy and league tables. We could even set up a mini petting farm. I'm sure I could round up enough rabbits, guinea pigs, chickens, goats and lambs – the possibilities are endless.'

'They sure are. But tell me about St Cuthbert's – is this the big school they'd bus your children to?' Lawrence asks.

'Oh no, it's the private school on the old Market Briar Road – their numbers are flourishing, so I know there are lots of children in the area. Mostly families that have relocated from larger towns where the schools aren't performing so well, but then St Cuthbert's has far better facilities than we do – Olympic-size swimming pool, all-weather sports arena and a proper arts theatre with a sound deck and professional lighting and all of that, somebody said. My little village school – with its patch of tarmac for a playground and regular rounds of begging letters to parents for donations of kitchen roll and shaving cream for messy play – really can't compete.' I shake my head.

'Ahh, but your school is ranked Outstanding on the government thingamajig.'

'Ofsted!' I offer, and he's right, and we're very proud of this fact.

'And what about Blue? Didn't you take him into school when you were doing the Beatrix Potter project? A real live Peter Rabbit. Surely the inspectors will be impressed by that initiative. And I bet they don't bring nature into the classroom at the big school in town,' Lawrence says hopefully, eyeing Blue, who is now snuggling on my lap, his little paws perpetually moving as he cleans his face.

'That's right, I did. And I'll be making sure he comes to school with me again so the inspectors can see how much the children love playing with Blue, and learning how to be gentle, how to care for him, how to take turns – all that emotional development is very important; it's a huge part of the whole child approach that

I try to apply in my school. But what I really need is more pupils. That's what will make all the difference. We can have the best curriculum for miles around, but it doesn't mean very much if the children aren't coming to my school.'

'And if the school were to close, where would it leave you?'

'I'm really not sure,' I reply. 'I might get a teaching job at another school somewhere. But it could mean I'll be travelling miles away too.'

'OK, but on a positive note, Meg, this could be an opportunity for you! You're a great teacher, we all know that, so you're certain to get something else, even if the worst happens. Or maybe you could do private tutoring for children with special needs. I know you really enjoy that aspect of your job. You could even set up a children's therapy centre . . . yes, the possibilities are endless.'

There's a short silence as I ponder on his suggestions.

'Hmm, yes, you're right, Lawrence.' Buoyed on the wave of his enthusiasm, I begin to see the possibilities. I was thrown off course this morning by the inspectors' visit but, as ever, Lawrence has helped clarify my thoughts. 'I am not going to sit here moping and worrying about what might never happen. I'm going to take advantage of the spare time I've got – now Jack's off doing his own thing – and right now I'm going to get stuck in to helping out with this year's village show. There'll be plenty that needs doing. Have you heard about it? Dr Ben is keen for us to have another go.' I smile.

'Oh yes,' Lawrence grins. 'Sybs popped by with one of her leaflets. I'm planning on getting involved too – do my bit for the community; and it sure would be helpful for my business if Tindledale were to get a mention in a national newspaper.'

Suddenly I realise how introspective I've been recently. 'Oh, I'm sorry, Lawrence.' I look at him with a furrowed brow. 'I thought things were going really well for you,' I say slowly, feeling remorseful. I've been so wrapped up in missing Jack, when Lawrence has obviously been worrying about his B&B business. And since his partner, Jason, died, he no longer has him for support.

'Let's just say that they could be better. Surely you've noticed a dip in the number of people in and around the village, the High Street, the Duck & Puddle, Kitty's tearoom? I was chatting to the vicar just a few days ago, and he said that even the congregation at his Sunday service is dwindling . . .' His voice trails off.

'Well, I hadn't,' I admit, 'but now that you mention

it, yes . . . it did seem quiet last time I popped into Kitty's for a scone and a mug of hot chocolate. Why is that?'

'I don't know for sure, but I guess it's inevitable with us having such a high number of elderly villagers – they pass on. And I reckon it's also something to do with the new retail park that's opened up on the other side of the valley, just past Market Briar. They have it all there – designer outlet shops, multiplex cinema, bowling, coffee chains, big-name restaurants; there's even a hotel with a swimming pool and spa – my cosy little six-bedroom home-from-home B&B just can't compete. And my guest numbers have definitely dipped since it opened.'

'But not everyone wants all that high-tech, bells-and-whistles stuff. Surely there are lots of people who still love the cosy quirkiness of a traditional village, the personal touch that you offer at the B&B – not forgetting your award-winning breakfasts,' I say, counting out the benefits on my fingers. Lawrence smiles. 'And there must be lots of people who want to amble along our little High Street and watch the world go by through the mullioned windows of Kitty's café, or thumb through some of the rare books in Adam's bookstore. I know I do.'

'I'm sure there are, but if they don't know about Tindledale and all that we have to offer, then they can't visit. A feature in a national newspaper is just what my B&B needs. And it's about time you had some fun too.'

'Exactly.' I nod in agreement. 'It'll do me good to get involved in the village show and keep myself busy.'

'Sure will. And broaden your horizons,' Lawrence says slowly, as if gauging my reaction to a plan that he's cooking up.

'What is it?' Silence follows. 'Come on, what are you up to?' I laugh, giving him a gentle dig in the ribs.

'Later,' Lawrence does a cryptic smile. 'Let's have some cake first,' he adds, carefully lifting a scrumptious-looking individual lemon drizzle cake from the bag.

I retrieve two bird-patterned tea plates from the dishwasher. Grabbing a couple of forks, too, I place them on the kitchen table and we sit adjacent to each other on the long padded window seat in the sun, arranging the assortment of homemade cushions behind us, plumping and patting until we're both comfortable. Suddenly I feel lighter and more opti-mistic than I have in ages. 'So, what's new, Lawrence?' I ask him, conspiratorially. 'Any interesting guests at the B&B?' I take a bite of the cake, which tastes divine – citrusy and sweet, but with just the right amount of sharpness too; Kitty sure is a cake-making queen. And Lawrence has been like a fairy godfather to me since he came to Tindledale twenty or so years ago – so, still a relative newcomer, compared to most of the other villagers whose families have been here for generations – and opened Tindledale's first bed and breakfast, which has proved to be very popular with tourists, and a welcome boost to Tindledale's economy. You'd be surprised how many pints of cider visitors can get through in the Duck & Puddle, and then there's the locally sourced produce they all go mad for in the butcher's and the fruit & veg shops in the High Street. And not forgetting Kitty's tearoom – tourists can't get enough of her afternoon teas with melt-in-the-mouth fruit scones, strawberry jam and deliciously thick cream, churned by Pete on his cattle farm down in the valley near Cherry Tree Orchard.

Lawrence takes another mouthful of wine before doing a furtive left-then-right glance.

'What is it? Or, should I say, who is it? Why are you looking so sheepish?' I ask, my interest instantly piqued. I bet it's someone famous – it must be; I've only ever seen Lawrence behave like this once before, and that was when the novelist Fern Britton checked in. They were doing some filming for a TV programme nearby in Market Briar, but she wanted to stay somewhere quieter. Lawrence said she was a true professional, very gracious and down-to-earth.

'OK, but you must promise not to tell a soul.'

'I promise,' I say right away, now dying to know who the famous guest is.

'Okaaaaaay,' Lawrence pauses. 'It's Dan Wright!' he announces impressively, as if I'm bound to know who Dan Wright is. Lawrence's face drops when he realises that I'm struggling to place him. 'Come on, you must know him, Meg.'

I lick my fingers before jumping up and running down the hall to retrieve my laptop. After lifting the screen into place, I go to type *Dan Wright* into Google and I get as far as the W.

'Look,' I tap the screen to show Lawrence. 'Google has found him right away. And he has a Wiki page,' I add, gradually piecing together a jumble of half-remembered facts and images.

Dan Wright, celebrity chef and owner of The Fatted Calf, three-Michelin-starred restaurant in London's Mayfair . . .

'Of course it has. He's famous. So, do you recognise him now?' Lawrence says, standing up and joining me at the end of the table.

'Yes, I think so . . . but when do I ever go to fancy restaurants in London?' I shrug, remembering the last time I went out for dinner – at the Oriental Palace, a Chinese restaurant and takeaway in Market Briar. Jack chose it, citing a desire for a lovely last chicken chow mein with his mum before heading to uni – it was such a fun evening, us and four of his friends, all laughing and being silly with our chopsticks.

'Fair point! You must have seen him on TV – he had his own show for a bit; though not for a while now, to be fair.' Lawrence swivels the laptop towards him, pulling up another chair and clicking on to YouTube. He does a quick search. 'Here.' There's a short silence while we both sit with our buffer faces on, waiting for the film to start. 'Isn't he handsome? In a filthy, Kit Harington about to do battle in *Game of Thrones* kind of way . . .'

A young guy pops on to the screen, sniggering about something the interviewer has just said, before sweeping a hand through a thick, unruly thatch of black hair.

I crinkle my forehead, staring at the image. 'Well, yes. I suppose. Blimey, he's very young to be a three-Michelin-starred chef, isn't he? Barely older than Jack,' I muse, but Lawrence smiles.

'Oh no, this film clip is ages old – twenty years, at

least. I reckon he must be mid forties perhaps, by now. Sorry, I should have explained.'

'Hmm, oh right.' I turn to face Lawrence and see a strange expression on his face. 'Hang on, you're not thinking I might fancy him, are you?' I laugh. I'm quite used to people trying to match-make for me, so I learnt ages ago to put my foot down right away. Mum is the worst culprit. Whenever I'm with her in Tenerife, she always tries to palm me off with some lost soul – usually divorced with a big chip on his shoulder and a long boring story about how the 'ex-missus stitched me up like a kipper'. Lawrence looks a bit guilty but faces me down, tilting his head to one side and giving me a curious look. 'Well, would it be so bad if you did?'

'*Weeeell*, I don't know, he just doesn't look my type.' I fold my arms and look away. The fact is, I've hardly had any good experiences when it comes to men – my own father did a disappearing act before my fifth birthday and Jack's dad, Liam, didn't even last that long. He left before Jack was born, claiming he wasn't ready to be a father – he needed to travel the world and find his passion before he could even contemplate settling down. But then when Jack was about eight, I met Will. Sexy, talented Will, who played in a band

and was rather gorgeous – but who ended up being almost as free-range and untrustworthy as Liam, and who finally decided he wasn't doing either me or Jack any good. And since then, five or so years have passed and I've just not had the heart to begin dating again, even though Jack has intermittently told me that I should put myself on Match.com before I get 'like *reeeeeally* old'.

Lawrence knew Will, and was really fond of him, and knows how hard his departure hit our little family at the time, and he looks suitably sympathetic. 'Look, I know it's really difficult, but Jack has moved on and so should you.'

'I know that,' I tell him, and I really do. 'It's more that I just can't be bothered with it all. Getting your heart broken, and all that. It's so overrated.'

'Ahh, I get it!' Lawrence persists, clearly still bemused. 'You've made an assumption based on watching just a few seconds of an old YouTube clip and now that's the end of it! Dan Wright isn't your type!' He holds his palms up in the air in an 'I-give-up' pose.

'No. But look, he's a celebrity chef from swanky Mayfair,' I pull a face. 'Worlds apart from me. I can't even remember the last time I went to London.' I pause to think and then it comes to me. 'I know, Jack was about ten years old and Will and I took him to see the sights – Big Ben, Tower of London, Madame Tussaud's, that kind of thing,' I start, feeling very provincial indeed.

'Marvellous! *Seeeee . . .*' And Lawrence smiles. 'You have the perfect icebreaker. You can ask Dan what his favourite waxwork person is.' He laughs to lighten the mood.

'Ha-ha, very funny,' I smirk. 'And just look at how he's sitting.' I tap the laptop screen where the film is paused, showing Dan on the TV sofa with his legs wide open.

'Sitting?' Lawrence laughs harder. 'What does that have to do with anything?'

'Everything! He's a spreader. And spreaders are inconsiderate, with no respect for personal space,' I inform him, sounding far haughtier than I actually intended to. I cringe inwardly.

'Ha! Well yes, I can see what you mean. But honestly, I've not seen him sitting like that at the breakfast table – in fact I think he had his legs firmly crossed, and on the few occasions when we've chatted, he actually seemed quite nice. Plus, you have to agree, you aren't exactly spoilt for choice when it comes to meeting a new man here in Tindledale.'

'Hmm, this is very true,' I say, loath to agree, but Lawrence has a very valid point. I grew up with most of the Tindledale men – went to school with them – so any charm or sexual attraction they might have had got lost somewhere along the way, likely when they were busy picking their noses in class or attempting a snog at the end-of-year disco, having scoffed all the prawn cocktail crisps from the finger buffet only moments earlier. Eugh. No, the mystique and magic just isn't happening. 'Anyway, like I say, I really can't be bothered with all that.'

'Truly? Isn't it what we all want? To love and be loved! Oh come on, Meg, wouldn't it be brilliant for you to be wined and dined? A gorgeous creature like you with your peaches-and-cream complexion and curves in all the right places . . .' He grins, sounding very corny indeed.

'Oh stop it, you old smoothy,' I laugh, giving his arm an affectionate bat.

'Weell, it's true, and how marvellous would it be . . . swept off your feet and whisked away to his restaurant in Mayfair? Very romantic! And he has three Michelin stars, so you'd know you'd be in for a gourmet treat,' Lawrence adds, brightly, for good measure.

'Maybe, but what's he even doing here in Tindledale?'

'Good point . . .' Lawrence pauses. 'I actually don't know . . .' He looks thoughtful.

'Ooh, you're slipping, Lawrence,' I tut, pretending to admonish him. 'I'd have thought you would have found out by now – you usually know everything that's going on in the village.'

'Are you implying that I'm a gossip?' He feigns hurt.

'Of course not, but it's true, you do often seem to know stuff.'

'That's because people confide in me – I can't help that,' he smiles, pausing to contemplate, and then adds, 'There is a rumour going around that Dan is here scouting out the village with a view to opening a new restaurant.'

'Really? And do you think that might be the case? Has he said anything about it? But where?' I ask, racking my brains to think of a suitable spot for a high-end restaurant somewhere in the village. There are a couple of empty places – the one next to the fruit & veg shop is probably too small, and there's definitely a rodent problem in there – I saw the pest control man's van outside there just last week. But then it's inevitable in the countryside with all the fields around us; I often have to put the mice powder down to stop them overtaking my cottage.

'The shop at the end overlooking the village green is reasonably sized,' Lawrence suggests.

'Oooh, yes. And it's double fronted, with lots of space to sit outside, which would be nice in this gorgeous warm weather, and very cosmopolitan, I imagine – sitting underneath a parasol enjoying an expensive bottle of wine with a ten-course tasting meal – that's what they have in London . . .'

'Hmm, but Tindledale is hardly Mayfair.' Lawrence pulls a face.

'True. And my fizzy elderflower wine is definitely not a fine Sancerre.' We both sit silently for a few seconds, pondering the possibilities. 'But, we have the village green right opposite – perfect for when the movie stars and celebrities helicopter in for their fine dining experience. And I'm sure your actor friends will come. You could call Dame Judi – or what about Helen? You said that she's a great dinner companion.'

'Ha!' Lawrence laughs. 'But we mustn't get ahead of ourselves,' he adds, always the voice of caution. 'Dan Wright hasn't actually said anything to me about a new restaurant. We are just speculating. But if he is planning on opening one here, then even better – he can appoint a manager, a head chef or whatever, at The Fatted Calf in London, and then move here. Then you can both live happily ever after together in Tindledale,' Lawrence finishes with a flourish, ever the romantic, having seemingly worked it all out.

'Hold on, slow down a minute. It's nice of you to be so concerned about my love life . . . or rather lack of,' I smile wryly. 'But honestly, I'm fine as I am. I love my friends, my home and my life. And anyway, neither of us will have any time for distractions for the foreseeable future. We have a village show to organise.'

'That's true,' Lawrence says thoughtfully, then suddenly leaps in the air, terrifying Blue, who scampers under the table. 'I have a plan!' Lawrence is now channelling John Gielgud – or is it Brian Blessed?

'You do?' I ask, eagerly.

'I most certainly do. Listen Meg.'

'I'm listening,' I say, rescuing Blue and stroking his velvety soft ear.

'Good. Here goes,' he pauses for impact, 'we make sure that Tindledale puts on the greatest show of its life!' Lawrence is pacing around the kitchen now.

'But what difference will that make to the school?' I ask, standing up too.

'*Meeeeeg,* don't you see?' He stops pacing, enthusiasm flooding his voice now.

'See what?' I ask, reaching for the wine to top us both up.

'This is the perfect opportunity.'

'What is?'

'*Weeeell,*' he starts elaborating slowly, as if formulating the plan in his head as he goes. 'If this year's village show is great, we'll make it into the top ten list in the national newspaper and the whole country will see how wonderful Tindledale is – the perfect place to live! Then everyone will be looking at your school on the Internet . . . you do have a website, I take it?' He looks panic-stricken for a brief moment. I nod. The council organised it years ago and it's very basic, but I reckon I could get it updated. 'Good, because, let's face it, every parent wants the best school for their child, sooooo everyone will then want to live here – FAMILIES, with LOTS OF CHILDREN to fill your school. Yes, it's the perfect solution.'

We stare at each other.

'And if there's a Michelin-starred restaurant here too . . . all the better!' I jump in, 'because everyone loves good food – and you could do gourmet weekend breaks, maybe culinary courses too; you could ask

Dan to help out – use his restaurant kitchen, perhaps. And soon your B&B will be booked up indefinitely, and with a very long waiting list to boot.'

'And Kitty and all the other businesses in the village will be thrilled too,' Lawrence nods, enthusiastically.

'Yes! Outstanding school. Outstanding food. Outstanding pub, tearoom, butcher's, baker's, and all the other stuff the great village of Tindledale has to show for itself . . . We have the lot,' I say, my voice brimming with excitement now, helped along by the fizz we've been consuming. 'They'll be beating a path here to Tindledale in no time, and the Great Village Show will save my great village school – you just wait and see!'

Three

As I duck down under the beam above the Duck & Puddle's gnarled old oak entrance door, I can see that there's quite a crowd gathered already – by the looks of it, most of the villagers are crammed into the compact but cosy space. Some are even hovering by the hatch in the snug at the end of the bar that doubles as the pub shop, selling essentials such as sweets, crisps, cigarettes, milk, magazines, eggs, bread, firelighters, logs, lighter fuel, that kind of thing.

'All right, Miss?' one of the farmer boys grins, giving me a big wink as I walk past, while his two mates snigger and nudge each other in the background. I try not to smile at their juvenility, and keep my scary teacher face firmly in place as I overhear them pondering the merits of adding TILF to their list of acronyms.

Cher, the landlady, repatriates a stray tendril of hair back into her treacle-coloured beehive before clapping her hands together and hollering from behind the bar in her Cockney accent.

'Ladies and gents, children and dogs.' Molly coughs from over by the inglenook fireplace where she's standing with her pet ferret in her arms – it's wearing a little leather harness and looks unfazed as it nestles into the crook of her elbow. Cooper, her husband, who owns the village butcher's, glances sideways at her before shaking his head with an exasperated look on his face, which we all know is just for effect as he absolutely adores his wife and would never begrudge her a pet ferret. 'Ooops, sorry . . . and ferrets!' Cher continues, and we all laugh before doing lots of 'shushes' and whispered nods of 'hi' and 'hello' as more people arrive. 'Welcome to the first Great Village Show meeting . . .' Cher twiddles a sparkly red-varnished fingertip around the inside of her huge gold hoop earring. 'There's plenty of space in our new beer garden . . . so if you'd like to go through,' Cher motions to a door with *GARDEN* written on it in swirly writing on a little wooden plaque, 'and Clive has laid on some nibbles which we'll bring out to you with our compliments.'

'Round of applause for Sonny!' one of the farmer boys shouts from over by the darts board – clearly

Cher's boyfriend's nickname is here to stay. I remember when Cher first arrived in Tindledale, not very long ago, to take over the running of the Duck & Puddle pub – of course the whole village was curious to see who she was (the older men of the village wanting to know if she was actually up to the job, what with her being a woman and all – they were used to Ray, an ex-policeman, running the pub for thirty years before he died). And they promptly renamed Cher's boyfriend Sonny, thinking it hilarious to sing 'I Got You Babe' at any given opportunity. So Clive, also known as Sonny, answers to both names now. Being the pub chef, he is probably one of the most popular people in the village, especially on a Sunday when the bowls of salted pork crackling and goose-fat roast potatoes appear on the bar for people to pick at over their pints.

'Now, what can I get you all to drink?' Cher shouts, and there's practically a stampede as the entire pub crowd surges forward to buy big jugs of Pimm's garnished with cucumber and strawberries and flagons of frothy ice-cold cider – it's such a lovely early summer evening, so it would be a shame not to make the most of it.

Twenty minutes later, and we're all milling around in the beer garden, the warm evening air full with the scent of citronella from the candles dotted around to keep the mosquitoes at bay. A variety of dogs are scooting about, and what seems like all of my school-children are bouncing up and down on the inflatable castle that Cher has kindly supplied to keep them occupied while the adults get on with the meeting.

'Hi Miss Singer,' several of the children chorus, as I walk past looking for a space at one of the wooden bench tables.

'Hello, are you all having a fun time?' I smile, lifting my glass of Pimm's out of the way to give Lily a big hug as she jumps off the bouncy castle and practically launches herself into my body; her skinny arms curled tight around me, clinging on to my sundress, seeking out affection. Waist height, I rest my free hand on her blonde, curly hair before gently unfurling her arms and crouching down to look her in the eye. 'Is your daddy here with you this evening?' I ask tentatively, wondering how Mark, our village policeman, is bearing up – it's only six months since his wife, Polly, passed away after losing her battle with breast cancer. Lily nods and points to the far side of the beer garden where a gaunt-looking Mark is standing with his hands in his jeans pockets and a lonesome look in his eyes. 'That's nice, isn't it?' I say brightly, pleased for Lily that she hasn't had to come along with one of her friends' mums again, because Mark wasn't up to socialising. Lily nods enthusiastically, giving me a big gappy grin.

'Daddy said Mummy is going to send the tooth fairy to collect my teeth tonight and take them up to her in heaven so she can look after them.'

'Oh,' I gulp, and then quickly add, 'well that's very kind,' followed by a big smile, not wanting the brave little girl in front of me to see my anguish for her. It's been a tough time for her at school, with many occasions spent crying in my office or with her class teacher asking my advice on whether or not to reprimand Lily for lashing out at another child – there was an incident shortly after Mother's Day, but the softly-softly, lots-of-love approach seems to be working fine: Lily is a lot less angry than she was, not so very long ago.

'Yes,' she nods some more. 'My mummy is the best one in the whole world and the good thing about her being in heaven is that she gets to see me all the time.' And with that, Lily squeezes my hand, turns on her heels and does a running body-slam back on to the bouncy castle, leaving me reflecting that children are often so much more resilient than we sometimes give them credit for.

Taking a sip of my Pimm's, I head over to Mark, who

looks as though he has the weight of the world on his shoulders. He lifts his head when I reach him.

'Hi Meg, how are things at the school?' he asks in a monotone voice, as if on autopilot and reading from a script he prepared earlier.

'Fine,' I hesitate momentarily, 'yes, all good, thanks for asking,' I reply, figuring a little white lie won't hurt; I imagine he has enough worries without me adding to them. 'Um, I just bumped into Lily, she seems to be having a lovely time on the bouncy castle with her school friends,' I add, gesturing over my shoulder, feeling unsure, really, of what else to say. I take another mouthful of my drink.

'Yes, it's nice to see. And how is she getting on at school these days?' He turns his head sideways towards me before lifting a hand from his pocket to sweep over his bald head. He looks tired, his eyes lacking lustre – rather like a neglected Labrador; in need of comfort and affection, just like his daughter. I resist the urge to put my arms around him and pat his head.

'Good, she's been much . . .' I pause to choose the right word, 'calmer,' I settle on, feeling relieved when Mark exhales and his shoulders visibly relax.

'Pleased to hear it. Pol and I—' He stops talking abruptly and lifts an empty pint glass from a nearby table. 'Sorry, force of habit,' he shrugs and stares into the glass.

'Hey, no need to apologise.' An ominous silence follows. 'I miss her too,' I manage, softly, remembering my friend with a deep fondness. We grew up together. Her dad was the pharmacist in the village chemist's until he retired and moved with her mum to a house by the sea.

'Sure, and I forget that sometimes,' Mark says quietly. 'You know, that other people loved her too.'

'We all did. And still do, very much.' I touch his arm. 'And how are things for you?'

'Getting better, thanks. I'm back at work now, which makes a big difference, occupies the mind. My mum is helping out with childcare and the job are being very accommodating – letting me take Lily to school and stuff,' he explains. *But how will he manage if school is suddenly seven miles away?* I wonder. *Or will Lily be expected to travel on the bus by herself?* 'And I'm glad Lily is OK at school – it's made the last year or so slightly easier to bear, knowing that she's just down the hill with people, friends of Pol's, who care about her, look out for her.' A short silence follows. 'It was Pol's wish for things to stay as "normal" for Lily as possible,' he says, smiling wryly.

'Of course,' I say, averting my gaze, desperately wishing the ones in charge of the purse strings at the council could take into account just how important our little school is to the community. It's so much more than just educating the children, my school is like a pot of glue, keeping the community intact – or helping to stick it back together again. 'Can I get you a drink?' I say, motioning with my head towards his glass.

'No, just the one for me, I'm on duty tomorrow.' He leans in to give me a polite kiss on the cheek. 'Better find Lily before the meeting gets under way.' And he goes to leave.

'Sure. And Mark,' I add. He turns back. 'If you ever want to chat . . . about how Lily is getting on, or Polly, or just, well, anything at all . . . you know where I am.' Mark nods before going to round up Lily.

Dr Ben steps into the patch of grass at the centre of the tables and coughs to get everyone's attention. The crowd immediately stops talking and turns their attention to the esteemed village GP.

'Firstly, I'd like to say thank you to you all for giving up your evening to come along—'

'Least we can do, doc,' someone interrupts, followed by lots of 'hear hears', which makes Dr Ben's cheeks flush slightly as he pushes his glasses further up his nose. He clears his throat before continuing. 'You're all very kind,' he says graciously, in his lovely lilting Irish accent. 'And this is the first time I've been fully involved in anything like this, so I'm really looking forward to seeing how it's done,' he says tactfully, pausing to glance reverently at the table where six or so stalwarts of the Women's Institute are seated, each wearing the obligatory uniform of pastel-coloured cardy twin-set teamed with easy-fit jeans. They each nod and give him knowing looks, as if confirming their allegiance, but most importantly, their solid experience in matters such as village fetes, fairs, shows and such-like – a nationally judged show clearly being like water off a duck's back for them, thank you very much – and they're only here to ensure proceedings are conducted in an efficient manner. I smile and look over at another table to see Mrs Pocket and the parish council contingency bristling when Dr Ben fails to glance at them as well, and groan inwardly. Ahh, so the battle has already commenced! WI versus parish council – each of them already assumes that they should head up the Great Village Show committee. Talking of committees, Dr Ben continues:

'I'm wondering if we should start off by selecting a committee panel to oversee each of the show's elements.' Sybs rummages through a folder in front of her before handing Dr Ben a sheet of paper. 'Thank you.' He winks at Sybs and I'm sure I spot a couple of my school mums bristling – they'd clearly been quite smitten when Dr Ben first arrived in Tindledale to take over the surgery from Dr Donnelly, and were then most put out when it became apparent that newcomer, Sybs, had '*snared*' him, as I overheard them describe it, having only been here '*for like five minutes*'. Oh well. I was delighted for Sybs: she deserves to find her happy-ever-after as much as the next person. 'I took the liberty of downloading all of the criteria from the National Village Show Committee website, and it seems that there are three main areas we need to focus on . . .'

'The three Cs,' someone shouts out. Followed by, 'That's right, I remember from last time – they stand for community, creativity, and, err, um . . . Oh, I can't remember the other one,' bellowed by Lucy, who owns the florist's in the High Street.

'That's right. The third C is civic duty,' Dr Ben says, reading it from the paperwork.

'We'll be in charge of that one,' harrumphs a pompous-looking man with a long nose and flared nostrils. He leans back from the parish council table to adjust his braces. I've never seen him before. But it's no surprise, as villagers old and new always come out of the woodwork whenever there's a big event like this to be organised.

'Hang on a minute. Wouldn't it be better to vote on it, get an idea of who wants to be involved in what?' Molly says, after glaring at the pompous guy. 'Take Sybs, for example: she should be in charge of the creative element . . . seeing as she runs the haberdashery shop and is good at knitting and quilting and making stuff look pretty . . . The High Street would look beautiful with some of her floral bunting buffeting in the breeze between the lampposts,' she adds brightly.

'What's that got to do with it?' the pompous guy pipes up again. 'Does she know how to thatch a roof? That's what I want to know. Nope! Now that's a proper creative master skill, not fiddling around with bits of bunting.' He flares his nostrils out a little further and some of the others seated at his table begin to bristle. 'The judges aren't going to be bothered by all those gimmicky things,' he ploughs on. 'What we need is to tidy up the verges. Have you seen the state of them? Tyre marks all over the grass outside my cottage! It's a disgrace.'

'Well, I agree with Molly,' Ruby from the vintage dress shop interjects, smoothing her scarlet, shoulder-length Dita Von Teese-style hair into place while treating the pompous guy to a very disdainful glower, her cherry-red lips poised for a comeback if he so much as dares to heckle further. I resist the urge to smirk by stirring my Pimm's and then drinking a big mouthful as I take in what's going on around me. The remonstrating and arguing about trivial details goes on until someone brings up the marrow incident, which doesn't help, and then Pete jumps in and it really kicks off.

'Those tyre marks will be from my tractor!' he states to nobody in particular, as if deliberately, and quite mischievously, meaning to escalate the matter, before draining the last of his cider. He wipes his mouth with the shoulder part of his shirt and then pulls open a bag of cheese & onion crisps, as if he hasn't a care in the world, which rankles the pompous guy further. He's up on his feet now, with the sides of his jacket pushed back so he can plant his hands firmly on his hips, showing us he's ready for action.

'Ahh, so you're the culprit. Well it won't do – I've a good mind to place some boulders around my borders,' the pompous guy retaliates. 'That'll stop you in your tracks.'

Cue a collective snigger from the farmers' table, followed by: 'I could supply you with a sack of coal if you like – you could paint all the lumps white and then pop them around your borders,' from John, who owns the hardware store on the Stoneley Road – and always has a mountain of logs and sacks of coal in the open lock-up adjacent to his place.

'Good idea, that should do the trick,' the pompous guy puffs, and I figure that he must be a newcomer as he's utterly unaware that they're pulling his leg now by goading him with their 'coal-painter' jibes, a local euphemism for the 'townies' who keep a country cottage in Tindledale for the weekends, but haven't a clue when it comes to rural life. Tractors mounting verges is just the way it is here; the lanes are just so narrow and winding in parts of the village that it'd be impossible for Pete, or any of the other farmers for that matter, to transport their cattle or crates of apples around the place.

'Or what about some nice painted pebbles?' Molly pipes up again, making the farmers chortle some more. But one of the WI ladies has had enough and butts in with:

'Never mind securing your borders, what the community would like to know is: when are you going to trim your bush!' And she extends a very accusatory index finger in Molly's direction.

A flabbergasted silence ensues. Even Pete stops crunching his crisps and stares open-mouthed.

'Um, I, err . . . beg your pardon,' Molly eventually manages to splutter, as Cooper shoves a fist into his mouth and silently laughs himself into a hernia, making his shoulders jig up and down uncontrollably.

'That bush of yours really needs attention.' Oh dear, Lawrence catches my eye and pulls an exaggerated aghast face. I have to look away before I burst into laughter too, and that would never do – I'm conscious that a reporter from the *Tindledale Herald* is sitting a few feet away from me, and the last thing I'd want is him reporting on the first committee meeting with tales of how '*even the headmistress laughed along to the juvenile, school-playground-style jokes*'. The WI woman ploughs on, seemingly oblivious to the mirth she's causing.

'Yes, it's so unruly, the path outside your house is practically impassable – my husband had to steer his motorised scooter right out into the road, just to get past. It's a wonder he wasn't mown down by one of Pete's verge-mounting tractors. No, your bush is a disgrace and must go before the judges arrive on show day!'

'Well, there's no need to be quite so "personal" about it,' Molly manages to squeak, barely able to speak properly for trying not to howl with laughter. But it's no use, and she caves in. And then Sybs joins in, and soon everyone is screaming, tears of laughter rolling down their cheeks as the WI woman stalks off inside, muttering something about needing a double whisky, for medicinal purposes. I take a deep breath and keep on observing – it was inevitable, I guess – thirty minutes in, and the villagers are already like squabbling ducks; they just can't help themselves from falling out, or making mischief. They're still laughing and the pompous man, it turns out, is a pensioned general, ex-army, and moved here last month for some 'much-needed R&R', according to Marigold, who's sitting opposite me.

Lawrence looks over and motions with his head for me to rescue Dr Ben, who is now hijacked in a debate about the therapeutic powers of wild honey and whether it might be a good idea to have a stall set up on the day with a working hive on display for the judges to try some out for themselves. The health-and-safety implications are being mulled over, with somebody actually suggesting the parish council would need to stump up a budget for 'protective clothing', which doesn't go down very well at all. Especially as Mrs Gibbs is still waiting for a decision about her request for a rubbish bin to be placed in the layby outside her house – it drives her mad when louts hurl their empty lager cans from car windows when passing through our lovely little village.

Unable to sit and watch the fiasco unfolding before me for any longer, I stand up and walk over to the crowd that's formed around Dr Ben, lift my elbows, and muscle my way in, before surreptitiously leaning into his left shoulder.

'Do you mind if I step in?' I ask discreetly.

'Be my guest,' Dr Ben says, giving me a very grateful grin as he hands the paperwork over to me. 'I'm so glad you're here; we really need someone used to taking charge,' he adds, wasting no time in joining Sybs back on the bench.

'OK, if I can have everyone's attention please,' I say in my best school assembly voice, and then count to five in my head. It works: the children on the castle stop bouncing right away, of course. Even the dogs seem to settle down, and eventually the adults stop bickering amongst themselves, the crowd dissipates back to the benches to finish the last of the cheesy chips and everyone turns their attention to me. 'Wonderful. And thank you. Now, as Dr Ben said, it's great to see everyone here and I can see how enthusiastic you all are, but we really have no time to spare if we're to stand a chance of Tindledale putting on a really great show this year! On . . .' I pause to scan the papers and see which date we've been allocated, and then I spot it. My pulse speeds up. Oh dear. 'July 11th!' *Right before the end of the school term, but Jack will be home then for the gloriously long summer holidays.* And my heart lifts at the prospect of having him around for a couple of months.

The crowd falls silent. Nobody moves.

'But that's only,' Lawrence pulls out his pocket diary, 'six weeks away!' he says after thumbing through the pages to check. There's a collective inward gasp.

'Um, yes, err, I'm very sorry, it's my fault,' Dr Ben raises his hand in the air. 'I sent off the application form quite some time ago and, well, I—'

'Don't you worry, doc,' Tommy Prendergast, who runs the village store, quickly pitches in, pulling himself upright with a very staunch look on his face. 'We won't let you down.' He's busy retucking his shirt back in around his rotund waist when everyone joins him in supporting the revered village GP.

'Hear hear! Can't blame the doc. He's a busy man. We'd be lost without him . . .' As ever, Dr Ben can do no wrong as far as all the villagers are concerned, and they certainly all seem committed to putting on a great show in record time. And what perfect timing, as now the school inspectors can really get to see what the village is all about. In fact, I'm going to invite them along to our Great Village Show – maybe we could get one of those boards with circle cut-outs for them to put their faces through while the villagers throw wet sponges, like they do at the seaside. I bet that would raise a few laughs amongst the community. JOKE.

'OK, everyone,' I say, refocusing us all. 'So I reckon we should just get on with it.' I glance around, and great, they're all listening. 'Let's have three committees working in tandem, with weekly meetings. Then we can convene a meeting for the whole village at regular intervals. I'm happy to put together and communicate a set of dates and times, locations, etc. I could pin a list on the notice board in the village square.' I quickly pause and look at Sybs for confirmation, not wanting to step on her toes, but by the look of the big grin on her face, she seems perfectly happy for me to take charge, so I carry on. 'Yes, and Tindledale needs to look its very best before show day, just in case the judges arrive a few days earlier, as they've been known to in the past.'

I stop talking and see them all staring at me, clearly bamboozled by my bossy, but – and if I do say so myself – extra-efficient approach. I spot Mrs Pocket in my peripheral vision, pursing her lips and doing her 'that's my girl' face, so she clearly approves. And if I have her on board, then getting everyone else on side should be a doddle. Spurred on, I scan the beer garden – Sybs is smiling and nodding, Lawrence winks and nods too, the WI ladies fold their arms and look to each other before doing a collective nod of agreement. Not to be outdone, the people seated at the parish council table demonstrate their support by clapping, apart from the general, who eyes me suspiciously before pulling out a pipe and sticking it into his moustachioed mouth. Molly and Cooper applaud too, having just about managed to recover from their hysterics – Molly is wiping her laughter tears away with a napkin. Taylor from the Pet Parlour, Kitty, Hettie from the haberdashery, and all the school mums join in. Everyone seems to be on board.

'Excuse me.' It's Hettie, with her spindly arms pressed into the table, trying to propel her wiry, frail body up into a standing position. Marigold and Sybs jump to her aid and, after a few seconds, Hettie is fully mobile and walking towards me. 'Sorry dear, I'm not as sprightly as I used to be. But I'd like to say a few words if I may?' She fixes her Wedgwood-blue eyes on to me.

'Of course Hettie, go ahead.' And the crowd falls silent – as one of the oldest villagers from a family that has lived in Tindledale going back several generations, she's automatically assured a certain level of respect.

'Thank you. As many of you know, I've lived in Tindledale my whole life – that's eighty years, give or take.' She pauses and pats her big Aunt Bessie bun. 'But what many of you don't know is that Tindledale has already won an award for putting on the greatest village show.' A collective hushed whisper ricochets around the garden. 'Yes, it was in 1965, on a gloriously warm day. So this will be the fiftieth anniversary of that win. It might be a nice idea to commemorate that victory – I'm sure a banner was made,' Hettie adds vaguely, her papery forehead creasing in concentration as she tries to remember what happened to the banner.

'Yes, that's right,' the vicar joins in, walking over towards Hettie and me. 'I was quite young, of course,' he laughs good-naturedly.

Lord Lucan wanders over as well. 'Me too. There *was* a banner, rigged up in the village square for everyone to see. And wasn't there talk of a commemorative stone? It was so long ago that I really can't be sure.' Lord Lucan shakes his head, baffled, as he tries to remember the details.

'Yes, but there just wasn't the money around.' Hettie clasps her hands together.

'Well, I think it's a splendid idea,' the vicar interjects, 'and would certainly set the right mindset for when the judges arrive – they'll see that Tindledale really is an old hand when it comes to putting on a great show. We must find the banner and resurrect it in the village square.'

'And install a proper commemorative stone! It could go next to the war memorial,' Lord Lucan says, pushing his shirt sleeves up enthusiastically.

'Absolutely, and one for the civic pride committee to take on, I reckon – six weeks is ample time to raise the funds for a carved stone,' I venture boldly. I actually have no idea how much carved stones cost, but it has to be worth a go, and I can see it now – a lovely picture of the stone in the centre of the Sunday supplement piece all about Tindledale, the village that has won again, fifty years after the previous triumph!

'And with plenty of space on the stone to add on this year's victory!' Pete gives the general a smarmy smile.

'I could help out with supplying the stone – cost price, and the carving for free,' the owner of the garden centre offers.

A woman I've not seen before is walking towards the crowd; willowy and beautiful, she's wearing floaty yoga clothes with a long, pretty cotton scarf trailing from her neck. She looks apprehensive, so I raise a welcoming hand to wave her over, but she doesn't see me and instead turns around and walks back into the pub. And, I'm not embarrassed to say, hmm, well . . . maybe I am a little, that the first thought that pops into my head is: I wonder if she has any children? I'm so determined to keep my school open that I'm half tempted to race after her like some kind of crazy looper to find out, and quite possibly insist that she brings them to my school, right away, so the inspectors can see that, actually, numbers aren't dwindling at all. Ha! But she's gone. Never mind. I make a mental note to approach her next time I see her around the village . . . She must be the lucky Mrs Cavendish with the charming, hot husband, as – apart from Dan Wright and the general – I've not heard of any other new people in the village, so I'm guessing she must be.

'So, how about a show of hands,' I say, turning my attention back to the meeting, where everyone is buzzing now, full of enthusiasm and benevolence. This is more like it; this is how we usually do things in Tindledale: together and with good grace. 'Thank you.' One of the parish councillors hands me the key to the tiny village notice board on the wall outside the village store.

Half an hour later, and we've divvied up the villagers into three committees, with various people taking charge of things that are particularly important to them. Everyone seems to understand that putting on a truly great show will be a wonderful thing for Tindledale, boosting local businesses and, hopefully, school numbers too. For the first time since Jack left for uni, I am fully focused on my life and future again, and I can't wait to get started on the preparations for the Great Village Show.

Four

Jessie pulled down the sleeves of her blouse to protect her arms, before pushing the brambles away from the door of the old, ramshackle potting shed at the far end of her new garden, and allowed herself a moment of quiet contemplation. She had hoped moving to Tindledale would be a fresh start for them all, and an opportunity to put London, in particular, Sam, her first love, out of her mind. But it hadn't been as simple as that. Sebastian had gone back on his word and insisted they consider St Cuthbert's, the private school on the outskirts of Tindledale, before making a final decision – so now Jessie felt deflated, duped even, that her wishes hadn't been taken seriously.

'Jessicaaaaaa!' Jessie smarted as she always did when Sebastian called her by her full name. He was the only one who did, despite knowing that she hated it. 'JESSICA. Where are you?' Sebastian thundered from the back door of the farmhouse. 'What the hell are you doing?' He strode through the long grass towards her and Jessie felt her back constrict on realising that Sebastian was in one of his moods. He came to a halt in front of her, glowering as he took the top of her arm and pulled her towards him. Jessie knew better than to antagonise him when he was like this, so opted for the position of least resistance and slipped her free arm around his waist.

'Exploring, darling. I thought I'd see what was hidden inside this old shed . . .' Jessie painted on her usual smile, which in turn had the usual effect on Sebastian; he released his grip on her arm and pointed to his cheek for a kiss. Jessie duly obliged and did as she was told. Anything to keep the peace. She really couldn't face another scene, not today, not when the sun was shining and the air was infused with birdsong and jasmine, and – most importantly – the children were happy, bouncing around on the new super-sized trampoline that Sebastian had installed soon after they arrived in Tindledale. Another of his grand gestures, this time to make up for having rehomed Banjo, their beloved cat, without warning shortly before the move. For compassionate reasons, he had claimed, saying Banjo would be confused so far away from London. But Jessie knew Sebastian hated cats, having merely tolerated Banjo on account of his mother buying the kitten as a surprise gift for the triplets. Sebastian was holding out to inherit her vast estate, so liked to keep his mother sweet, hence he hadn't protested when Banjo's adorable black fluffy head had popped out of the cardboard box on Christmas Day and the triplets had whooped with joy.

Jessie smiled fondly at the memory, but then tensed on remembering how heartbroken Millie, Max and Olivia had been on finding out that Banjo had 'been left behind'. They were in the car, following behind the removal van, when Jessie had realised that Banjo's crate wasn't in the boot. But it was too late by then; Sebastian refused to turn back and wouldn't even reveal the name of the neighbour he'd given Banjo to. Jessie had tried to console the children who were crying in the back seat, but then Sebastian had dug the fingertips of his left hand into her thigh, leaving a little row of bruises as he berated her for mollycoddling them. They had all spent the rest of the journey in tense silence.

'Well, stop it and listen to me.' Sebastian let out a long puff of air. 'It seems you'll be getting your own way after all . . . St Cuthbert's called.'

'Oh?' Jessie said, purposely making it sound vague, knowing better than to show delight on hearing that perhaps her wish was coming to fruition after all.

'Full up!' Sebastian pulled a face. 'Can you believe it? The only prep school for miles around and they don't have space for three more. It's preposterous. I knew I should have registered them in utero.' Sebastian shook his head and shoved his hands deep into his pinstripe trouser pockets.

'Never mind, darling. You didn't know then that we would be living here; it really can't be helped,' Jessie soothed, figuring a show of solidarity and understanding was exactly what was required right now.

'Hmm, true! Well, perhaps it's for the best in any case, St Cuthbert's doesn't even feature in the "Top 100 Best Schools Guide", which is exactly what I told them! *And* that if they ever do manage to achieve such status, which I imagine to be highly unlikely, then perhaps we'll reconsider!' Sebastian postured, while Jessie withered inwardly, figuring it wouldn't bode well for them integrating successfully into village life. Word got around rapidly in small communities, Jessie knew that, and the last thing she wanted was to be known as the wife of the rude banker down from London.

Jessie really wanted to fit in, make new friends and

be community-spirited, and the Great Village Show was the perfect opportunity for her to do so. She'd had every intention of going along to the meeting in the Duck & Puddle pub garden – Sebastian had been working late in London, so had chosen to stay in the company flat – and with her dad visiting overnight to see the new house and help with the unpacking and the childcare, Jessie had a rare opportunity to venture out on her own. But it had been harder than she had anticipated, with so many people there. And then when the pretty, friendly-looking woman chairing the meeting had waved her over to join them, Jessie had panicked. With all eyes on her and the bruises on her thigh, not to mention the scrape on her back from a previous altercation, a continuous reminder of how inadequate and raw she felt for not having the courage to call Sebastian out and challenge him, the little confidence left in Jessie had waned entirely.

'So what are we going to do then?' Jessie asked tentatively, glancing at the grass. Yes, far better to let Sebastian feel in charge; let him think a change of plan was his idea.

'Well you need to get them into the village school, of course!' Sebastian instructed. 'And sharpish, because it seems a state school education is de rigueur these days, according to today's *FT*.' He paused to do quote signs in the air. 'Yes, "state till eight", it said, so before you know it, every bugger will be jumping on the bandwagon . . .'

'Is it really?' Jessie replied carefully, with just the right amount of surprise in her voice.

'Indeed. So don't fuck it up and forget or they'll miss out on that too. I'm not paying for home tutors. Not after the fortune I forked out on that useless Norland nanny.' Sebastian turned to walk away, leaving Jessie with an enormous sense of satisfaction as she ducked down out of sight behind the potting shed to do a silent high five. And it had never been Jessie's wish to employ a nanny, anyway. Sebastian had selected her, saying it was the norm in the section of society that he came from, further highlighting the chasmic difference in their backgrounds. Jessie had been relieved when the nanny had declined to come to Tindledale with them.

As Jessie was inwardly celebrating this unexpected triumph, something caught her eye – a white wooden object, covered in mud. After quickly checking over her shoulder to ensure the triplets were still happy and OK inside the safety net of the trampoline, Jessie pulled on her gardening gloves and carefully reached in amongst the overgrown mass of stinging nettles.

A hive!

Jessie's heart lifted even higher as she brushed away the worst of the grime, making a promise to herself to try again to get involved in village life. Perhaps she could offer to make some honey? If she got a move on she could harvest a small batch of jars to sell at the village show. All she needed was to catch a swarm, and she could do that with her eyes closed – well, perhaps not like that exactly, but certainly with a net curtain, a dustpan brush and a cardboard box, she recalled, having achieved this feat as a teenager when a swarm descended on the village fete and she had rounded up the bees before gently coaxing them into the box and taking them home to live in one of her hives, earning herself a hearty round of applause from the gathered crowd.

With Sebastian off to Zurich soon for a few months, she wouldn't have to put up with his mood swings, and then when the children joined the village school, Jessie would meet new people. Maybe there'd be a friend she could confide in, someone to talk to about her sham of a marriage, an ally to draw strength from. Jessie had contemplated a life without Sebastian, but she knew with absolute certainty that he would never let her take the children, and she refused to leave them alone with him. So, for now, she had no option other than to try to make a happy life for herself and the children.

Jessie took a deep breath and wandered over to the trampoline to show the children the hive, pondering that perhaps coming to Tindledale really was the perfect move after all.

Five

The following morning, Saturday, and I'm up early and raring to go. I'm already in the High Street, having enjoyed a very pleasant stroll in the magnificent morning sun, taking the long route round past the pond and village green, stopping to offload my leftover stale bread for the greedy geese and ducks, something I haven't done since Jack was a little boy, but only because Jack's enormous appetite means there just hasn't been any leftover food in my house for quite some time. But that's all changed, and the ducks can now enjoy the remnants of a large seeded bloomer from the Tindledale bakery.

I'm about to pop into all of the shops to make sure they're happy about committing to the tasks we agreed last night – such as making sure the display windows are pristine, and in keeping with the 'Traditional Tindledale' theme that we've decided on for this year's show. And to see if there's anything I can do to help, as apart from my current cross-stitch project, and of course my school work and my plan for impressing the inspectors, I reckon I could still spare some time on Sundays when my cottage feels emptiest and I miss Jack the most. I've already roped in Hettie and Sybs to run some crafting classes with my children, having spoken to them last night after the meeting, and they were more than happy to help out.

I'm also trying to find someone to tend to the little lawn area in the village square, and perhaps the village green. I saw earlier that the duck pond certainly needs attention; there's algae and weeds sprouting at all angles on the farthest side – which reminds me, the dilapidated two-berth caravan in the station car park has to go. With the roof sawn off and the brambles growing inside 'left to nature', it's an eyesore, and hardly the best first impression of Tindledale should one of the judges choose to arrive by train – although, that seems a bit unlikely, as the walk from the station to the village is over two miles, up a very steep and winding hill, so unless they're lucky enough to time it right and hop into Tommy Prendergast's taxi after he's dropped some-body off – hmm, highly unlikely, as he only does taxi runs after four p.m. when the village store has closed, but anyway, best not to risk it: perhaps Pete can tow the caravan away with his tractor? I pull out my pad to make a note.

I've made up a poster listing the dates, times and venues for all of the meetings – the Creative committee is going to meet in Hettie's House of Haberdashery; they have lots of sofas and chairs in there and, to be honest, it's where most of the creatively minded villagers tend to spend most of their free time in any case, doing the varied array of classes that Sybs and Hettie run. The Community committee are going to meet in the Duck & Puddle and the Civic committee has opted to use the village hall. I've made sure my phone number and email address is on the poster, too, just in case there are other villagers that couldn't make last night's meeting but still want to get involved – the more the merrier, I say! And I've been thinking about my conversation with Lawrence, and have come up with another idea, a triple whammy – something that will not only impress the school inspectors, and help Lawrence's B&B business, but also boost our chances on show day, so I'm heading over to the Country Club this afternoon.

I've just finished pinning the poster to the notice board, when Taylor from Paws Pet Parlour, on the other side of the High Street, appears at my side.

'Hi Miss Singer,' she grins, bobbing from one foot to the other, while fiddling with a yarnbombed bollard which I have to say looks very pretty indeed now that it's been made to look like a giant knitted daffodil complete with long green knitted petals protruding jauntily on wire stems. Very original and inventive.

'Hi Taylor, how are you?' I ask, 'and you know, you can call me Meg these days – it's a long time since you were a pupil at my school.' I tilt my head to one side and smile kindly. I know I shouldn't have favourites, but Taylor was such a lovely schoolgirl, funny and kind, keen and willing to learn, even though she was also quite rebellious at times too, always up to some prank or another. I remember one time she tipped a pot of glitter into the classroom fish tank so we had to do an emergency goldfish evacuation. Taylor loves animals, and was so upset that she cried herself to sleep that night – according to her mum, Amber. And then she came into school the following day with an apology card covered in stickers of Nemo that she had made herself. I still have it pinned to the cork board on the wall in my office.

'Ahh, sorry Miss Sing—, oops, sorry, *Meg*. Feels weird saying Meg,' she grins and I laugh. 'Um, I just wondered how Jack was doing?'

'Oh,' I say, a little taken aback as I wasn't aware that they were friends. As if hearing my thoughts, Taylor adds,

'We played pool together in the Duck & Puddle, last time he was home.' And I'm sure I spot a flush in her cheeks. 'I let him win,' she shrugs, and sweeps her long Elsa-from-*Frozen*-style plait over her shoulder, clearly smitten.

'Well, um, that was very kind of you.' I lean towards her and lower my voice. 'He can get very huffy if he loses a game,' I say conspiratorially. Taylor laughs and pats my arm like we're best friends, and it warms my heart; for a moment I'm reminded of Jack, tapping my arm to get my attention – and then I realise that physical contact is one of the main things I miss most about him not being here, in addition to his smile and jokes and advice on just about everything, from dating to what the latest street-slang words actually mean, to trying to goad me into doing impressions of rappers so he can roll around on the floor laughing at me. Taylor smiles and inspects her paw-print-patterned acrylic nails before asking again how Jack is. 'He seemed fine, last time we spoke,' I reply, curious to know why she's enquiring, and she seems very insistent on finding out – I make a mental note to ask Jack next time he calls.

'Good. That's really good,' Taylor says, distractedly, but she seems vacant now, nervous even. 'Um,' she hesitates. 'Sorry, I . . .' Her voice fades.

'Are you OK, Taylor?'

'Yes . . . I just wondered if . . . um, that when you next talk to him, if you could ask him to get in touch with me, please? It's quite important – I've messaged him but he hasn't replied.' She looks at her hands and my heart goes out to her. An unrequited crush is always quite devastating, but especially so when you're only seventeen years old. I know I'm biased, but Jack is a very good-looking boy, all dark curly hair and gypsy eyes, takes after his dad, whose grandmother was a Romany gypsy, and Taylor isn't the first girl to go gaga over Jack. Taylor pulls her long cardy closer around herself before folding her arms as if shielding her body. Oh dear, she's got it bad. She's clearly feeling vulnerable.

'Sure, I can do that,' I smile.

'Oh would you?' Taylor beams. 'That would be awesome!'

*

A couple of hours later, and I'm sitting in Kitty's tearoom, having already polished off a delicious round of locally sourced cheese and homemade chutney sandwiches, and now have a perfectly plump huffkin bun in front of me, with caramelised cherries cascading from the hole in the centre, and a mug of hot chocolate with a very generous swirl of marshmallow-topped squirty cream on top.

'What do you reckon?' It's Kitty, and after wiping her hands on her ditsy floral-print apron, she points to the cake. I slip my almost finished cross-stitch project back inside the cloth shoe bag to keep it clean and free from crumbs, or a possible hot chocolate spillage. I've already had to unstitch part of it three times because I made some silly mistakes with the detailing, so it really is becoming a labour of love and it would be a real shame if it got ruined at this stage when I've very nearly finished it.

'Very impressive! It looks amazing and I bet it tastes as good as it looks too,' I say, smiling up at her.

'I thought I'd get a head start on the Traditional Tindledale theme and practise baking some local favourites so they're perfect for show day.' Kitty dips down in the chair opposite me, her aqua eyes bright with enthusiasm. 'And Ed loved huffkin buns, so it seems right, seeing as it would have been his thirty-third birthday on the eleventh of July.' She glances across at a framed photo on the wall of her late husband, Ed, wearing a khaki uniform and kneeling down with an arm around his military dog, Monty, a gorgeous, shiny black Labrador. Ed was a soldier, killed by a landmine in Afghanistan, and the news came through just a few days before he was due home, the village square having been decorated with bunting and balloons, so we all knew. Well, we all knew Ed in any case, as he grew up in Tindledale, drank in the Duck & Puddle, and played in the cricket team when he was home on leave between tours. It was heartbreaking, seeing poor Kitty, pregnant at the time with her baby girl Teddie, left utterly devastated, her whole world ripped apart. I place my hand over Kitty's and give it a gentle squeeze. She pats the top of my hand with her free one and smiles wistfully. And Teddie is three years old now and truly adorable. I glance over to the big playpen packed with soft toys, Lego and a painting easel, at the back of the café near the door that leads to the flat upstairs where Kitty and Teddie live.

'Can I say hello?' I ask Kitty, giving Teddie a big grin and a wave. She lifts her toy cat in the air and jiggles it around in reply.

'Of course,' Kitty smiles, and walks over to open the playpen gate so Teddie can run out into the café.

A few seconds later, and I'm enjoying a glorious cuddle with Teddie on my lap, giggling along with her as she dabs her chubby finger into the jammy part of the huffkin bun, before popping it in between her little rosebud lips and saying 'Mmm, wuvvly,' over and over. Pressing the tip of my nose down gently into her hair, I draw in the divine smell of Johnson's baby shampoo. It reminds me of Jack when he was this age, so snuggly and loving; he would curl up next to me on the sofa on a Sunday and we'd watch films together and eat popcorn in our pyjamas all day long. Ahh, those were the days. Hard work at times, too, but very special and I really wish they hadn't raced by quite so quickly.

I give Teddie another gentle squeeze, and stroke her hair, before taking a bite of the bun. I break off a chunk for Teddie who opens her little mouth in anticipation. Kitty gives her a look as if to say, 'Come on, you're a big girl now,' to which Teddie responds by taking the piece of bun from my hand and stuffing it into her mouth whole, giving it a couple of chews and swallowing it as fast as she can, clearly eager for more. It makes Kitty and me laugh, which seems to delight Teddie as she throws her little head back and does a big belly laugh before clapping her hands together.

'Well, I'd say you've already mastered the traditional

huffkin bun, if Teddie's testimonial is anything to go by,' I say, in between chewing and swallowing. I take another bite. 'Mmm, this is truly scrumptious,' I add, placing my hand over my mouth to ensure crumbs don't pop out. I can't resist devouring the sweet-tasting doughy delight. 'And the judges are going to love popping in here to try them, as will all the other visitors on show day,' I smile enthusiastically, scanning her tearoom and café – a double-fronted, mullion-windowed shop on the corner of the High Street, central and prominent, with its higgledy-piggledy mix of old dining chairs and tables, and pretty, real china teapots and chintzy cake stands. It's very olde worlde in an appealing way. Coming in here is like stepping back to a bygone era – like much of the rest of the village, I suppose.

'Ahh, do you think so?' Kitty asks, leaning into me, but then her expression changes. 'To be honest, I'm really hoping we'll win the village show competition this year.' She pauses, before dropping her voice. 'Things have been a bit slow so far this summer. I'm usually jam-packed in here with afternoon cream teas by now, but the tourists just aren't coming this year. I didn't like to say anything in front of everyone at the meeting last night . . .' She shakes her head and looks really anxious, so I place my hand over hers again and give it another quick squeeze.

'I'm sure it'll pick up, Kitty,' I smile, keeping my voice light and optimistic. But the smile soon freezes on my face when she whispers, 'But are the rumours true? That the school is going to be closing down?'

A cold chill trickles down my spine followed by a warm, prickly sensation in my hands. I open my mouth and then close it again before coughing to clear my throat, sincerely hoping that Mark hasn't heard about this yet – I should explain to him. Yes, I make a mental note to do so right away as I don't want him to be concerned unnecessarily. Or Lily to be unsettled – she's had enough to cope with and there really is no point in them worrying about something that may never happen, certainly not if I've got anything to do with it. I'm determined to do everything within my power to keep the school open. I push a brave-it-out grin on to my face.

'Um, well . . . Where did you hear that?' I ask, stalling for time while I formulate a proper explanation, but instantly know that it's futile, and that I was naïve to think I could possibly keep the inspectors' visit a secret. Damn them for just appearing out of the blue, worrying and upsetting everyone in the village like this. Kitty looks so anxious – she went to my school too, was a few years behind me, being younger than I am, and is planning on Teddie coming as well. She's friends with some of the school mums, so of course she knows, the whole village probably knows. News like that was never going to wait until Monday. I should have realised and said something last night, as now everyone might be thinking that I've deliberately tried to conceal things. Oh dear.

Kitty looks as if she's just about to answer when the bell above the door jangles, announcing the arrival of another customer. Kitty and I swivel our heads to see who it is.

'Oh, here, let me help you,' Kitty says brightly. She jumps up to hold open the door with an enormous grin on her face, seemingly pushing her woes aside to make her next customer feel warm and welcomed.

'Ooh, hello,' I say, on seeing the woman in the floaty yoga gear from last night, who I'm pretty certain must be the newcomer, Mrs Cavendish, leading three children into the café. The two little girls and a boy all look very nearly school age – about four, I'd say. And I wonder if they're triplets? They certainly have the same fair hair, cornflower-blue eyes and sprinkling of freckles across their noses, just like their mother. Marvellous.

And a very welcome boost to the next academic year's intake. I must let the inspectors know.

'Um, hi,' Mrs Cavendish smiles tentatively, clearly not used to strangers greeting her so warmly. She turns to Kitty. 'Do you have a table for four please?' she asks politely. Kitty smiles kindly before gesturing with her free hand around the near-empty tearoom. Apart from a couple of farmer boys at the corner table who are enjoying the all-day breakfast, I'm the only customer in here.

'Why don't you take that nice big table over there in the window?' Kitty offers, steering the children across the room, while the woman hesitates momentarily before nodding politely and unravelling a pretty purple butterfly print scarf. I wonder where it's from? An expensive shop in London, I imagine; it even has little diamanté studs dotted all over it – I wonder if I could buy one online? 'There you go, I'll bring you some crayons and paper,' Kitty says to the children, who all look mutely at their mother, as if waiting for permission to be excited, and I can't help thinking that it's unusual for children of their age to be quite so pensive. Maybe it's just taking them a little bit of time to adapt to living in a new place where some of us locals have a habit of chatting to newcomers as if they're old friends.

We aren't all wary of strangers – well, I'm certainly not; especially ones with children who, hopefully, will come to my school. Mrs Cavendish is gazing at the floor while twiddling an enormous diamond-encrusted platinum ring. Wow! I don't think I've ever seen an engagement ring as impressive as that; it must have cost a small fortune. 'That would be lovely. Thank you,' Mrs Cavendish says quietly, stowing the scarf in her expensive-looking leather duffel bag. Kitty expertly plumps the cushions on the chairs and quickly tidies the condiments on the table and then hands the woman a menu.

'Can I get you some drinks to start with?' Kitty asks cheerily.

'Oh, um, yes please,' the woman glances apprehensively across at me and I smile, nodding at the big yellow china mug in front of me. 'I can highly recommend the honey and almond hot chocolate, even on a warm day like today.'

There's a short silence. Mrs Cavendish's eyes look watery, as if she's been crying; she swiftly drops her face down to study the menu.

'How about milkshakes for the children?' Kitty quickly says, picking up on the now suddenly awkward atmosphere. The woman nods and mutters 'yes please', absentmindedly, without even looking up from the menu. The children, still mute, stare wide-eyed at Kitty, as if she's a fairy princess waving a magic wand to make all their dreams come true.

Before long Kitty re-emerges from the kitchen area with three tall glasses brimming with swirly cream-topped pink milkshakes scattered with rainbow sprinkles. She places them on the table in front of the children, who each mumble their thanks before taking the straws and tucking in, just as there's a loud 'bang-bang' on the window. I glance up to see who on earth is making such a racket – even the farmer boys have stopped eating to see what's going on. Teddie almost jumps out of her skin and I stroke her back to soothe her as she looks around anxiously for her mum.

A tall, suave-looking man in an expensive grey pinstripe suit is outside gesticulating, pointing at the woman in between tapping his watch and shaking his head. Mrs Cavendish, clearly startled to see him here, quickly dashes outside.

And I have to resist the instinctive urge to go after her.

Because, a few seconds later, the man is gripping her arm. Just a little too tightly. Mrs Cavendish is wincing – or maybe I'm mistaken. It's hard to be sure as the sun is dazzling against the window, making it difficult to see clearly, and she doesn't have her sunglasses on, and her eyes *were* watery and red when she arrived, so maybe she's just squinting. And she clearly knows the man. Maybe he's Mr Cavendish, but if he is, then he certainly doesn't seem very charming right now; in fact I'd go as far as saying that he's being the complete opposite: utterly forbidding. Even though I can't hear what he's saying, it's quite clear from the way he's pointing and getting in her face, as Jack would say, that he's giving her a right telling off. I glance at the farmer boys, who don't seem bothered as they've all resumed eating, and Kitty is soothing Teddie over by her playpen.

I'm not sure what to do. Nobody likes people who interfere and perhaps I'm worrying unnecessarily. I take a sip of my hot chocolate – the children are still enjoying their milkshakes, not even looking out of the window at their mother – yes, I must be reading something into the situation. And, when I take another look, I'm reassured, because the man has both arms around the woman's body, and she's resting her head on his shoulder – I can't see her face, but surely she wouldn't be hugging him if things weren't OK. I let out a little sigh of relief and finish the last of the huffkin bun.

Mrs Cavendish (I assume) returns to the café. She rummages inside her bag before locating a bunch of keys, which she takes back outside. Ahh, so that's what the commotion was all about; he's obviously locked himself out – we've all done that and it sure does induce panic. It all seems to be fine between them now. He's pointing to his cheek, which she stands on tiptoes to kiss, before coming back inside to be with the children, who wave impassively as the man walks away.

Six

I'm on the bus on my way back from the Country Club and we're just about to go past Hettie's House of Haberdashery, so I swivel to the window to see what's going on. The shop looks truly beautiful, bathed in sunshine, with buttery gold miniature sunflowers lining the little path leading up to the front door, and I can see Sybs sitting in a yarnbomb-covered armchair in the window with the rest of the Tindledale Tappers, the local knitting club. Beth, one of my teachers is there, with her classroom assistant, Pearl, and Basil is sprawled out on his usual spot, a padded window seat covered in a flowery print; it's perfect for seeing who's coming and going. Sybs gives me a big wave, knitting needle still in hand . . . and is that a little lemon-coloured bootie hanging from the other needle? I press my nose to the bus window to try and get a better look. Maybe she and Dr Ben are already planning on starting the *big* family that Lawrence mused about. I sure hope so!

Lawrence's is the next house on the lane, so I decide to jump off and call in to share the good news from my meeting with the manager at the Country Club. He is definitely up for doing a deal with Lawrence's B&B. I thought a special weekend pampering package, just like they do at the spa hotel on the industrial estate, would help boost business for Lawrence. He can provide the country cottage escape and the award-winning home-cooked food part of the deal, and the club can do the spa experience. And the manager also instantly saw the benefit of the club doing its bit to help the community by sponsoring the village show, figuring a mention in a national newspaper would be just the thing to entice well-heeled people to sign up for golf membership. He even agreed to let my school children have use of the pool for some much-needed swimming lessons, which is bound to impress the inspectors when I tell them first thing on Monday morning. So it's a win all round.

After stowing my cross stitch away, I stand up and press the bell before making my way downstairs, gripping the handrail to stay upright, as the bus swerves suddenly to avoid an errant peacock from the

Blackwood Farm Estate. The impressive bird is standing proudly in the middle of the road, its iridescent blue and green feathers fanned, the tips wafting nonchalantly in the afternoon breeze. And the peacock is clearly in no hurry to move, so we sit and wait until it eventually struts into a gap in the nearby hedgerow and the bus chugs on before coming to a shuddery halt right at the end of Lawrence's driveway.

'Thanks Don,' I say to the driver – he's been doing this route since I was a little girl, so everyone in Tindledale knows him. I step off the bus, giving him a cheery wave, and start crunching across the gravel parking area and down the long path towards the picturesque black-and-white Tudor beamed cottage with a tall chimney at either end of the thatched roof.

I've just stepped on to the narrow little wooden bridge to cross the stream in Lawrence's front garden, when a man, head bent down, furiously tapping away on a mobile phone, comes barrelling towards me.

'Oh, um,' I start, surprised to note he's making no attempt to move out of my way, despite the fact that I was on the bridge first. But I'm just about to give in, figuring it's the easiest thing to do, and step aside, when his left leg catches on my new, and very lovely Cath Kidston basket – green wicker with a polka-dot fabric interior – making it jolt sharply. He stops moving and tuts overdramatically.

'Well, *excuse me*,' I puff under my breath, before pushing the basket back into the crook of my elbow and turning to walk away. But the man doesn't move.

'*Pardon?*' he grunts, without even bothering to glance up, still mesmerised by his phone.

'I think you mean *sorry?*' I say automatically, in my best teacher voice, but the minute the words are out of my mouth, I wish I could push them straight back in, for two reasons: firstly, this man is not a child – no, he most definitely is not; and secondly, I realise belatedly that he's the celebrity chef Lawrence was telling me about, Dan Wright. I'm sure of it. Much older than he was in the YouTube clip, of course, but with the same unruly black hair and sardonic set to his jaw. I was right, though – he is a spreader; he's taking up the whole bridge with no regard for my personal space. He even has his enormous Timberland-clad foot planted in front of my shoes, blocking my way.

Buuuut, if we want him to open a fine dining restaurant with ten-course tasting menus in Tindledale, which would really help put us on the map and attract new blood with lots of children to the village and ultimately my school, he has to be made to feel welcome . . .

Sooooo, I take a deep breath and think of the greater good and attempt some damage limitation.

'What I actually meant was, that I, um . . .' I fiddle with a stray tendril of hair and flick my eyes away, willing my cheeks to stop flaming, 'err, I meant that I'm sorry,' I just about manage, hating having to apologise when he's the one in the wrong.

'Forget it!' he grumbles distractedly, still staring at his phone.

'Oh,' I say, taken aback by his sheer audacity and lack of grace.

A short, very awkward silence follows. Eventually he gives up on the phone and shoves it inside his jeans pocket.

'Bloody place. How do locals cope?'

'Cope?' I repeat, bemused.

'Yes, cope!' he says irritably. 'You know, being so cut off from the rest of the civilised world?' And it sounds more like a statement than a question. He runs a hand across his beard, which is a little bushier and unkempt than is currently fashionable.

'Um,' I start. Dan actually seems to be waiting for an answer. 'Weeeell, I guess us *locals* manage somehow. Pigeons make very good messengers, and you can't beat a good old-fashioned letter with a stamp on.' I shrug my shoulders in what I hope is a nonchalant way. 'And only last week I was telling all my children about that modern phenomenon, the World Wide Web. Have you heard of it?' I tilt my head to one side, trying not to sound too sarcastic.

'*All your children?*' he says, sounding aghast. He even takes a small step backwards, recoiling, as if imagining a tribe of children, all from different fathers, all making appearances on *Jeremy Kyle* as we sort out our latest spats and feuds. His face is even screwed up now. I can feel myself bristling so I pull my shoulders up to ease the tension.

'School children!' I tell him firmly. 'I'm the acting head teacher at the village school,' I add, just a little too primly, and he actually shrinks his head back a bit and arches his eyebrows, like I'm some kind of wicked witch who's about to give him a hundred lines for being rude. I cough to clear my throat as I straighten my navy bolero cardy, wishing I'd opted now for my usual jeans and stripy T-shirt instead of this shapeless but very comfortable, faded flower-print tea dress and battered old floppy sun hat with sweat stains around the rim that I usually only wear when gardening (I couldn't find my sunglasses so it was better than nothing) which, on reflection, probably makes me look like a scatty old spinster to him, with only her pets to keep her company. And then, to my horror, I spot a selection of Blue's caramel-coloured hairs, stark against the navy wool, clinging to my left shoulder from where I gave him a cuddle this morning, which just confirms my theory.

'Riiiiight.' And he gives me an up-and-down look, before passing judgement, 'Well, that explains it . . .' And I'm perplexed: what does that even mean, *explains it*? I open my mouth to reply, but on second thoughts . . . I close it again, and then pull off the sun hat and shove it sharply inside my basket. What on earth was I thinking, putting that on my head and venturing outside? I really should have gone without. Another short silence ensues, and I take the opportunity to glance at his foot, wondering if he might actually get the hint and move it so I can carry on my way; but no such luck, he's oblivious, so I end up having to say, 'Excuse me,' followed by a loaded look downwards to the wooden panels beneath us.

'Yeah, sure.' He finally moves his big-booted foot out of my way, and then goes to walk on, but hesitates and turns back, as if he's just thought of something else. He rubs his beard again, as though he's trying to remember. Eventually he says, 'What network are you on?' And *please* is what immediately happens inside my head. Honestly! If he were one of my school children, I'd be telling him right now to remember his manners.

'Network?' I arch an eyebrow.

'Yes, mobile phone network.' He sounds exasperated. 'And why are you repeating everything I say?' he adds, creasing his forehead again and shaking his head slightly, as if he's talking to the village idiot. My back bristles some more. He really is the most infuriating man I have ever met, and that is really saying something, after the way Jack's dad carried on.

'I'm not, but if you ask nicely, then I might tell you!' I snip, wishing to God that I had just gone home now and called Lawrence with the news about the Country Club deal, rather than detouring to tell him in person. I feel deflated now. And ridiculous. And Dan Wright is to blame.

'Err . . .' Dan pauses, and now it's his turn to look taken aback. He's clearly not used to people pulling him up on his communication skills – or lack of. Most likely they're all very reverent and just mutter, 'Yes chef', in between doffing their forelocks all the time like they do on that Gordon Ramsay TV programme. An amused smile creeps on to his annoying face as he nods his head really slowly. Ha! Take that, rude celebrity chef man.

'Fair enough,' he says quietly. 'I probably deserved that.' He shrugs and shoves his hands into his pockets.

'You did!' I nod back. 'And just so you know . . . we don't have proper mobile network coverage in the village. Broadband, yes! But mobile phones are pretty much redundant here in Tindledale.'

'*Whaaaat?*' He looks incredulous. 'You're joking! You mean to say that I've been wasting my time wandering around waggling my phone at all angles like some kind of lunatic for absolutely no reason?' He stares at me intently.

'Well, um, yes, I suppose so, if you put it like that.' I smile, despite myself, but have to admit, very frustratingly, that Lawrence was right. Dan is actually quite attractive when he isn't being hostile. There's a glint, a sparkle almost, in his dark, leonine brown eyes; or maybe I'm mistaken and it's mischief or sheer blooming bloody-mindedness. Either way, it's quite appealing. Damn it! And I reckon he probably has a very firm, athletic-looking jawline if he got rid of the silly beard, or at least trimmed it back a bit. He looks like a Viking! A big, chunky, tall Viking – all he needs is a club, a horned helmet and one of those swingy leather skirts. And, on glancing at the gap where his shirt is fluttering open in the warm breeze, I see that he already has the mandatory hairy chest, so maybe he belongs to one of those re-enactment clubs where they meet up in muddy fields and do pretend battles. It's entirely possible.

'Right. Well, in that case, I won't be needing this!' And Dan actually whips out his phone and flips it over the side of the bridge before pushing his hand back into his pocket like a petulant child. He shrugs, like nothing just happened. I stare at him momentarily, unable to believe my own eyes.

'Um! Err . . . what on earth are you doing?' I ask, incredulously, glancing into the stream. But it's too late. The phone lands with a triumphant splash, sending a cascade of water up on to the bank and all over a nearby duck, which quacks disgruntledly before flapping its wings and waddling away.

'Something I should have done a very long time ago.' And a half-smile slips on to his face.

'Oh!' I cough, unsure of what else to say.

Sensing a bit of a thaw in the previously frosty atmosphere, I decide to seize the moment and ask him – soon the village show will be in full swing, so Dan is going to have to get cracking if he *is* planning on opening a restaurant in the village. Plus, I want to talk to him about coming to my school, too – and if I don't ask, I won't get! So, I take a deep breath and decide to go for it, imagining the look on the inspectors' faces when I tell them tomorrow that celebrity chef, Dan Wright, is popping in some time this week to teach Year Six. *Oh yes, didn't you know? That's how we roll out here in the sticks. And the big school in Market Briar doesn't even do domestic science after their teacher left and they weren't able to find a suitable replacement. Ha!* I sort out my hat hair in preparation.

'Can I ask you a question please?' I smile, properly this time.

'Sure,' Dan shrugs.

'Well, I know that you're a chef,' I pause, and he looks at his watch, 'a very famous, award-winning chef of course,' I quickly add, figuring a bit of flattery won't hurt, but he folds his arms. Oh no, I should have realised; he's probably in a hurry – important meetings to do with the new restaurant – so I quickly cut to the chase. 'Is there any chance you could spare a couple of hours to run a cookery class with my school children please?' I widen my grin.

Silence.

'It really would be very much appreciated,' I add, gripping the handle of my basket a little tighter in anticipation of his answer.

Dan's face hardens. He gives me another all-over look before delivering his verdict.

'NO!'

My mouth drops open. He turns around and strides off back into the B&B.

Rude.

I swallow hard and, after reuniting my jaw with the rest of my face, I realise that I was right – initial impressions sure do count. The YouTube clip of him was spot-on. Dan Wright *is* a child! In fact, that's actually an insult to the children in my school, as they wouldn't even *dream* of behaving as badly as he just did. And I hadn't even got to the 'teaming up with Lawrence's B&B for cookery course weekends' idea!

Well, never mind! Tindledale can certainly do without the likes of him. And Lawrence would be making a grave mistake if he so much as contemplated any kind of joint business venture with Dan Wright, because if he's as rude to his customers as he has just been to me, then the B&B would probably end up having to close down completely, when potential guests see its shockingly low rating for hospitality, or severe lack of, on travel sites such as TripAdvisor and the like. And I do an actual harrumph as I bat Blue's veritable bale of hair right off my shoulder.

With my resolve never to speak to Dan Wright ever again firmly in place, I snatch the sun hat back out from my basket, slap it on to my head, tug it down sharply, and storm off back to the lane to wait for the next bus home. I'll call Lawrence later, which is exactly what I should have done in the first place.

Seven

Back home, and after dumping my basket on the window seat in the kitchen and letting Blue out of his cage, I pull open the fridge door and grab the bottle with the last of the elderflower wine in. After bypassing the pouring into a glass part of the process, I pop the cork out, which bounces across the table before landing angrily against the side of my open laptop, and I stick the bottle up to my lips.

As I go to retrieve the cork, my hand brushes over the mouse pad, bringing the screen alive, and just to rankle me further, I'm sure of it, Dan's smirking face pops up. The YouTube clip is still freeze-framed on the screen. I hesitate, my finger hovering, and then curiosity gets the better of me and I click the arrow. The film continues playing. Dan is slouched back on the inter-viewer's sofa, his legs still spread wide. He slings an arm across the back of the sofa. God, could he look any more arrogant and over-entitled . . .? I take another mouthful of wine as I listen to him rattling on about his childhood in Maida Vale, wherever that is, and about how his passion for food started at a very young age when he spent the summer holidays with his grandparents. Ooh, he's laughing now, the audience too . . . some in-joke about his granny ruining him with her dripping on toast and full-fat unpasteurised cream straight from the farm served with plump strawberries from the fields at the back of their garden. I put the wine bottle down and turn up the volume.

'Yes, she's an old-fashioned cook. Sticks to plain and simple "country bumpkin" fare,' Dan smirks, swinging his left foot up on to his right knee, forming a triangle of crassness as he makes silly quote marks with his fingers round the words 'country bumpkin'.

'And plenty of it, I assume . . .' The interviewer laughs.

'What are you saying? That I'm fat?' Dan pats his flat stomach, grinning at the audience.

A woman shouts out, 'No, you're not Dan. You're lovely!' and they all clap; someone even does a wolf whistle.

'Nooo, certainly not. It's just grannies always seem to serve up enormous portions,' the interviewer laughs, before composing himself and asking: 'So, Dan, have you ever considered a permanent move to live in the village with your grandparents – it sounds as if you enjoyed some very idyllic school holidays there?'

'What, move to Tindledale?' Dan clarifies, and I gasp. His grandparents live here? Is that why he's here? Do I know them?

Well, whoever they are, they surely can't be impressed by his attitude. But then I remember what Lawrence said, that this film clip is years old, so they may not even be alive any more. But it does explain his presence in Tindledale – he has a family connection. That's nice, I suppose, but he's going to have a job on his hands if he carries on behaving the way he did with me earlier. The villagers certainly won't entertain such rudeness, and nobody will want to sit under one of his parasols watching the world go by as they pop an olive into their mouth.

Back on the show, Dan is cooking his goose in impressive style: 'God *no*! Not even the discovery of the finest truffles in the Tindledale woods would make me want to live there. School holidays are one thing, but *every day*?' and he pulls a horrified face as he cocks his head to one side, loops an index finger in a circle around his neck, mimicking an imaginary hangman's noose, before lifting his fist up high in the air as if he's pulling a rope tight. He even pokes his tongue out of the side of his mouth for added comedic effect.

And I'm aghast.

So he thinks Tindledale is truly dullsville. That living here is likely to send him so close to the edge that he'd take his own life just to escape the boredom! Ridiculous. And he really is insufferable. And the sooner he goes back to Maida Vale, or whatever wonderfully vibrant and life-affirming place he lives in now, the better! I assume he'll open the new restaurant and stick a manager in to run it for him then, as it's quite clear that he hates being here. Maybe that's why he was so obnoxious to me – he's already losing the will to live. He just can't wait to escape this godforsaken little village and get far, far away!

I slam the laptop shut and sit stunned for a few minutes.

I've just glugged the last of the satisfyingly fizzy liquid and wiped my mouth with the back of my hand when the phone rings. Jack! It might be. I was planning on calling him tomorrow in any case – I'm intrigued to know what's so urgent about him contacting Taylor, but maybe my plan has worked after all. I backed off and now he wants to call his mum. And what wonderful timing, as I sure could do with hearing his cheery voice after Dan's quite frankly terse and belligerent one.

I dump the bottle on the side and dash into the lounge to retrieve the handset from the base.

'Hello.' It's not Jack, but a voice I don't recognise.

'Oh, um, hello. Is that Meg?'

'Yes it is,' I reply, momentarily concerned that something has happened to Jack. But someone from the university wouldn't just casually call and ask for Meg. Surely it would be a more formal request to speak to Miss Singer; my rational, sensible self quickly kicks in.

'Err, I hope you don't mind me calling . . . my name's Jessie, Jessie Cavendish, and I saw your poster on the notice board in the village square with this number to call for information on how to get involved. And well, I'd like to,' there's a short pause, 'um, get involved, that is.'

'Oh hi!' I manage to say, before she carries on.

'I was hoping that I might be able to help out with the village show in some way. I've just moved to Tindledale and I . . .' Her voice falters nervously. I catch sight of my reflection in the mirror above the mantelpiece and quickly rearrange the still-disgruntled scowl on my face. It's not Jessie's fault that Dan is a giant arse. It must be very hard uprooting from everything you know to move to a brand-new place. My mood softens as I walk across the room and sink into the enormous squishy sofa by the window. Gabe, next door, is dead-heading his lipstick-pink roses in the front garden, and when he looks up and across to my cottage, I give him a neighbourly wave.

'Wonderful,' I say to Jessie. 'I think we've already met – well, not properly. I was in the Spotted Pig café in the High Street earlier and I think you popped in with your lovely children.' An ominous silence follows. 'I'm the acting head at the village school,' I quickly add, to plug the gap, and then groan inwardly for oversharing. Oh dear. And she's going to know there's been gossip now, about the newcomer, as how else would I presume to have already met her earlier?

'Err . . .' I can hear her inhaling, 'yes,' she coughs to clear her throat now, 'yes, that's right, we were there earlier. Were you the lady who recommended the hot chocolate?'

'Yes, that's right.' Ahh, so she did hear me. 'And sorry if I was intruding, I was just . . .' I let my voice fade, figuring it best not to mention her seemingly vacant demeanour, or indeed her watery eyes. A short silence follows.

'I'm very sorry about my husband . . .' There's another short silence. 'For scaring your little girl like that. He,

126

err, is under a lot of pressure . . . with his work and stuff.' Jessie sounds anxious.

'Oh, Teddie isn't my little girl. No, she's Kitty's daughter, the woman who owns the café.'

'Ahh, I see. Well, I had better go back and apologise to her then.' And I can't help wondering why, if it's such a big deal, her husband isn't doing the apologising.

'I'm sure there's no need. Teddie just jumped when he banged on the window, that's all,' and not wanting Jessie to be as concerned about it as she sounds, I swiftly decide to change the subject. 'So how are you all settling in to the village?'

'Oh, yes, good, thank you. The children and I are enjoying finding our way around. And everyone has been so friendly and welcoming.'

'That's nice,' I say, and then without thinking I add, 'and I hope your husband is settling in well too?'

'Um, yes,' she says, not elaborating further, and then immediately gets back to the purpose of her call. 'I'd like to help out with the show if I can. I thought it might be a good opportunity to get to know some people in the village.'

'Yes, we'd love to have you on board. There really isn't very much time, so any help you can offer would be very much appreciated. What did you have in mind?'

'Oh, I hadn't really got that far . . .' There's a short silence and I'm wondering about suggesting she comes along to the next meeting with me – I could introduce her and we could take it from there – when she continues, 'I used to keep bees back in the day. Perhaps I could do a talk about that . . . although I'm sure you already have someone in the village who makes honey in any case. I probably shouldn't intrude.' She laughs nervously.

'That's an excellent idea, and quite coincidental . . .' I say encouragingly

'Oh, why's that?' Jessie asks.

'Your farmhouse! The old boy, Victor, who used to live there – he kept bees too.'

'Really? How lovely, and explains the old hive that I found behind the potting shed,' she says, sounding brighter already.

'Yes, he's long gone now, of course, died ages ago. The farmhouse was empty for a number of years until his family finally sorted out the probate and decided to renovate it and make it lovely, all ready for you to live in.' I smile, remembering when I was in The Spotted Pig café one time, several months ago, and a group of school mums on the next table were huddled around an iPad, having found the house on Rightmove. I caught sight of some of the pictures, and it really is a beautiful home. Jessie is very lucky indeed. I then overheard the mums saying, 'It's all granite counters and solid oak flooring with a master bedroom suite *and* a walk-in dressing room.' They were very in awe of whoever bought the house, seemingly having it all!

'Sounds interesting!' Jessie says. 'I'd love to hear more about the history of this house,' she adds enthusiastically, but then I hear a muffled sound as if she has her hand over the phone. Maybe one of the children is after something. Jack always used to do that – he'd be playing nicely, but the minute I picked up the phone he'd be all over me, patting my leg and bellowing for something or another, or jumping on the sofa when he knew very well that he shouldn't, just to monopolise my attention. But this is different, I can hear a man's voice – Mr Cavendish, I assume, and he's shouting. Then there's a soft, thudding sound and his voice is quite clear, 'How many times have I told you?' Then silence. 'The car is coming in twenty minutes!' He must be telling one of the children off . . . surely he doesn't talk to Jessie in this way? I wait patiently and then Jessie is back on the line. 'Sorry.' But she offers no explanation. I cough to clear my throat and carry on the conversation.

'Oh, um, where were we?' I ask, feeling a bit flummoxed.

'You were telling me about the house,' she recaps, quietly.

'Ahh, yes. Well I'd be happy to tell you what I know, and I could put you in touch with Mrs Pocket. She's the historian in Tindledale and has charted Tindledale right back to the Domesday Book, so I'm sure she'll know all about your farmhouse.'

'Thank you. I'd like that very much.'

And then I have an idea.

'Great. Can I ask a favour please?' I start, not wanting to make the same mistake that I made earlier with Dan, by diving in too quickly.

'Sure,' she says, pleasantly.

'How would you feel about popping into my school? Maybe do a short talk about keeping bees for the children?' Silence follows. Oh no, I hope she isn't going to decline like Dan did.

'Ooh, um, yes, I could do that,' she says, and then asks, 'But would you mind if I bring the triplets along? They won't be any bother; it's just that I don't have any childcare in place yet, and—'

'Of course not. Please do,' I reply enthusiastically and then, remembering my conversation with Lawrence, I add, 'we're doing a teddy bears' picnic on Wednesday – the perfect time to explain how honey is made. Maybe you could do the talk then, and your three children would be most welcome to join in. How old are they?'

'Four, five in October.'

'Lovely, so they'll be starting school in September? My village school?' I probe, mentally crossing my fingers.

'Yes, I'm really hoping so . . . but it all depends on . . .' Jessie pauses. 'My husband said . . .' Her voice wavers before trailing off. And then she surprises me again. 'Do you have space for three more? I know it can be tricky with triplets; it took me ages to find a nursery in London for them . . . the good ones get booked up years in advance,' she sighs, and I'm staggered, as I had no idea competition was *that* fierce for places in the big cities. All the more reason for Tindledale to put on a good show and entice people away from all that.

'Oh, I'm sure we can squeeze them in,' I say in an unashamedly breezy voice, but then immediately think, what if the school does have to close? Oh dear, it's such a mess. I really need clarification from the inspectors, and soon. People need to know what's happening now, not at the end of the academic year.

'Really? Well, that would be wonderful. I've been meaning to organise it all, but what with the move, and um . . .' Jessie pauses and I can hear her letting out a long breath, as if she's really stressed, 'err, every-thing else,' she continues.

'Well, not to worry. I can help you sort it all out,' I assure her, hoping she's OK. Moving house can be such a difficult time, it's no wonder she's feeling the pressure. But I feel bad now, I really shouldn't have added to her burden by asking her to do a talk about bees for my children.

'Great. Can I ask you about something else, please?' and she sounds more relaxed now, more down to earth too. Oh well, maybe I've got it wrong.

'Sure. I'm happy to help if I can,' I say brightly, waving at the window again as Gabe lifts a trowel in the air to signify that he's finished his gardening for the day. Vicky appears on the footpath with a mug of tea and a packet of custard cream biscuits for him. He gives her a kiss on the lips as she hands him the mug. Ahh, they're such a lovely couple, but sadly no children yet, and not for want of trying, Vicky had her fourth miscarriage last Christmas and it was terribly sad; she had just got past the three-month stage and was tentatively beginning to believe it would happen this time. She had even asked if I might do a cross-stitch sampler for the baby's bedroom, which Gabe had started decorating.

I inhale sharply and shift my focus back to Jessie.

'I heard that there was a knitting group in the village – do you know anything about it? Like, who I should contact about joining?' she asks.

'Oooh yes, the Tindledale Tappers, they meet in Hettie's House of Haberdashery. It's a little way out of the village, but very popular; in fact it's not far from you – just along the lane, on the way to the Blackwood Farm Estate. They run all sorts of crafting classes as well and, to be honest, the shop has become a bit of a social hub recently. Some people just pop in for a cup of tea and a chat . . . a gossip, and to buy a gift or whatever, not to do any actual craftwork,' I laugh, remembering the last time I was there for the cross-stitch class. There was barely room to swing a small feral farm cat, there were that many of us squeezed on to the sofas and armchairs. Sybs even had to turf a very disgruntled Basil off his favourite spot on the window seat to make room for Marigold, who was standing stoically, trying to be a martyr, until her sciatica kicked in. 'I'm sure you would be made to feel very welcome. Just call in whenever you're passing and ask to talk to Sybs – she's the manager.'

'Oh, that sounds perfect, thank you. Maybe I'll sign up for a class too . . . as soon as I have some proper childcare in place.' And I'm sure I hear her sighing again.

'Well, how about bringing the triplets to the nursery? It's attached to my school, so it'll be the perfect opportunity for them to meet the other children from the village, especially as some of them will be in their class come September,' I say, hoping she doesn't pick up on the uncertainty in my voice.

I shall have to get some answers from the inspectors or, better still, I'll call the council and insist on talking to the decision-makers. I might even get on the bus to Market Briar and go into their offices. Ha! They can hardly keep me waiting around if I'm standing right there in front of them. And then my imagination spirals – I could stage a sit-in, force them to give me more time to show what Tindledale and my lovely little school is all about – or persuade them to at least wait until after the village show. If we make it into the top ten, it'll have a massive impact, I'm convinced of it.

'Can I just do that?' Jessie asks.

'Sure. Pop into school tomorrow and ask for me, and then I'll introduce you to Becky. She runs the nursery.'

'Wonderful. And thanks so much. I'm so pleased I called you now,' and she sounds really relieved. 'So, getting back to the village show – would it be OK just to turn up for that too, do you think?' and the anxiety in her voice is back once more. She sounds reluctant to do this, which I guess is perfectly understandable. I remember Jack telling me about the time when Sybs first arrived in Tindledale – he was doing a shift collecting glasses in the Duck & Puddle and she staggered in through the door covered in snow, dragging an enormous wheelie suitcase, and everyone stopped and stared for a good two minutes at least. Typical Tindledale villagers, they can be very wary of newcomers until they get to know you. But I've instantly warmed to Jessie, even though there's something about her that I can't quite put my finger on. I'm sure we could be friends. And didn't Lawrence say that I needed to broaden my horizons? Well, here's my chance to do just that and be a good neighbour.

'We could go together if you like,' I suggest, and there's a short pause. 'Why don't we meet outside the pub? There's a meeting on Friday, it starts at six, so how about I see you just before then by the benches opposite – near the duck pond?' I finish.

'Oh yes, I know. I took the triplets there to feed the ducks. It brought back such lovely memories . . .' Her voice fades.

'Memories?' I venture. I'm intrigued to find out a little bit more about her.

'Yes, I grew up in a village – quite similar to Tindledale, it was. My mum used to take me to the pond near the village green with a hunk of stale bread under my arm. And we always had such a good time.'

'Mine did too!' I tell her. 'How did you come to be living in London then?'

'My husband is the Londoner,' she tells me.

'I see. But he came to his senses then?' I laugh, but Jessie doesn't join in.

'Does your husband work near here then?' I continue, wondering if I've offended her, insulted her husband somehow. Oh dear. I push a chunk of hair back behind my ear and plough on, 'Sorry, I don't mean to be nosey . . .'

'No, it's fine, really . . .' she says graciously. 'My husband is abroad for a lot of the time. Zurich, mainly; he works for a Swiss bank.'

'Oooh, that sounds exciting. Does he bring you back lots of chocolate?' I ask her, that being the first thing that springs to mind when I think of Switzerland.

'I'd love to go to the meeting with you,' she says, completely sidestepping my question. 'That would be wonderful, if you're sure?'

'Um, yes,' I say firmly, still feeling a bit thrown by the swerve in conversation. 'Absolutely.'

'Oh, but what about the children? I'm guessing the nursery is closed at that time,' and Jessie actually laughs – it's a soft, short laugh, but a laugh nonetheless.

'Oh bring the triplets with you – everyone else brings their children.' I laugh too. 'They can bounce on the inflatable castle with all the other children from the village.'

'Thank you! In that case I shall really look forward to it. And I'll be sure to pop into the school tomorrow to see Becky.'

I smile as I put the phone down, pleased to have done my good deed for the day and feeling much better than I had earlier. I was right – Tindledale doesn't need the likes of egotistical celebrity chefs. Jessie and her triplets are much more the type of people the village needs – and she's obviously making an effort to get involved in village life and help the community. It's more than can be said for Dan Wright – huge hypocrite that he is. Coming here to open a restaurant, when he absolutely hates Tindledale! Well, it's not on, and I fully intend on telling him so next time I have the misfortune of bumping into him!

Eight

Feeling buoyed up after going for it and making the call, Jessie smiled and pondered on the amazing difference being involved in the Great Village Show was about to make to her and the children's lives. She loved the idea of the teddy bears' picnic in the woods as well – talking about bees in a rural idyll would really make her feel the way she used to, growing up in the countryside – and such a wonderful experience for the children to enjoy too. And Meg sounded so lovely, warm and welcoming, and it was going to be so much easier walking into the meeting with a friendly face beside her – the acting head teacher, no less. Jessie knew how village life worked, and when the villagers saw her, the newcomer, with a longstanding Tindledale resident, they were bound to make her feel welcome.

Jessie glowed as she pencilled 'Village Show meeting'

into Friday's slot on her kitchen wall calendar after placing the phone back on its base.

'About time!' Sebastian appeared back in the kitchen doorway. 'Only ten minutes now until the car comes! And who were you talking to?' he grilled her, tugging at the sleeves of his turquoise cotton shirt in an overly dramatic way. Jessie opened her mouth to reply, but Sebastian battled on, huffing and puffing as he inspected the sleeves once more. 'It's no good. This shirt looks like a used dishrag and hardly a good first impression for me to give to the new CEO in Zurich. Are they all like this?' And he strode over to the neatly folded pile of shirts on the central marble island and started rifling through, shaking each shirt out in turn to scrutinise it.

Jessie inhaled sharply, determined to hold on to her upbeat mood, but it quickly dissipated when Sebastian dumped two of the shirts back in the laundry basket on the floor beside the ironing board.

'They need doing again.'

'*Please*,' Jessie muttered to herself, flicking the radio back on so the music masked her voice, before lifting the first shirt on to the ironing board as Sebastian went to walk out of the kitchen. Ten more minutes! That was all. And he'd be on his way to the airport, and then Jessie could relax and really get on with integrating into village life and making everything nice for her and the children.

Jessie allowed herself a small smile as she carefully poured more water into the steam iron, wondering if Sam would call her again this evening. She really hoped so – chatting to him gave her courage; made her feel strong, and much more like her old self. And with Sebastian so far away in Switzerland, it would give her some much-needed space to work everything out in her head – work out how she really felt about Sam and everything that had happened since he had come back into her life, now refusing to give up on her.

'What's this?' Sebastian's voice cut through her thoughts. Jessie turned to see him tapping an index finger on the wall calendar.

'Oh, the village show . . . there's a meeting on Friday evening, so I thought I'd pop along and see if I can get involved,' she said cautiously.

'Get involved!' he replied, incredulously. 'What on earth for?'

'Um, well, I thought it would be a good way for us to make new friends . . .' Jessie pressed the button on the iron to release the steam and smoothed out the sleeve of the first shirt.

'And what about the children?'

'They can come along too. There's a bouncy castle and—' Jessie stopped talking as Sebastian silenced her with a raised palm, standing squarely in front of her.

'Seems you have it all worked out,' he stated, staring at the ironing board between them.

'The head teacher at the village school invited me to go along with her, so we're going to meet outside the pub,' Jessie replied, hoping this might appease him, seeing as it would also be the perfect opportunity to find out if there were three spaces for the triplets at her school, but it seemed to have the opposite effect.

'The *pub*?' he expostulated. 'You mean to tell me that you are dragging the children along to a *pub*, on a Friday night, just so you can gossip with your new best friend?'

'Darling, it's not like that,' Jessie started. 'The meeting is in the pub garden; most of the villagers will be there, with their children . . . it's how things are in the countryside,' she quickly explained, and swept the iron over his shirt, taking care to create a sharp crease down the centre of the sleeve, just as he preferred.

'Well, I don't like it, and it's irresponsible. And for the love of God, will you *please* stop ruining my shirts.

Here, I'll show you again,' and Sebastian went to grab the iron from her hand, but Jessie was momentarily distracted when Millie ran into the kitchen, and the tip of the scalding hot iron landed angrily on Jessie's arm.

'Aggggghhhhh,' Jessie shrieked, instinctively shrinking away. Millie stopped running and stood motionless, staring at her parents before promptly bursting into tears and turning to run back the way she had just come. Sebastian bolted after her, leaving Jessie all alone.

As Jessie held her arm under the soothing cold water, she closed her eyes and let a silent tear trickle down the side of her nose as the realisation really sank in. No matter what changes she tried to make, how she tried to make life good for her and the children here in Tindledale, all the time she was married to Sebastian, nothing would ever properly change. Jessie knew she had to break free, but how? What would Sebastian do? Could he really take the children away from her? And, if he did, what if he somehow stopped her from seeing them? What if he sent the triplets off to boarding school, as he had always planned, when they were six years old? What would that do to them? Sebastian said she was too soft on the children, but Jessie loved them, knew them – their foibles, their favourite foods, their funny ways, their fear of the dark, their fondness for a cuddle when they first woke up in the morning . . . she knew everything about the triplets as only their mummy could. But with his finances, not to mention his vast inheritance, which was only a matter of months away now that his mother had been moved to the hospice, Sebastian could afford the very best divorce barrister.

Sam had suggested Jessie seek legal advice of her own, and had even offered to go with her to see a solicitor, to support her, just as a friend. He knew how she felt about being unfaithful, even though Jessie knew Sebastian was having another affair. She had found a receipt folded in amongst his clothes. He was usually more discreet, careful, but Jessie knew exactly what it meant. Maybe she should take it with her to the solicitor – a night in an expensive hotel room with champagne, dinner and breakfast for *two* people was quite conclusive, especially when it was dated for the same evening he had claimed expenses for the overnight stay in the company flat. She knew, because Sebastian's PA had called to clarify the total, and Jessie had overheard him telling her to add on a couple of hundred pounds to 'cover a modest dinner', because he'd had to dine out. So he was also fiddling his business expenses – maybe Jessie could tell that to her solicitor too.

Jessie turned off the tap and felt her face contort into a crumpled grimace, heartbroken that her life had come to this, and then it was all she could do not to laugh – a horrible, sad, desperate laugh on remembering that Sebastian had also told his PA the 'kitchen in the company flat was barely big enough to swing a kitten in', which was ironic, really, given his hatred of cats . . .

Nine

I'm at school in my office. It's almost home time, thankfully. The inspectors have been getting in the way and upsetting all the teachers for most of the week with their constant questions. Why do they need to know how much money Mary spent on toilet tissue for the school loos? Honestly, if it's coming down to the price of a packet of Andrex, then I'll just bulk-buy online, from my own pocket, rather than see them close my school. And they've told me that I really shouldn't be doing the twenty-minute sessions with Archie Armstrong, because I'm not a trained speech therapist. As acting head teacher, my time would be better spent overseeing the running of the school, by which they mean writing reports and filling in forms. This was followed by a sharp intake of breath and a squiggle on a clipboard when the cost of bringing in a properly trained speech therapist was mooted.

Added to which, the parents are up in arms about the possible closure of the school, which is probably a good thing as they can be a very vocal group and it'll put pressure on the council to let us stay open. They want to discuss it properly at the next village show meeting on Friday; as one parent quite rightly pointed out, 'We haven't a hope in hell of putting on the best village show if the heart of our *community*, one of the big three Cs, has been ripped away before our very eyes.'

I'm packing up my bag, when there's a knock on my office door, and before I can walk across the room to open it, the door flies open and Mary dashes towards me with a huge, girlish grin on her sixty-something face. And a very nonchalant-looking Dan Wright is leaning against the doorframe of my office. Oh no! What does he want? My heart sinks.

Mary steps right up close to me, and with her eyes all googly, she mouths, 'He's off the telly!' before giving him a simpering look back over her shoulder.

'I was just leaving,' I say under my breath, reaching for my bag and hoisting it over my shoulder. The last thing I want to do today is have to deal with Dan Wright. I'm just not in the mood for round two. I wanted to make a start on writing the new school newsletter before my cross-stitch class this evening, so the inspectors, and all the parents, can see what wonderful things the children have been up to recently. They've been crafting with Sybs on Monday afternoon (Hettie had to bow out gracefully as someone needed to stay in the haberdashery shop), and she's got them making some kind of tapestry display of Tindledale through the ages – very intriguing and top secret, apparently. The adults aren't allowed to see it until it's finished and the children are beside themselves with excitement about it. And I must remember to mention the most impressive new addition to our curriculum . . . swimming lessons! Years Five and Six had their first one today at the Country Club and it was a phenomenal success. And I'm sure I saw a flicker of a smile on one of the inspectors' faces when I explained why their classrooms were empty this afternoon, *and* at no additional cost to the council. I'm now pondering on how we might raise enough funds for a school minibus, as taking twenty-two children in a walking bus line to catch the actual bus from the stop in the village square, which only runs on the hour every hour, was quite some feat. Especially at this time of year when all the bramble bushes are bulging with blackberries that the children just can't resist picking to eat – popping them into their mouths and covering their fingers and faces in the inky juice.

'But you can't *gooooo*,' Mary exclaims, 'what if Mr Wright wants to do a TV show here in the school? Can you imagine? It would be just like that series Jamie Oliver did about school dinners.'

'I doubt that very much,' I say, far too quickly, and instantly regret it when Mary's face looks so crestfallen. But what is he even doing here in any case? How does Dan know that I work here? And then I remember – I told him! Hmm. Well, he still has no business just turning up, unless he's come to apologise. Maybe that's it. I dump my bag back on the floor and fold my arms in anticipation.

'But he's *Dan Wright*. The famous chef,' Mary gasps in an exaggerated stage whisper, clearly baffled by my attitude.

'Yes, that's right, we've already met. And perhaps you could, err . . .' *What exactly?* I'm not sure what to say – ask her to send him packing, ask her to tell him in no uncertain terms that he isn't welcome here. Or I could tell her that he hates Tindledale, I bet she wouldn't be so impressed by him then. But then I realise that I'm being ridiculous, immature and emotional. It was a run-in, that's all. Adults get off on the wrong foot all the time.

'It might make all the difference if the inspectors see him here – and think the school will be on the telly . . . could be brilliant publicity,' Mary says persuasively, giving me a gentle, covert nudge with her elbow. Ha! If only she knew, but rather than burst her bubble further, I relent.

I cough to clear my throat as I straighten my necklace, a little silver rabbit on a chain that Jack bought for my last birthday, before gesturing towards Dan. I take a deep breath and say,

'OK. He can come in.' And Mary turns and practically hoicks Dan from the doorframe, by slipping her hand inside the crook of his elbow and propelling him towards me.

'Great, thanks love,' he says, patting the back of Mary's hand before extracting it from his arm. *Love? That's a bit familiar.*

'Not at all,' Mary gushes to Dan, clasping her hands together in glee. 'Shall I bring some tea, Meg?' She turns her flushed face towards me, her eyes all sparkly and fluttery.

'Oh no, I don't think that's necessary; I wouldn't want to keep you back late. It's home time,' I say, thinking it's highly unlikely that Dan and I are going to cosy up over a pot of tea – and besides, I know that Mary has Brownies tonight in the village hall – she's Brown Owl – plus she'll want to be getting home to sort out her elderly mother's dinner. She's her carer, so she really has enough to do without waiting on Dan and me too.

'There might be some of Becky's Victoria sponge birthday cake left. I could slice it up for you, if you like,' Mary continues, extra-eagerly, before turning to look at Dan. 'It's a just a shop-bought one, left over from when her daughter popped in at the weekend – she iced it herself – but Becky couldn't manage it all on her own so she brought it into school to share, which is very kind, but some of us need to watch our figures.' And Mary does a jovial pat of her rotund tummy, 'and it won't be up to your exquisite culinary standards of course, Mr Wright, but it's no bother.' She fixes her dazzling smile on to Dan before switching it to me. I open my mouth to reply, but Dan leaps in.

'Your hospitality is very kind, *Mary*. But I've just eaten, so I'll pass, if you don't mind.' And I'm flabbergasted. Who is this well-mannered, attentive man in front of me, kindly managing to remember the clearly besotted school secretary's name? Certainly not the one I bumped into on the little bridge in Lawrence's front garden, that's for sure. I glance at Dan and he looks totally different. He's smiling, warmly and openly, and it makes him look – dare I say it? – quite appealing. Hmm. I glance at the wall clock.

'If you're sure,' Mary breathes reverently before backing out of the room.

As soon as she has closed the door behind her, Dan strides across the room and plonks his bottom on the corner of my desk. He folds his arms in a very casual, relaxed way, clearly comfortable in his own skin. So why then does he have this stifled anger thing going on?

'Err, excuse me, was there something I can help you with?' I ask, and then immediately wonder why I sound so prim again, just like Mrs Pocket, all of a sudden. I actually think I may have arched an eyebrow, too, just to complete my scary teacher face. I turn away and pretend to be busy rummaging in my cloth school bag. It's Dan, the effect he has on me; his demeanour is very . . . confident, gregarious, larger than life. It makes me feel quite guarded – even a little intimidated, perhaps.

'There's no rush. I'll wait for you to find whatever it is you're searching for,' and he gestures with his head towards my bag. There's an amused smile on his face.

'Sorry, have I got a leaf in my hair or something?' I can't believe I just said that, but why is he looking at me in this way, as if he's about to burst into a fit of uncontrollable laughter?

'A leaf?' he repeats, pulling a face of confusion. There's a short silence before he adds, 'Why? Do you often have leaves in your hair?'

'No! Of course not.' I stop rummaging and pat my hair, just to be sure, as it can actually be a hazard when cycling around country lanes, especially on a windy, autumnal day – I once found part of a prickly conker shell tangled up in my ponytail.

'Why did you say it then?' He tilts his head to one side.

'Because there's obviously something amusing you!'

'Is that so?' The corners of his mouth tilt upwards.

'I don't know, you tell me? You're the one sitting on my desk with a daft grin on your face . . . so I just assumed . . .' I place a hand on my hip, wishing I had stuck to my guns and gone home now.

'Oh, well, that's very nice! Charming indeed.' He laughs. 'I came here to tell you that I've been thinking about your request, and to say that maybe I could help out after all . . . Why not? Kids love me.' He does a big shrug, holding up his palms to emphasise his claim, 'and it would certainly keep my manager happy . . .' He stands up and studies the swirly pattern on the carpet. 'It would need to be kept hush-hush of course, no publicity. You know, no pictures on the school website, talking to the media, or any of that stuff. My people would want it all contained. They like to oversee everything. Control it all.' Dan shakes his head before rubbing his beard, and I can't tell if this is really him talking or a pre-rehearsed persona. It's weird. Like he's playing a part, almost.

'Pardon?' I crease my forehead.

'Which bit?' He looks up and fixes his leonine brown eyes on me. I feel compelled to glance away.

'What are you talking about?' I ask, now feeling infuriated by him all over again.

'A cookery class for the kids. Here's my card – give Pia a call and she'll sort it all out.' He hands me a cream-coloured business card.

'Pia?'

'My manager!' Dan says it as if it's the most widely known fact in the Western world. I take the card and turn it over a few times before going to hand it back to him. 'What's up?' he says, standing up and pushing his hands into his jeans pockets.

'I'd rather not call Pia.' I pull a face, but then stop talking, as Dan has his head thrown back and is laughing hard. 'What's so amusing now?' I ask, placing the card on my desk.

'You! You're hilarious.'

'Oh?' I say, a little wounded. I can't tell if he's laughing at me or with me.

'Yep. Truth be told, Pia scares the crap out of me too!' And he laughs some more.

'Um, no, I didn't mean . . .' I shake my head.

'Just call her and I'll turn up alongside the crew when I'm told to,' he says in a very matter-of-fact voice.

'Crew?'

'That's right.' He gives me a look, and then elaborates when he realises I have no idea what he's talking about. 'Oh, you know . . . camera and sound guys, assistant chefs – choppers and peelers I call them, and mustn't forget the make-up girl – she dollops stuff on to my face to give it a glow.' He rolls his eyes. 'Pia will deal with it all,' he finishes, sounding a bit weary now, like he can't really be bothered.

'But it doesn't need to be a huge thing,' I start. 'And I'm not sure about filming the children – that would take a very long time to get organised, get the right permissions in place, and so on,' I say, panicking. This isn't what I had in mind at all, and he doesn't really seem to be keen on the idea in any case. I'd rather not have him teach the children if he's going to come across as bored or, worst still, here under sufferance. You can't pull the wool over the children's eyes – they are bound to pick up on it right away. And what will the inspectors think when they see him? Dan Wright, the reluctant chef! 'Can't I just call you and arrange for you to do something low key – I thought you could pop in and perhaps show the children how to make a shepherd's pie or something.' A flicker of disdain darts across his face. I guess he's used to cooking fancy cordon-bleu stuff, not boring, basic shepherd's pies. But my children love a shepherd's pie – me too; everyone has second helpings when it's on the school lunch menu. 'We have an oven in the school kitchen,' I offer, feeling feeble and very provincial.

He doesn't say anything as he mulls over my suggestion.

'You can't call me direct,' he eventually replies, turning his back on me to study the corkboard on the wall.

Rude. Again!

'Oh, why not?' I ask, feeling even more irked when

he taps something on the board and does a sort of snigger to himself, his shoulders bobbing up and down. 'Am I too much of a "country bumpkin"?' I ask, remembering his line in the YouTube interview. I even do the same silly quote marks with my fingers, which, even though he can't see me, is still actually quite ridiculous, so, feeling like an idiot, I immediately drop my hands back down by my sides.

'What are you talking about?' Dan turns back to face me, and looks confused. 'Don't be daft . . . you can't call me because I threw my phone in the river, remember?' he clarifies casually.

'Um.' I can feel my cheeks reddening. 'Yes, well, err . . . of course, I know that . . .' I say, trying to sound breezy and indifferent, on realising that he's seemingly got one over me.

'So are you going to call Pia or not?' He looks me up and down, and it unnerves me again. And why does he have to be so . . . bold and direct? And, oh I don't know . . . larger than life, I guess! It's intrusive. Yes, that's what it is.

'I don't think so,' I reply, feeling put on the spot.

'Fair enough. I'll be off then . . .' and he goes to leave.

'I think that's probably a very good idea,' I retort,

feeling stubborn and petulant and immature now. But he started all this.

'Fine.' He strides across my office, and then just as he reaches the door, he stops and turns back. 'You know if they do close down the school, you should call a film studio and get a job as a fight director; you'd be really good at that!' And he's gone.

And yet again, I'm left flabbergasted.

Speechless. My hands are tingling with indignation. How dare he? I didn't start the so-called fight, so what does he mean? Fight director! Is there even such a thing? And why does he think we're fighting? I declined his offer to use my school as some kind of publicity stunt, that's all. I can only assume that he's not used to being turned down. Or thinks I'm the one being difficult, deliberately setting out to pick a fight with him. Why would I do that?

I close the door behind him and walk into the middle of my office. I don't know what to do. I actually don't. So I do nothing. I just stand still, with my eyes closed, as I concentrate on breathing. In and out. Over and over. I even count to ten as I taught Jack to do when he was just a little boy with a large fiery temper.

That's better, I feel calmer now. I go over to the

wall, curious to know what Dan was sniggering over, and scan the corkboard. There's Taylor's picture of the goldfish, numerous thank-you cards from children and parents, collected over the years. There are a couple of pictures that Jack drew – an alien, a sunflower, a wooden hutch with Blue and Belle inside, each chewing on a carrot. There's a space-hopper-shaped scribbly circle with stick arms and legs, which is supposed to be me – Jack had just turned three years old when he drew it, so it would be incredibly unfair if Dan was sniggering at this. And then I spot it.

I lean in closer and my heart actually stops mid-beat, momentarily.

Noooooo! Oh no!

And of all the people to see it, it had to be Dan *flaming* Wright. It's my completed cross-stitch project. I took a photo of it before dropping it off to be framed at the bookshop in the High Street – my beautiful cross-stitch sampler to celebrate my lovely village school. I thought I could hang it on the wall in the hall so that the inspectors could spot it; see how long the school has been here – over a hundred years! I even managed to stitch a fairly reasonable image of the school with the clock tower on too.

But it's all ruined, and I'm an enormous idiot! Because the words say,

Tinbledale Village School
Established 1841

Spot the error! I didn't. And I don't know how many times I checked it. A lot, that's for sure. I guess my eyes saw what they wanted to see. How infuriating. And embarrassing. No wonder Dan was sniggering. And I hate how I feel now, like he's got one over me . . . again! More so, that I seem to be bothered. What is that all about? I really wish I didn't care, but for some reason I do. Damn it! Dan Wright has really got under my skin.

Once again, I find myself hoisting my bag over my arm and storming off, wondering how on earth I managed to misspell TINDLEDALE, the name of the village in which I have lived my whole life.

Ten

At last, the end of a very long week has arrived, and when I get to the village green for tonight's show meeting, Jessie is already here. The triplets are sitting in a neat row on the wooden bench, while she stands, shielding her eyes from the early evening sun.

'Hi Meg. How are you?' Jessie asks as I sit down next to her.

'Great,' I fib, still reeling slightly from my last terse encounter with Dan. I called in to see Lawrence on my way home after my class with Hettie on Wednesday evening, and he already knew all about the defective cross-stitch sampler – said it was no big deal and that Dan wasn't laughing at me. That, in fact, he had asked Lawrence to let me know about the misspelling, as he felt mean later, not having pointed it out to me at the time, but reckoned I was already wound up enough without him antagonising me further. Hmm, likely story. He was definitely sniggering – well, his shoulders were jigging about. I didn't actually hear him doing a sniggery sound, but . . . anyway, he was right about one thing, he had certainly wound me up! And I realised afterwards that he hadn't even apologised for barging into me on the bridge. I reckon he only came to see me as, on reflection, he thought a televised trip to the quaint little village school would make him look good. He even said as much by telling me it would keep his manager happy. I bet they talked about it and saw an opportunity – all that spiel about wanting control over publicity, yep, so they could sell a story to the papers. Do another interview on TV perhaps, with Dan telling silly jokes about the 'country bumpkins' – have you heard the one about the teacher with the sweat-stained sun hat, who thinks she has leaves in her hair and can't even spell properly? Hahahaha!

But Lawrence also pointed out that in a way, I suppose, I actually do have Dan to thank, as at least now I can get the sampler back from Adam in the bookshop – the framer doesn't come to collect the new stuff until next week. Then I can correct the error and save myself the humiliation of letting the inspectors see how the acting head of the village school they are assessing for viability can't spell 'Tindledale', her own village's name.

Anyway, Lawrence agreed with me that Dan wanting to turn my school into a publicity stunt to promote himself wasn't really on. No, so I've come up with an alternative plan to broaden the curriculum – Years One and Two are going to visit the Spotted Pig café to see how a proper professional kitchen works, and Kitty will show them how to bake their own bread, followed by a couple of batches of huffkin buns, which they can eat for their tea. The parents have all given permission; some have even offered to come along to help out. When I made the inspectors aware, they seemed very interested: there was lots of ticking and note-making going on, especially when I explained that the huffkin buns are a Tindledale tradition and will be featuring at our village show, so not only are the children learning about food and how to cook it, they're also finding out about their heritage too. I call that a win-win. And I bet they don't have trips out to commercial kitchens on the curriculum at the big school in Market Briar.

'How are you, Jessie?' I ask, stepping back, and then I see her nervously twisting her fingers around the tassels on the end of her scarf. 'Hey, it'll be fine . . . come on,' I loop my arm through hers. 'Nothing to be worried about, you're with me – the villagers wouldn't dare make you feel unwelcome, not if I put my scary teacher face on.' I laugh to lighten the mood, but Jessie looks away. 'Hey, is everything OK?' I ask. Then something catches my eye. There's a guy, standing by the pond, wearing a faded grey T-shirt, jeans and trainers. He pushes his sunglasses up over his blond curly hair, and waves across in our direction.

'A friend of yours?' I smile gently at Jessie, wondering what's going on.

The man looks pleasant enough, harmless; an ordinary, down-to-earth guy. Definitely a newcomer, though, as I've never seen him here before in Tindledale. And I'm sure the playground mums would have spotted him already and started swooning, as he's very easy on the eye, so I definitely would have overheard them gossiping about the new 'mystery man'.

'Oh, um, yes,' Jessie hesitates, 'he's an old friend.' She busies herself with helping the children off the bench, clearly not wanting to elaborate further. Then, Millie, the only one of her children who actually spoke when they came to the teddy bears' picnic, spots the man and shrieks, 'Saaaaaam! Look, Mummy, it's Sam,' and she grabs Jessie's arm in excitement, but I'm sure I spot Jessie wince as she quickly pulls her arm away. 'Has he come to see us?' Millie is bobbing up and down now; in stark contrast to the way she was that time in the café. She's clearly thrilled to see the mystery man.

'That's enough Millie,' Jessie snaps, just a little too harshly, and then looks horrified, scared almost, as she glances over her shoulder at the man, who is walking away now, his head bowed despondently as he pushes his hands deep into his pockets. 'Sorry sweetheart,' Jessie says, her voice softening as she turns her attention back to little Millie.

'Never mind, Mummy. Shall I kiss it better?' And Millie places her little hand, very gently, on the top of Jessie's arm.

'No, it's OK darling, but thank you.' Jessie turns to me. 'He's a gardener,' she explains, motioning with her head towards the mystery man, before lifting Millie's hand away, quickly adding, 'I caught it on the corner of the iron. Damn thing, hurts like hell,' she explains, doing an awkward kind of laugh, which doesn't sound right. In fact, it makes me feel quite uneasy. But before I have a chance to analyse further, Lawrence appears with a glass of Pimm's in each hand.

'Hello ladies,' he smiles, 'I was wondering where you had got to; I thought I'd bring these out to you.' He hands Jessie a drink before handing me the other one.

'Oh, mmm, thanks Lawrence,' I say, in between taking a couple of sips of the refreshing, fruity drink that instantly makes me feel warm and relaxed as the alcohol hits my bloodstream. 'I don't think you've met Jessie yet,' I say gesturing with my free hand, 'or her lovely children, Millie, Olivia and Max.'

'No, I've not had the pleasure yet,' Lawrence says. 'Welcome to Tindledale,' he adds politely, doing a little nod in his usual gentlemanly way. 'How are you settling in?'

'Yes, good, um . . . thank you,' Jessie says, sounding flustered now.

'Lawrence is my oldest and dearest friend,' I jump in, feeling a need to put her at ease. But I make a mental note to try and chat to her later, make sure everything is OK, at least, because I'm not entirely sure it is.

'Err, excuse me! Less of the old,' Lawrence laughs, bringing my thoughts back to the moment.

'Oh, you know what I mean.' Grinning, I bat his arm playfully, and steal a surreptitious glance sideways in Jessie's direction – she has her sunglasses on now, but is staring ahead into the middle distance, in the direction that Sam went. And her fingers are trembling, only slightly, but I spot it nonetheless.

'Here, Jessie, let me help you with your Pimm's,' I say, cheerfully, taking the glass from her. 'You'll need both hands for the children.' I smile. And Lawrence, sensing something is awry, I'm sure of it, quickly steps in to help out too.

'Yes, silly me, I wasn't thinking! Why don't I carry both glasses back across to the pub garden and then you can follow on with the children . . .' he says calmly and reassuringly as he nods at me. 'That's better. There we go.' Lawrence takes the Pimm's and starts wandering off across the lane towards the Duck & Puddle pub. After seeing the children link hands in a little line, with Max then holding on to Jessie's hand, I walk along next to Lawrence, with Jessie and the children following behind. 'So, how's it all going with the inspectors?' Lawrence turns his head towards me.

'So-so,' I shrug, 'but they did seem pretty impressed with my teddy bears' picnic initiative – Jessie and the triplets joined us and she told us all about bees and how they make honey. She even brought along a proper white wooden hive – an empty one, but the children were still fascinated. Jessie found it behind an old outbuilding, figuring Victor's family must have overlooked it when they cleared out all his stuff.'

We make it into the pub garden, where Jessie and I

manage to bag a comfy cushioned corner sofa under a pergola next to three giant wooden trugs crammed with wild lavender. The scent is truly divine. And with the still-warm sun glistening on the grassy horizon, I can imagine it really is like being in the South of France, if you ignore the crunch of crisps and whiff of frothy beer mingled with garlic bread and cheesy chips from the farmers' table to our left.

The triplets are happy on the bouncy castle with all the other children, and Becky has volunteered to be a community babysitter for the evening, so there's a lovely, fun and relaxed atmosphere from the off, which makes a change from last time, or maybe it's the copious amounts of Pimm's that have already been drunk. I cast a glance around the garden and see that most of the tables have at least one – some have two – already empty jugs on them.

Various parents have been asking me what exactly I know about the school closing down and I try and assure them that, as far as I'm concerned, the school most definitely isn't closing, not if I can help it, but also tell them it would really be helpful if they all sent emails to the council outlining their concerns. Someone from the parish council agrees that it's an outrage and they have already had 'words' at the highest level, before Mrs

Pocket says she's scheduling an emergency governors' meeting to explore all the options. Good! Because I'm beginning to feel like a one-woman army against the team of inspectors. The sooner they go, the better, and my school can get back to normal.

The meeting looks as if it's just about to start as Sybs is standing up and trying to get everyone's attention. She's chinking the side of a glass with one of her knitting needles. I finish my drink and am about to go and join her, when Taylor appears from behind one of the lavender bushes.

'Miss Sing—. Sorry, Meg,' she smiles and scoots into the seat beside me as I bat away a bee that goes to nosedive my drink.

'Hey Taylor, how are you?' I say kindly. I bet Jack hasn't been in touch; she looks very forlorn. Not calling me because he's having too much fun is one thing, but I don't like him treating girls badly.

'Not too bad. I just wondered if you had managed to speak to Jack? I still haven't heard from him.' I hesitate and then, to spare her feelings I tell her, 'Oh Taylor, I'm very sorry, I've been so busy, what with the village show and the inspectors at school every day . . .' I discreetly cross my fingers to guard against the repercussions of telling a white lie.

Her face drops, and I'm somewhat surprised to see tears glistening in her eyes. Gosh, she really has got it bad. It makes me wonder if there's something more serious going on between them, but then why didn't Jack mention it? He's always been quite open in chatting to me about dating and girlfriends and all of that. 'Taylor, is everything OK?' I ask softly, and she studies me momentarily, seemingly gauging whether or not to talk to me about whatever it is that's troubling her, when the moment vanishes as Sybs calls me over to chair the meeting and give everyone an update on the state of the station car park and the duck pond.

An hour later, and I've suggested we take a break, seeing as we've managed to whizz through the agenda and cover a lot of ground. The village show plans are coming together splendidly and everyone in the village has got on and tackled whichever tasks they agreed to take on at the last meeting. Pete is planning his usual ploughing competition in the fields of the Blackwood Farm Estate – Lord Lucan opens the estate up on every show day – and Pete has roped in over twenty other farmers. Some of them even have heavy horses to pull the old-fashioned manual ploughs, to see who can win his most proficient ploughman's prize, a barrel of beer from the Duck & Puddle, which sets the general off again with yet more complaints about the 'utter disregard' for his mangled borders.

The commemorative stone has already been paid for by the parish council at a heavily discounted price, and is being carved 'as we speak', apparently, which I find hard to believe given that the guy who owns the garden centre is currently in the Bahamas for his daughter's wedding, but we all agree to trust that it'll be ready and erected in the village square for show day. The WI women have come up with an 'innovative idea', their chairwoman says, before treating us all to a very thorough explanation, complete with dance sequence diagrams with little paw prints on – a synchronised dog show! Taylor perks up at this point as, together with her mum, Amber, they've agreed to groom all the dogs ahead of the show, and then provide a doggy marquee on the day, with water bowls and beds and treats and stuff. Lord Lucan and his wife, Marigold, are organising hot-air balloons to take off from one of the fields on the estate, and then float over Tindledale on show day, which will be amazing, and such a treat – especially if they can get the right insurances in place so that people, the show judges in particular, can enjoy a ride. I'd love to go up in a hot-air balloon. And we all agreed that this initiative could really set us apart from all the other village shows.

It turns out Jessie is a keen gardener, so she has kindly volunteered to tidy the station car park, duck pond and little lawned area in the village square, and also came up with a great idea to organise an allotment food bank. And everyone agrees this is an excellent way to show Tindledale's commitment to helping the wider community, especially the allotment owners, who are all delighted at the prospect of their surplus crops going to a worthwhile cause. Apparently they've seen a bumper harvest already this year, with the weather being as wonderful as it has been, and they have already passed on as much produce as they can to family and friends. Nobody likes to see good food going to waste. So Mrs Pocket is marshalling a team of volunteers to collect the excess from the twenty or so allotments down the lane near my school, to take to the food banks in Market Briar.

I've just finished chatting to policeman Mark and his daughter Lily – she's delighted with her newly decorated bedroom and insisted on showing me a picture of it on Mark's phone. They've had one of those colourful canvas prints done using pictures of Polly, laughing and pulling silly faces, which now hangs on Lily's wall.

I'm walking over to join Jessie on the corner sofa, when . . . Oh no. My heart sinks.

What's he doing here?

Dan is striding across the grass.

That's all I need. Another run-in with Dan *flaming* Wright.

And what on earth does he look like? A big, pirate sailboat – his long black shirt is hanging out of the back of his jeans, billowing in the breeze as he gathers speed. His beard has reached ridiculous lengths now – and what's he done to his hair? He's clearly going for the 'bird's nest' or 'bonkers professor' look, as it's truly wild: more Ken Dodd than Kit Harington. But he smells nice; a mixture of almonds and oud lingers in the air behind him, which I suppose makes up for the monstrous Cornish-pasty-shaped green Crocs on his feet. I've never seen the attraction myself, and can honestly say that they do nothing for Dan – he looks as if he's just rolled in from a wild weekend-long yacht party. Wired and dishevelled.

Well, I'll just ignore him. Everyone else is pretending to, even though I can see some of the mums nudging each other and grinning like pubescent schoolgirls. One of them has even got a mirror out of her handbag and is hurriedly topping up her lipstick and fluffing her hair about, obviously attracted to the brutish type.

I reach Jessie and sit back down beside her.

'Well done, Meg,' she says brightly, popping a straw into a carton of juice before handing it to Millie, who practically imbibes it in one enormous gulp, she's so eager to get back to her new friends on the bouncy castle. 'I wish I could be as forthright and organised as you,' Jessie smiles as she busies herself with wiping Millie's mouth and sending her on her way.

'I'm sure you do just fine,' I say, wondering if now might be a good moment for me to find out a bit more about her. But just as I open my mouth, the general appears in front of us.

'Good evening! I hear that you are the lady to deal with,' he says very directly, whilst doing a sort of rocking movement on his feet, his arms ramrod straight behind his back.

'Oh, um, maybe,' I reply hesitantly, lifting a hand to shield my eyes from the dazzling orange evening sun as I rummage in my handbag with the other to find my sunglasses. The general, surprisingly thoughtfully, shifts a little to the left to block the sun so that I can see him without squinting. 'Thank you.' I smile. 'Do you need my help with something?'

'No. It is I who can help you!' he says slowly, punctuating each of the words distinctively. He rocks some more.

'Is that so?' I ask, curiously. Ahh, I find my sunglasses and pop them on.

'Indeed. I'm outraged by all this hot air flying around – stuff and nonsense about closing the village school. It's preposterous! You know, my father was educated there . . . before winning his place at Sandhurst. And his father before him.' The general nods firmly.

'Oh, I didn't realise you had a family conn—'

'Yes, that's right. It's the reason I came to Tindledale. Inherited the old place – my father's childhood home. Anyway, I found this in the attic and want you to display it in the school hall. I'll have a tradesman come by to install a proper cabinet.' And the general hands me a small blue box. I open it carefully. 'Don't be afraid, dear – have a proper look, it's a remarkably fine piece of craftsmanship,' he informs me.

'Oh gosh, it's an OBE medal!' I say, impressed, as I touch a finger to the scarlet and grey striped ribbon, and then down, momentarily tracing over the gilt crown and floriated cross beneath it.

'That's right. It was my father's. He was awarded the Most Excellent Order of the British Empire for his sterling contribution to business,' he informs me, using the proper, full name for the medal.

'Wow! But I can't possibly take this,' I say, closing the box and trying to hand the medal back to him.

'You must. I've already informed Mrs Pocket. She will trace all the other people of note that attended your school. Right back to the beginning.' The general straightens the collar of his navy blazer. 'Tindledale village school is steeped in history, and we must be proud of this fact! Did you know that your school hall was commandeered during the war by the Home Guard *and* took responsibility for educating a very respectable number of evacuees?' and he pulls his pipe from a pocket and points it in the air to punctuate the words.

'Um, no. No, I didn't,' I say, shaking my head. 'How fascinating!' And my mind is already working overtime, wondering how we can utilise the school's impressive history to put even more pressure on the team of inspectors.

'Yes it is! And this is why we must not allow the buffoons at the council to close it down without a second thought.' He points his pipe in the air some more. 'The heritage of this fine country is not to be sniffed at.' And he's rocking again now, as if gearing up for one of his rants. I smile politely, and spot Dan in my peripheral vision from behind my sunglasses – he's chugging a glass of what looks like whisky. 'I shall get on to my pal in the house if it comes to it,' the general harrumphs.

'The house?' I ask, lifting an eyebrow.

'Of Lords,' he states.

'Well, that would be wonderful,' I say, figuring a connection in Parliament might be just the thing to save my little school, if the teddy bears' picnics, animal petting afternoon, swimming, cookery and crafting lessons – and our Great Village Show – aren't enough.

'Indeed. Right you are. No time to waste in getting a proper commemorative display organised, photos and details giving a potted history of the school and all the distinguished pupils. Not forgetting the invaluable contributions the school has made to our country through two world wars. Good day to you, miss.' And he marches off to sit back with the parish council people.

'Gosh,' says Jessie, grinning, 'he's certainly a force to be reckoned with.'

'Isn't he just. But nice of him to donate the medal to the "save our school" effort,' I smile.

'Sure is. Mind if I take a look please?' I flip open the case to show her. 'Do you really think this will help to save the school?' she asks.

'To be honest, Jessie, I have no idea . . . but it has to be worth trying,' I say, stowing the medal in my bag for safekeeping and feeling a fresh sense of determination to see this mission through.

Eleven

As I finish the last of my Pimm's, I notice that Jessie hasn't touched hers yet. Oh well, maybe she's not a fan – it is quite potent.

'Is your husband coming this evening?' I ask her, looking around vaguely, as if expecting him to hove into view at any moment.

'No. He's in Zurich,' she says in a monotone voice, sitting upright now.

'Ahh, well, he'd be hard pressed to be in two places at once, wouldn't he?' I laugh, feeling an urge to lighten the mood all of a sudden.

'Thankfully.' Jessie mutters the word as she turns her face away, but I know I'm not mistaken.

I frown slightly, and turn to her. 'You know, if you ever want to chat about anything,' I say, gently touching the top of her arm to avoid the iron burn – feeling my way for fear of overstepping the mark. There's another short silence while Jessie fiddles with her scarf. She turns to look at me, and goes to say more, but then hesitates and dips her head.

I change the subject. 'Sooo, the guy earlier . . . on the village green, he looked nice. How do you know him?' I ask cheerfully, to cover my own feelings of awkwardness now.

'Ahh, we grew up together,' Jessie says, staring straight ahead, avoiding eye contact. 'In the same village.' She doesn't elaborate, and then Kitty is calling for us all to be quiet as she has something to ask, so I miss my chance to find out more about the mystery man.

'Obviously, I'll be laying on the huffkin buns and a selection of other traditional foods,' Kitty informs us. 'Afternoon tea with finger sandwiches, strawberries and cream, Eton mess and cakes, etc., but I thought it might be nice for us to be a little more adventurous this year. I'm sure the judges must get tired of sampling the same food at all the village shows around the country. So, I wondered if anyone has any ideas?' she smiles sweetly, rubbing her hands together and glancing around the crowd. 'Cher, I know we've already chatted and you suggested venison burgers with sweet potato chips.' Cher, with two empty Pimm's pitchers in each hand, nods in agreement. There's a collective circuit of 'oohs and ahhs' and 'that's a jolly good idea' from the villagers. The farmers' table seems especially keen, and then Cooper, the butcher, pulls himself up into a standing position, aided by Molly, who gives him an affectionate slap on the backside.

'I can sort out the meat for the burgers, no problem.' Cooper whips out a black pocket pad and makes a note before sitting back down. Molly squeezes his right cheek and then gives him a very generous kiss on the lips, at which their youngest son, Ollie, who's in Year Six, yells, 'Ugh. Muuuuuum,' from over by the fence, where he's with a group of other children, feeding grass to the five greedy goats in the field next door.

'Venison is a splendid idea!' the general puffs.

'No it isn't!' Taylor says, swivelling in her seat and turning her attention away from her mobile, which is a waste of time in any case as there's no signal in the beer garden. And I'm not even sure why I have a mobile phone, but someone at the council insisted, so they could contact me in an emergency – just goes to show how little they know about Tindledale!

'Why the devil not?' he goads.

'Because it's cruel. You can't kill Bambi!' Taylor shrieks.

'Nonsense. Blasted deer are a menace,' and the general is off on one now. I roll my eyes behind my sunglasses, thinking he sure doesn't help himself. Taylor looks as if she's about to burst into tears. 'Vandalising my garden . . . wandering in willy-nilly whenever they feel like it,' the general continues. 'No, cull the lot of them, I say!' And Taylor swings her legs over the wooden bench seat before jumping up and running into the pub. Oh dear. I contemplate going after her, but Amber grabs her purse from the table and darts off, so I leave it.

'OK, maybe we should do pork and apple burgers instead,' Cher concedes, but the crowd all seem quite content with the venison idea.

'And venison burgers would be perfect with a celeriac remoulade.' It's Dan. And my hackles are immediately up. What's it got to do with him? And he's doing his usual cocky, comfortable-in-his-own-skin stance, leaning against the brick wall of the pub with his arms folded across his wide chest and a casually confident look on his moody, thunderous, bearded face.

'Ooh, that sounds fancy,' one of the school mums pipes up, 'I bet I'd love that,' she then adds, quite suggestively, before muttering, 'What is it?' to her friend.

'Posh coleslaw,' Dan offers, laughing pleasantly, and

the school mums all join in. There's a tutting sound from the WI table. Ha! At least they aren't being bamboozled by his fake display of charisma. Maybe I should mention the YouTube film; the school mums wouldn't be enjoying jolly banter with him then. I take a deep breath and try to get a grip – I'm being petty, I know, but he riles me so much. And what's he going on about now? Something about food trucks being dotted around the village on show day – he has a friend who can loan us some lovely, retro, chrome trucks with candy pink and white striped awning, for a very reasonable fee, which, hang on . . . Dan is even offering to cover the cost of. Wow! Well, OK, that's very generous of him.

But, I can't help thinking, how come he's now so keen to help support the village community, when he wouldn't come to my school and do a low-key cookery class without his entourage? It's quite a U-turn. Talk about mercurial! Hmm. He's now suggesting teaming up with the village bakery to sell artisan loaves to the hipsters down from London. Dan reckons they'll be flocking to our Great Village Show when they hear about the veritable gourmet food fair that we have planned. And now he's talking to Sonny – the chef from the pub – about all of them pulling together and selling a selection of traditional food, mingled with some ideas he has for modern innovative fayre. Well, let's just hope the villagers' food isn't too 'country bumpkinish' for his exquisite culinary tastes. I stick a cheesy chip into my mouth and cross my arms.

'But how about my café? Business is hard enough, without your Michelin-star food trucks everywhere,' Kitty quite rightly points out.

'No problem, you could have a truck too . . . We could all cash in,' Dan suggests.

'Weell, I like the sound of that,' Kitty joins in, her forehead furrowing as she mulls it all over. 'But wait, hang on a minute, how can I run the café and serve food from the truck at the same time?' she then asks.

'How about a joint venture – you supply the buns, cakes, sandwiches, etc., and I'll flog them alongside the other stuff. We can split the revenue, or maybe we can have some volunteers to help out, sell the food in a selection of vans, and I can whizz around keeping an eye on them all and generally lend a hand. What do you reckon?' Dan throws the question out to the crowd, and there's an immediate show of hands teamed with lots of eager nodding heads. 'And don't worry, I'll call into your café beforehand and we can thrash it all out together.' He winks at Kitty, prompting all the school mums to drop their arms and narrow their eyes at her. But I reckon they're safe enough – Kitty is still mourning Ed, her school sweetheart, her first love. She told me once that he'd be her last love, too, which I remember thinking was just so sad, so I hope she does manage to move on one day. Maybe I should have done so too; maybe I should have tried harder to meet another man. To have been more open to the possibility, if only for Jack's sake, instead of dismissing his and Mum's attempts at matchmaking after Will left. Oh well, too late now. Jack is all grown up and gone away, and I'm settled.

Besides, I like stability, things to stay the same. And in the short space of time since Jack has left, I've managed to acquire some foibles. I rather like taking my tea and toast back to bed in the morning now – crumbs in the bed don't bother me, and I quite like leaving my clothes on the bathroom floor – I never did that with Jack around or it would have been impossible to get him to tidy up after himself if I didn't set a good example. I especially like having the remote control to myself, channel hopping as I please. And having hot chocolate and a packet of custard creams for my dinner, should I fancy doing so, not always having to prepare a proper meal as I did when Jack was around . . .

'What other stuff?' someone shouts out, bringing my thoughts back to Dan and the meeting.

'Right! Well, we can all throw in some suggestions,' Dan begins slowly. 'And this is just off the top of my head. But how about something like handmade scotch eggs, fiery beetroot salad, butternut squash tostadas, rice noodle cups with chilli prawns, mini chorizo pizzas . . . as long as people can eat it easily enough with a napkin and a fork, the possibilities are endless.'

OK. So that could work. I suppose. I find myself nodding along with everyone else. And, as much as it peeves me to think so, given that it's Dan's idea, I reckon the families with lots of children, reading the Sunday supplement review of the top ten village shows, will like it too – food trucks are a thing; there was a discussion about it on the radio last Sunday. Street food. It's actually very 'on trend', as they say.

'And how about a pop-up juice bar?' Dan goes on, but then Lucy, the florist, sitting next to an elderly woman, nudges her and chimes in with, 'We could flog some of your parsnip wine, Granny Elizabeth.' And everyone laughs. I resist the urge to smirk. Jack and I tried out Granny Elizabeth's recipe a few years ago, and it is certainly an acquired taste. Or *rank*, as Jack described it after swigging a mouthful. He had to spit it out into the kitchen sink before grabbing some milk from the fridge to take the starchy taste away. I don't think I had let it ferment for long enough though, to be fair; I've tried it again since at the last school fete, and it was surprisingly pleasant. Sweet and nutty with a hint of orange.

'Yes! That's a great idea,' he keeps on. 'Parsnip schnapps!' Dan embellishes. He looks totally focused, younger and more relaxed somehow. This is clearly what he was born to do; his métier, as Lawrence described my teaching.

'Don't you mean "snips"?' someone laughs.

'Yes! Even better. Parsnip "snips". Has a ring to it. How many litres do you have?' Dan addresses Granny Elizabeth. 'We wouldn't need vats of the stuff, not if it's strong – small measures would suffice. I take it all the temporary event licences have been applied for?' he asks no one in particular, and seems to really be in his element now. Dan pushes a hand through his messy hair.

'Of course, everything is in order. We have all the correct permissions to sell whatever we want to – cakes, alcohol, rides on machinery. You name it, we have it in place; I've made sure of it,' someone very serious on the parish council table states, and Mark nods firmly in confirmation.

'And we could serve the "snips" in jam jars, like they do in the cocktail bars in London,' Cher offers, 'and add some garnish, lovely!'

'Yeah, stick a parsnip on the side of the jar,' one of the farmer boys yells, and everyone laughs again, including Dan. Hmm, so he has a sense of humour. 'Well, it seems like a waste of a decent jam jar to me,' Granny Elizabeth quips, 'but if that's what the young people want these days, and the judges are going to be impressed, then . . .' She shakes her head in disbelief and Dan leaps forward to give her a hug. Granny Elizabeth bats him away with her bony hand, but not before giving him a peck on the cheek and grinning like a lovestruck teenager.

Dan turns to Lawrence, coughing to clear his throat. 'Yes, and Lawrence, that sparkling elderflower wine you serve would work well. Needs tweaking a bit, of course.'

Whaaaat did he just say? Needs tweaking! I push up my sleeves and brace myself, while Lawrence looks nervously in my direction.

'What do you mean?' Lawrence replies a little defensively. Bless him; he's always been such a loyal friend.

'Well, it's a bit *blah*!'

Blah? What does that mean? Flaming cheek. And I have to wonder if Dan is actually setting out to deliberately get my back up. 'But it could be amazing – livened up with a hint of ginger, or a mint infusion, the possibilities are endless.' Dan nods and smiles.

'Or how about with a twist of cucumber and poured over ice?' Lawrence suggests with a hint of irony, his lips twitching into a sideways smile in my direction, making me laugh inwardly, given that this is exactly how I serve it.

'Yes, now that would really bring out the fresh floral notes of the elderflower. What do you reckon, Lawrence? How many bottles do you have?' Dan asks.

'Well, I only have one bottle left,' Lawrence starts, and I know exactly what's coming next. I take a deep breath and put on a sweet smile, because, suddenly, all of the villagers are looking at me, then swivelling their heads back to gawp at Dan like he's some kind of juice-bar genie. A proper legend, as Jack would say.

'Oh no!' Dan scratches his head, deep in thought. 'But you can get more, right?' He looks genuinely concerned, like he really does care about making the pop-up juice bar a success for the Tindledale show. 'Who makes it?' he asks. 'Who do I need to be nice to?' Dan glances around the pub garden. *Ha! Might be too late for that . . .*

'She's sitting right here,' and Lawrence points across the garden in my direction. 'I think you've already met, but I'm happy to introduce you properly, if you like. Dan Wright, meet my lovely friend and Tindledale's finest winemaker, Meg Singer.'

Dan turns towards the pergola. I do an awkward little wave and fix a grin on to my face before self-consciously lifting my drink to my lips, and I can feel Jessie's elbow nudging me gently in the side. And then Dan realises. He does a double take. It's slight, but I spot it nonetheless. He's disappointed, I think, but I can't tell for sure as he's definitely a professional, used to being in the spotlight and dealing with every eventuality, it seems, as he quickly composes himself and strides towards my table with a big smile on his face.

'Fantastic! Meg, you and I are going to have *loads* of fun together.' And I almost choke on the last mouthful of my Pimm's.

'We are?' I splutter, snatching a tissue from my bag to wipe away the embarrassing froth of bubbles currently clinging to my top lip.

'Yep. Just wait and see!' *Oh. I can barely contain myself. Much.* He winks and grabs my hand to shake, so vigorously, it almost dislocates my arm from the socket. 'Sorry,' he says quickly, clocking my pained expression, 'I'm getting excited,' he grins, letting go of me. Hmm, I'd never have guessed, '. . . and also for,' he waves a hand in the air, '. . . you know.' I lift an eyebrow and then instantly drop it, realising that I'm doing my scary teacher face. 'The bridge . . .' he prompts, creasing his forehead and nodding purposefully, as if telepathically transmitting the meaning of his words, before heading back across the lawn towards the crowd who are all staring at me – the school mums looking as if they're about to implode.

And, I can't be sure, but did Dan just apologise? I think he might have!

And despite all my misgivings about Dan Wright, culinary bad boy, I can feel my resolve starting to weaken, because his ideas are all pretty good, even if this does mean that I'm now going to have to spend some proper one-to-one time with him having 'loads of fun together'. But I have to admit that his enthusiasm and effervescent energy is actually very appealing. Not for me *personally*, of course, oh no! But if he helps us put on a Great Village Show, which in turn puts Tindledale firmly on the map as a 'top ten most desirable place to live and bring all your children to the lovely village school', then that's good enough for me . . . I'm sure I can put up with Dan Wright's insufferable rudeness and big personality for a little while longer.

Twelve

Saturday, and I'm in the High Street updating the community notice board. I feel delighted on seeing that the village is starting to get its show hat on. The village square is undergoing a 'dress rehearsal' ahead of the big day, and has been swept clean, literally, by the WI women with their wooden, wire-bristled brooms. All the shop windows are looking super shiny and colourful, each with their traditional Tindledale themes. The bookshop in particular deserves additional merit as my favourite, with its collage of black and white photos depicting Tindledale through the ages. The picture of a horse and cart in the tiny village square – just a patch of dirt really, as it was back then – is incredibly poignant; the owner is dressed in shabby, ill-fitting trousers, worn-out boots and what looks like a scratchy shirt made from an old sack. The horse has a nosebag hung around its head.

Even the old Victorian lampposts have been swathed in Sybs' polka-dot bunting; she's standing on Pete's tractor as we speak, on the other side of the road, securing the ties into place. And, talking of displays, the general stayed true to his word and had a cabinet installed in my school hall, which now houses a fascinating arrangement of various war medals and other merits donated by the villagers from over the years – he placed an advert in the *Parish News* magazine that gets delivered by volunteers to every home in Tindledale, asking for any kind of memorabilia to be loaned to the school. The villagers came up trumps and produced loads of fascinating artefacts – photos mainly, but also trophies for various sporting events won by the pupils over the years. We even have an old Tindledale school cricket jumper, circa 1940, which was donated by Hettie after she found it in amongst a pile of stuff in her back bedroom. There's also a girl's green gingham 1950s summer uniform dress, that Ruby, who owns the vintage clothes emporium, had donated by an anonymous person, who left a bag full of stuff outside her shop door one night.

There's a wall montage too, showing the school right back to the beginning. In the centre there's a glorious, whole school picture, of the Victorian children all lined up and looking very serious – not like nowadays; when we had the photographer in to do the leavers' picture last summer, it took the best part of ten minutes for us to stop the children laughing and fooling around and to make them stand nicely and smile without doing silly faces. This contrast in children's behaviour can also be seen in the 'then and now' section – a wonderful collection of photos taken in the same spot outside the main school door: Victorian children shivering as they shovel snow, versus our modern-day children wrapped up warm in padded anoraks, all laughing as they throw snowballs at each other, including us teachers.

God, I really hope the inspectors' report comes back in favour of keeping the school open. It'd be like losing a dear friend if not, and I'm not entirely sure the village would cope . . . I, for one, will be devastated. I've been putting on a brave face, my default setting, but what else can I do? I can't let the children or parents see me worried or upset about it. That would never do. And if last week's school governors' meeting is anything to go by, then there really is a serious possibility that the school will have to close. The treasurer had been through all the figures and said it didn't look good, and someone backed this up from the council, explaining that the dwindling numbers means my staff aren't being utilised to the max. I tried to say that the school is more than that – it's the heart of the community, part of Tindledale's history, I even mooted the idea of us getting a preservation order – the school building must be listed or something, or what about the fields surrounding it? Surely they're worth some money; maybe we could sell one to a farmer and raise enough cash to keep the school open. To which I was told, the school building wouldn't be demolished in any event. No! Most likely sold to a developer and 'rejuvenated' into modern apartments. Silence ensued after I pointed out that people who live in apartments have children too, that need to be educated. And nobody wants a seven-mile-by-bus school run. But my pleas seemed to fall on deaf ears.

Hmm, but there is some good news – I've heard a rumour that a small housing development has been proposed on the outskirts of the village. Let's just hope the busybodies on the parish council don't put a stop to that. They have before, forming a protest to protect our village services; they were concerned about appointment availability at Dr Ben's surgery, the queuing time in the post office and chemist, etc. They worry about these things being affected when outsiders come to live here, but then complain when business is dwindling, the shops are empty and my lovely little village school is threatened with closure. If Tindledale is to thrive, then it needs new blood, otherwise we'll end up like Little Branhill, the village on the far side of Stoneley that's now a glorified drive-through after the tiny row of shops closed and became houses and the petrol station was bulldozed before being turned into a council refuse depot that the villagers are constantly complaining about. They say that, on a bad day, the stink is worse than when a septic tank is emptied, and that's saying something . . . Jack actually threw up one time when Vicky and Gabe, next door, had their tank emptied; he was off school with a tummy bug which probably didn't help, but even so . . . The smell permeates the air for ages.

After popping the key for the notice board back into my handbag, I walk across the cobbled road to see what developments might be taking place in the double-fronted empty shop – the one where I'm assuming Dan will open his high-end restaurant. It's all very exciting. And it definitely looks as if things are progressing, as there's one of those pink planning notices pinned to the timber doorframe, but I can't see what the words say as they have faded from being outside for too long in the sun. Oh well, this all looks very promising though, and my anticipation heightens when I press my nose to the window and see that the inside has been stripped, the walls freshly plastered and there is a stack of dining chairs in the middle, swathed in bubble wrap. Well, that settles it, Dan is opening a fine dining restaurant. I must remember to pop in and update Lawrence as he'll be thrilled too – such a bonus for his B&B guests, a Michelin-starred restaurant within walking distance . . . Well, almost, as it is a bit of a hike from his place, but then the bus runs on the hour every hour, and I'm sure Lawrence could come to some arrangement with Tommy and his taxi service.

I cross back over the road and continue on past the florist's, chemist's, antiques shop, and I've just reached the butcher's, when the door opens and Jessie troops the triplets out on to the pavement, one by one, in front of me.

And my heart stops! Momentarily, I'm convinced of it. Adrenalin laced with panic surges through me so fast it makes me feel nauseous.

'STOOOOOP!' I yell, flinging my arm around little Millie as she goes to bounce off the kerb into the road, narrowly missing a mud-splattered old Land Rover trailing an empty sheep transporter with a black and white collie dog inside, enjoying the sunny breeze as it pops its head out in between the metal-grilled side. 'Hold on sweetheart.' I pull Millie into me, just in time. The trailer, travelling far too fast, very nearly ran her right over.

'Look at that doggy,' Millie gasps, her index finger still pointing, as she cowers in to me.

'*Millie!* What have I told you about that? Don't you dare run into the road!' Jessie screams, slinging her handbag over her shoulder and dropping the carrier bag containing newly purchased meat from the butcher's on to the pavement in her panic to get to Millie. The other two children stand silently, staring at their shoes. 'That is really naughty! Really, really naughty. Do you hear me?' But Millie can't hear anything because she's sobbing so hard as she tries to hide behind me, her little hands clutching the back of my cord skirt, and I'm reluctant to intervene and make Jessie feel undermined in front of her children, but she seems to be disproportionately furious. Her face is rhubarb red and she's gripping the strap of her handbag so tightly, I can see the whites of her knuckles, like pearls ready to pop right through the skin. 'And stop hiding behind Meg, she doesn't want her skirt ruined with all your tears . . . why do you always have to spoil everything?' Jessie goes to grab Millie away from me.

'Please, it's fine Jessie, honestly no harm done . . .' I start, shocked by the ferocity of her loud outburst. And people are looking – the WI women on the other side of the street have stopped sweeping and are now staring, some with concerned looks on their faces, nudging each other and wondering if they should intervene, while the others are shaking their heads in disapproval. 'Don't worry about my skirt, it's just an old—'

I stop talking.

Jessie is crying. Full-on tears are tumbling down her face. Her shoulders are slouched in surrender. She slumps against the wall. Defeated.

Instinctively, I herd the children into the little alcove in between the butcher's and Ruby's vintage shop, and then turn to Jessie.

'Hey, come on . . . whatever it is, we can sort it out,' I say in a low voice as I put my arm around her, shocked at how taut and tense her back feels, but even more so by the way she flinches away from my touch.

I take a deep breath, and then take control of the situation.

'OK. How about we all go to my house and play in the garden?' I turn back to face the children and rub my hands together enthusiastically. 'It's a glorious afternoon – we could even go for a paddle in the stream, what do you say?' I ask, putting on an overly cheery voice for the children's benefit; all three of them are standing silently now, and it's odd. They don't respond. They don't even look at Jessie to see if my proposal is OK. It's as if they're quite used to seeing their mother break down and sob. It's truly hard to tell what they're thinking as each has their head bowed. Motionless and still. And it's sad. And then I spot Olivia and Max, standing either side of Millie; they slip their tiny hands around hers, as if silently trying to comfort their sister. Clinging together, the three of them for reassurance. And I'm in no doubt whatsoever now that I must get to the bottom of what is upsetting Jessie. Whatever it is, whatever is bothering her . . . surely it can't be irreparable? Every time we've met up, it's as if she wants to tell me something, to confide in me, but she seems to be too afraid or guarded, and then we always seem to get interrupted. So if we can just have some quiet time together, then perhaps Jessie will feel able to confide in me.

After gathering up Jessie's shopping, I slip my right arm through hers, very gently, and tell the children to carry on holding hands and for Max on the end to hold on tight to my skirt so we can go in a little convoy together to the bus stop, safely, so nobody inadvertently darts into the road again and nearly gets run over by a speeding trailer with an appealing-looking sheepdog inside. I look ahead across the village square and see to my relief that the bus is there, about to leave. I catch Don the driver's eye and he nods to show that he'll wait for us. Wonderful. As I really can't imagine Jessie is in any fit state to drive her old Mini through the village and down the hill behind the church to my house right now. No, we can sort the logistics of all that out later, and my bike too, but it'll be fine leaning against the bench by the war memorial for a bit . . . as long as the WI ladies don't mistake it for scrap metal, which is entirely possible, given the state of it, and sweep it away with their unforgiving brooms.

Thirteen

B ack at my cottage, and we're lounging in striped deckchairs in the garden. The children are playing happily in the long grass, barefoot and tummies full, after devouring several rounds of sandwiches filled with my homemade blackberry jam, followed by Party Ring biscuits and packets of Iced Gems. I figured it might not matter just this once for them to have a cobbled-together lunch. I know Jessie is quite particular about their diet, but seeing as she was rather fragile when we arrived, hurriedly taking herself off to the bathroom to 'get myself together, if you don't mind', I thought it best to just get on with it. So after quickly rummaging through the pantry, I found some of Jack's treats. He might not be a little boy any more, but that doesn't stop him from still being fond of a Party Ring or two and, despite my misgivings about Tommy in the village store selling so much sugar to my school children, he does keep all the old favourites in stock. Which reminds me:

'Who'd like an ice cream?' I say to the triplets, who are rolling around on a blanket now, taking it in turns to feed Blue, who we've put into an upturned empty wooden wine crate as a makeshift pen, with some hay and several large dandelions that the children found for him earlier, along with a fresh crop of crunchy carrots – the children particularly love feeding them to him, giggling when he twitches his nose and tickles their fingers as he munches the carrots down in record time.

'Me! Me!' they all shout, springing to their feet and jumping up and down.

'Sorry,' I turn to Jessie in the deckchair next to me. 'Is that OK with you? I should have asked first,' I say, realising she most likely won't thank me for overloading the children with sugar. It'll be their bedtime soon and they'll still be working off the sugar high.

'Yes, fine. And thank you,' she says solemnly, lifting her mug of tea, 'for everything this afternoon . . . I'm so sorry for crying on you like that. And for being so bad tempered and aggressive with Millie, I feel so asham—'

'Hey, please . . . Jessie, it's fine. Like I said earlier,

no need to apologise. We all have our limits, we all snap sometimes. You're only human, and children can be extremely challenging at times. Trust me, I know, I see it every day – parents at the end of their tether, telling their darlings to "behave or else . . ." through gritted teeth, smiles firmly in place, hoping nobody notices how exasperated they really are. And you must be exhausted – moving house is a major life event,' I say diplomatically, while thinking her husband, the charming Mr Cavendish, clearly isn't very charming at all. No, in fact, he's an utter shit. He's responsible for the burn mark, it turns out. Yes, Millie told me what she saw when Jessie was in the bathroom. She said, 'Daddy got cross because his shirt was creased up; he tried to help Mummy, but when he took the iron from her it dropped on Mummy's arm. Because she's so clumsy, Daddy told me that.' Poor Millie, she seems to have the weight of the world on her little shoulders, her face was very earnest, her little brow furrowed in concern as she asked me if this is the reason why Mummy cries all the time. 'Even at night, when she's supposed to be asleep.' Millie said she's heard her and is worried about it.

I think I managed to hide the feelings of anger and shock from my face. And now I need to work out what I should do with this information, because as a teacher I have a duty of care to the children. They attend the nursery that's attached to my school, and if they're witnessing domestic violence, which might explain their withdrawn behaviour, then I can't pretend that I don't know ... I should tell Becky, she's the designated person for safeguarding the nursery children. Jessie may not thank me if she thinks I'm interfering, but I trust Becky implicitly – she'll know what to do.

'Strawberry or vanilla?' I ask the children, before turning to Jessie. 'Would you like one too?' And she hesitates before replying, 'Um, yes please . . .' and she smiles, albeit a weak, watery one, but it's a start.

'Good. So hands up who wants vanilla . . .' I lift myself out of the deckchair, and none of the children moves. 'Strawberry?' I laugh, figuring it important to lighten things up a bit for them. They don't appear to have had much fun for a while, and Becky has told me, in confidence of course, that the triplets also seem very withdrawn when they come for their sessions with her at the nursery. Three spindly short arms fly up. 'With sauce and sprinkles?' and the arms reach up even higher, accompanied by three very wide grins and bobbing bodies, bouncing up and down in excitement. 'Perfect.' I smile too, thinking how nice it is to see them behaving like ordinary, happy, bubbly children for a change. 'Shan't be a minute then.' And the children run off down to the long grass, laughing and whooping as they go.

Jessie smiles properly for the first time this afternoon, grinning proudly as she watches the triplets tumbling around happily. Earlier, when the children were at the end of the garden and out of earshot, Jessie told me how unhappy she is in her marriage, how controlling Sebastian is, how she allowed herself to be swept away by him at first, only to feel lost and isolated later when she found out about his affairs . . . but she couldn't elaborate further as just then Millie came rushing up to show her a nice hairy caterpillar she'd found.

Ten minutes later, I emerge from the house with a tray holding five bricks of strawberry ice cream, each wedged between two wafers and slathered in raspberry sauce and rainbow sprinkles. I've added a couple of glasses of my fizzy elderflower wine for good measure – we might as well go the whole hog. Talking of elderflower wine, Lawrence called by last night to pass on a message from Dan – can he spend the day with me tomorrow to go through my wine cellar? He's very keen for us to put together an 'eclectically appealing selection of beverages' for show day, apparently, which should be interesting. I'm going to try not to revert to my scary teacher persona, seeing as the village does actually need his help – so as long as he behaves himself, then everything should be fine. I'm sure I can put up with Dan Wright for one day . . .

The children come running and, after I've dished out the ice creams and set them up with a length of kitchen roll each to mop their fingers and faces, they go and sit contentedly back on the blanket with Blue.

'Here you go,' I say to Jessie, offering her the tray. She takes an ice cream and tears off a piece of kitchen roll. 'And after that, there's a glass of chilled elderflower wine for you.'

'Not for me, thanks. I don't feel like drinking. But the ice cream is lovely.' Jessie licks her lips after running a finger down the side of the ice-cream slab. 'I haven't had one of these for years.' She pauses to ponder. 'I must have been a kid, last time, back home . . .' she nods. 'Yes, Dad used to make them. He'd buy a box of these wafers in our village shop. They were happy times.' Jessie's face softens.

'Ahh! Well, guess where these came from? Yep, the village store,' I laugh, tapping the side of my wafer, remembering last time Jack was home – he was getting over the end of freshers' flu and asked for an ice-cream sandwich – said it was the only possible thing to make him feel better . . . He was exactly the same as a little boy. 'Heaven knows how long the wafers have been on the shelf, I'm not sure Tommy is very particular when it comes to checking the stock.' I shake my head and take a bite of the deliciously creamy treat.

'Well, it tastes fine to me,' Jessie says, slipping her ballet pumps off and wiggling her toes in the warm grass. 'Mind you, the wafer is a little chewy come to think of it.' And we both giggle.

We finish eating, and I hand Jessie some more kitchen roll. She has a blob of raspberry sauce on her floaty white long-sleeved T-shirt.

'Thanks,' she says, dabbing the sauce. 'I'm so clumsy . . .' She smiles wryly and a short silence follows.

'Clumsy? Are you really?' I ask her gently. And Jessie looks at me before lowering her eyes. We both know what I'm referring to.

'No, I'm not,' she eventually says, in a quiet voice. 'How did you guess?' She glances at her arm, where the burn mark is. I pull my top lip down and bite hard, stalling for time, as I don't want to break Millie's confidence.

'Well, the burn is on your left arm and you're left-handed, aren't you, so I figured you probably didn't catch the iron on your arm all by yourself . . .' We sit in silence for a few minutes more, watching the children making a sticky mess with their ice creams. 'I don't have all the answers,' I say eventually, 'but I'm a good listener.'

She turns away. 'Yes, sorry, I do want to talk, but not about that . . . It isn't what you think, anyway – I was ironing and things got out of hand. He got cross because I hadn't ironed his shirt the way he likes it, so he grabbed the iron intending to show me, and I went to stop him, figuring I wasn't going to let him take control of me all the time, and well . . .'

'I'm so sorry.' I smile sympathetically, and wait for her to continue, but she doesn't, so I do. 'Jessie, you don't have to explain to me. I just want to help. Please tell me what I can do for you.'

'Thanks Meg, that's very kind, but I really don't know yet . . . I need some time to think – at least I can do that while he's away. And he was sorry after the iron incident – he said so as he left for the airport. Yes, he can be controlling, but he's not violent. Not really . . . It's not like that.' She looks away. 'Honestly, it isn't,' she adds, when I keep quiet, unsure of what else to say, but why then did she flinch when I tried to console her earlier?

'So when does he get back?' I ask tactfully. There's a short silence.

'Will you think I'm ridiculous and pathetic if I tell you that I don't actually know for sure?' Jessie leans forward in her deckchair and clasps her hands together, as if willing herself to draw strength. 'It'll be at least two months this time, but I only know this because his PA's secretary told me – I think she feels sorry for me.' She shakes her head, while I wonder what a big cheese her husband must be if his personal assistant has her own secretary.

'I don't understand, how come?' I ask. It seems odd.

'He doesn't tell me the exact day that he'll be back. He says the element of surprise is exciting, stops marriages from becoming dull; that it'll keep me on my toes . . . whatever that means.' Jessie pulls a face and shakes her head.

'Oh Jessie, I'm so sorry,' I say, unable to imagine a life like that, always on tenterhooks, dangling on a string like a puppet. It's clearly no way to treat the person you're supposed to love. 'What are you going to do?'

'Do?'

'Well, you seem pretty stressed and unhappy . . .' I begin carefully, looking into her eyes as I try to gauge how far I can go in projecting my own opinion on her personal situation. At the end of the day, we haven't known each other very long, and I also don't want her to feel I'm wearing my head teacher's hat and being interfering, but it's clear the situation is putting her and the children under a huge strain.

She seems to come to a decision. 'To be honest, if it were just me, I would leave him. But there's the children to consider . . .'

'What do you mean?' I ask. From my perspective it seems likely they'd be happier out of the current situation. They're clearly unhappy, and it can't be good for them to see their mum so miserable.

'Sebastian would stop me from taking them, I know he would. He said as much, when . . .' Jessie pauses. She presses her lips together and inhales deeply through her nose. Her hands are trembling again. 'When he found out that—' She stops talking abruptly as Max yells from down by Jack's old tree house.

'Mummyyyyyyyyy!'

'Um, I'd better see to him.' And Jessie shoots out of her deckchair and darts off down the garden, a mixture of relief and anxiety etched on her face, leaving me to sip my wine and wonder about what she was going to say next.

An hour or so later and the children are exhausted. It's been fun seeing them play in the garden. I found Jack's old paddling pool in the shed and used my bicycle pump to inflate it; they splashed around in the water in their pants before wrapping up in some beach towels, still warm straight from the airing cupboard. I've really enjoyed having a house full of children again; it reminds me of the long summer days gone by, when Jack and all his school friends would rush in from school, pull off their uniforms and make camps or dens in the garden until the sun went down. It sometimes felt like an extension of my school, with around twenty or so children here at any given time. Running in and out of the garden, asking for lollies and drinks and 'please can I use your toilet, Miss Singer?' and generally keeping me busy and very happy. Ahh, those were the days . . . Noisy and chaotic, and my home feels so quiet in comparison now.

I glance at my watch and see that it's nearly six o'clock.

'We should go,' Jessie says, gathering up the children's clothes.

'I'll come with you, if you like,' I say, thinking about

Sebastian making one of his sudden appearances. And if he does, then I'm not sure I won't want to have a word with him. I shan't, of course, it could make things worse for Jessie and the children, but he can't just carry on making their lives miserable.

'Thank you, but there's no need, really, we'll be fine. If we go now, we can catch the bus from the stop opposite – *on the hour, every hour,*' she says, already sounding like a local, having picked up a familiar Tindledale saying. 'I'll pick up the Mini from the village tomorrow.'

'OK. If you're absolutely sure?' I ask, figuring she's a grown woman who knows her own mind and I mustn't treat her like one of my school children.

'Definitely. I'm absolutely sure.' She touches my arm as if to emphasise her point. She pauses for a second, before saying, 'Meg, can I tell you something?'

'Sure you can. What it is?'

'I've felt so isolated since moving here.' She pauses. 'Well, and before then actually – Sebastian has never really liked me having friends; he says he likes to keep me all to himself. So I lost touch with all my old school friends soon after the wedding, and then if I got close to any of the baby mums, or women from my yoga class, they tended to drift away once they met him.'

She stares at her hands. 'And it's hard to put yourself forward and get involved, make new friends . . . and, well . . .' Her voice fades.

'I bet it is,' I nod, thankful that I've never had to move away and start all over again. Familiarity and a sense of belonging suit me. 'But you've settled in so well – the children are in nursery and you're making lots of friends in the village; getting involved in the show and so on . . .'

Jessie grins back, and suddenly I get a glimpse of a much younger, more carefree woman – a girl, almost. The contrast in her is remarkable. Her skin is slightly flushed from the heat of the sun and her hair mussed where she was leaning back against the deckchair – the country girl look suits her so much more. And suddenly, her expensive blonde highlights, perfectly polished manicure and fashionable yoga clothes with designer shoes seem so misplaced, like they aren't really hers; like they belong to somebody else . . . a trophy wife – one of those women I've seen on the telly, a lady who lunches and looks after herself in salons and spas and so on. A 'real' housewife. Although they never seemed very real to me . . . the stay-at-home school mums I know don't spend hours on their make-up before setting off on the school run.

'Thanks, Meg. That means a lot to me,' Jessie continues. 'You're so strong and together, and meeting you has made me feel . . . well, empowered I guess.'

'Oh well, appearances can be deceptive,' I laugh, feeling flattered but a bit embarrassed too. I'm not used to people saying stuff like this about me. 'And it can't be easy running an efficient household and looking after three young children under five – it's obvious you are a pretty determined woman yourself.'

'Perhaps I was, a very long time ago, but all that seems to have drifted away somehow . . .' She falls silent for a moment before adding in a quieter voice, 'I have some big decisions to make about my life, I know that.'

I squeeze her hand and we stand together, each of us mulling over the implications of her words. 'I'll be here . . . to help, however I can – feed you ice-cream sandwiches and such-like. Or look after the children – I've loved having them here today,' I grin, glancing over at the triplets. 'It's brought back such wonderful memories of when Jack was their age, playing in the garden with his friends.'

'Ahh, you must miss him,' Jessie says.

'Yes, it's taken some getting used to, but he seems to love uni, so that's OK,' I grin.

A few seconds later, and Jessie busies herself with dressing the children. 'Thanks so much for having us. They've loved it,' Jessie says. I pick up Olivia's dress and give her a hand to put it on. 'And so have I,' she adds, and then, after the children have said goodbye and thank you to me, she chivvies them out of the front door, with instructions to wait by the gate, and definitely not to open it. Jessie turns to me. 'I know we haven't known each other very long, but I'm so pleased we are friends.'

'Me too,' I step forward and give her a gentle hug before she turns to walk down the path, 'and Jessie.' She looks back over her shoulder. 'I'm here, any time. Just call me or pop in, whenever,' I tell her, smiling warmly.

'Thank you, I really appreciate it, Meg.' She hesitates. 'And I'm sorry for keeping on about myself. Next time we'll talk about you . . .'

'Ahh, don't be silly. To be honest, there's very little to know about me . . . my life is really quite ordinary,' I laugh and pull a funny face. 'School, cross stitch, wine-making, gardening – Jack when he's home – and now the village show. See, nothing very remarkable at all.'

'Well, the effort you're putting in at the school is

219

amazing, and it was your drive that chivvied the show committee along . . . making sure everything was on track and nobody bickered.'

'You're very kind,' I say.

'And I don't think I'm the only one you impressed . . .' she adds quietly and hesitantly.

'What do you mean?' I crease my forehead in curiosity.

'The chef . . .' Jessie looks me straight in the eye. 'Dan Wright – I have to say that I went a bit fan-girl when he strode in. And did you see how none of the villagers even batted an eyelid? Apart from that small group of women from the school . . . So I reckoned I should act the same – unmoved by his celebrity status.'

'Ha! Yes, the Tindledale villagers can be a hard bunch to impress, being off the telly won't cut it around here, unless you're presenting *Countryfile* or one of those gardening or allotment programmes – they go mad for those,' I say, wondering what Jessie is going on about.

'Well, Dan Wright didn't really look at anyone else. He couldn't take his eyes off you,' she says, seeming impressed.

'*Whaaat?* Oh, don't be daft,' I tip my head back and

laugh, wondering how on earth she can think so. 'Dan?' Jessie nods. 'Really?' I make big eyes. 'You have to be joking.'

'No, seriously, I saw him watching you, studying you, when you were talking to the crowd. I'd go as far as to say he was spellbound. His gaze didn't leave your face the whole time . . . and he seemed pretty pleased at the prospect of you two having lots of fun together – getting everything organised for the juice bar. And he is very good looking . . .' She grins.

'No way!' I shake my head. 'Not that he isn't good looking – that part is true,' I nod, as he is, there's no denying that, 'but he hates me. And, to be honest, I'm not very keen on him either. He's so rude and, well, incredibly bumptious!' I fold my arms across my chest.

'*Bumptious?* What does that even mean?' Jessie laughs, creasing her face in amusement.

'You know . . . full of himself. Or to be exact, "irritatingly assertive",' I say, rolling my eyes and remembering the dictionary definition I gave out in Year Six's English class a few days ago.

'Hmm, maybe so . . . but what if that's just bluster? You know . . . it could be a cover-up. Not all men are naturally confident when it comes to women; maybe he's shy underneath all that bumptiousness,' she says knowingly, and I wonder who she's referring to . . . surely not Mr Cavendish, I'm sure he has no problems when it comes to confidence. Maybe she's talking about the mysterious Sam? And I wonder, too, if that's what she was about to tell me earlier, before Millie came over – how Sam fits into her life, or not, as the case may be. I'm assuming Sam helps look after the gardens around Jessie's farmhouse; they are far too much work for one person with three children and a house to look after. But I saw the reaction his appearance provoked in her on the village green that time, so I can't help wondering if they're more than just employer and employee. And what if Mr Cavendish knows? What if that's why they argued over the iron?

Stop it, I say inside my head, feeling bad. I'm making up stories about Jessie without knowing any of the facts, and that's not nice. I inhale sharply before letting out a long breath, bringing myself back to focus. Speculating is no better than gossiping, really.

'Ha! Dan shy? I don't think so. If you saw the way he bowled into my office and made himself at home, then I'm sure you wouldn't think so either . . .' I shake my head.

'Your office? Ooh, so he came to see you at the school then?' she asks, excitedly.

'Yes, but . . .' I pause, and Jessie lifts an inquisitive eyebrow. 'Oh no, it was nothing like that, definitely not,' I protest, cringing all over again at the memory of the misspelt cross-stitch fiasco.

After waving Jessie and the triplets off, and waiting by my front door until the bus arrives to make sure they're all safely on it – Don waves from the driver's cab as the bus judders off up the steep lane towards the High Street – I close the door and figure that I should probably go and collect my bike in the morning.

As I go to walk through to the kitchen, shaking my head and laughing inwardly – *Shy? Bluster? Ha I don't think so . . . sheer swagger, more like,* as Jack would say – the phone rings. I dash into the lounge and take a look at the caller display.

Ahh. Spooky coincidence. It's Jack. Wonderful.

We've spoken a few times since Taylor last asked if I had heard from him, but whenever I've mentioned her, he's changed the subject, which feels a bit strange. Call it mother's intuition, but there's definitely something he isn't telling me. I make a mental note to find out what is going on this time.

'Hello darling, I was just thinking about you!'

Fourteen

Jack is going to South Africa for the summer holidays. I'm really pleased and proud that he's capable, independent, and keen on doing his own thing. After all, I wouldn't be much of a mother if I hadn't brought him up to stand on his own two feet. But a part of me can't help but feel a little tinge of sadness that an era has come to an end and that Tindledale, his home, and his mum will no longer be featuring highly in Jack's priorities.

'I'm so pleased for you,' I tell him, honestly.

'Are you sure, Mum?' he asks, suddenly sounding far more mature than his eighteen years.

'Of course I am, Jack. It's an amazing opportunity,' I say, trying to convey my enthusiasm without sounding falsely jolly.

'It is, isn't it? And I've managed to save enough for the flight . . .' He sounds so animated, excited and alive.

'Wow, well done.' I am seriously impressed. I know he's been working evenings and weekends in a trendy bistro attached to an upmarket hotel, but I had no idea he'd manage to earn enough for a return flight almost to the other side of the world. And I'm sure it wasn't that long ago that he asked to borrow twenty pounds, telling me he was skint . . . hmm.

'And I've done a bank transfer for that money you lent me,' he adds, right on cue. Ahh, that's nice. He's being responsible. But nevertheless it feels strange that he doesn't even need my money any more. 'The tips I get are really good, Mum; the people who stay in the hotel must be loaded. Everyone leaves at least a fiver, sometimes a tenner; I've even had a few twenties. You know . . . if it's a big party and they're celebrating. And I can cover ten tables in a night, easy.' He laughs. 'And Stevie's dad is *such* a top guy . . .'

'Stevie?' I ask, trying to take it all in. I don't remember Jack mentioning a friend called Stevie before.

'Yep, you know, his room is next to mine. I told you about him. He's doing biochemistry. Boring. But he's actually all right.' But Jack doesn't even pause to draw breath. 'He's from Liverpool, but his dad lives in South Africa, Cape Town . . . left when Stevie was a kid, but he always spends the summer with him. So cool. And

I spoke to his dad on Skype and he's going to take us out on his yacht and he said that he'll teach me how to sail. We might even get to swim with some dolphins too, if we're lucky.'

Jack sounds really excited, and I've heard him like this before – the time he went on a school trip to the Natural History Museum in London, and when he went with Josh – Cooper and Molly's eldest son – to the cinema for the first time on their own in Market Briar, with a couple of girls. But this is something more. Something I can't quite put my finger on.

'And we are going to surf, hang out, that kind of thing.' Jack sounds so charged, so high on life. 'Yeah, it's going to be awesome.' And then I get it! I know what's so appealing about this trip – Jack can spend time with Stevie's dad!

For a moment it makes me feel inadequate, as if I'm not enough. Like I should have tried harder to make it work with Liam, Jack's dad. For Jack's sake. So he could have all that father and son time. Play football, mess around in the garden, instead of feeding the ducks with his mum. Isn't that what people do? Stay together for the child? But then I think of Jessie, and I realise that I'm being ridiculous. Sometimes it just isn't possible, or what's best at all for the child.

Life isn't like that. Black and white. No, it's mostly grey. I did my best. And Will was wonderful with Jack, until he left.

I wonder if Liam thinks about Jack? Misses him? Or, more pertinently, does Jack miss Liam? I wonder if I let my own feelings of hurt and disappointment cloud what was best for Jack. I know that's why I don't let people, men mostly, get close: I didn't want to let myself – or Jack – get hurt like that again . . . But Jack is a grown-up, he has his own life now. Maybe Lawrence was right; perhaps it is time I broadened my horizons . . .

'Do you miss your dad, Jack?' The minute the words are said, I panic. An ominous silence follows. 'Um, err . . . sorry sweetheart, I shouldn't have just blurt—'

'Mum, it's cool. I spoke to him and . . .'

'What do you mean?' I had no idea Jack was in contact with Liam. I sink down into the sofa, feeling . . . actually, I'm not entirely sure how I feel. It was all such a long time ago, and Liam is Jack's dad . . . he has every right to a relationship with him. Of course he does. I feel dizzy from the sudden surge of mixed emotions.

'It's no big deal, Mum. He messaged me . . . to see how I was getting on.'

'Oh!' I breathe, calming down a bit. 'And what did you say?'

'Yeah, I said I was doing OK,' he tells me casually, like it's no biggy, as he would say. 'I told him uni is awesome, and he showed me some pics of his fam. That was it really . . . Oh, and he asked if you were all right, and how Gran was, if she still lives in Tenerife. Just the usual, polite chat stuff. I said you were both doing great . . . never better.'

'His family?' I ask, trying to process it all quickly, and wondering if I really want to know the finer details of Liam's life.

'His kids. My half-sisters, I guess. He has two . . .' Jack informs me and, somewhat to my surprise, I don't feel very much at all. It's funny, how sometimes the thought of something is far, far worse than the actual reality. What I really feel is indifference. Obviously I'm happy for Liam that he isn't on his own, that he has a family. And what about Jack? I wonder how he feels about this news.

'That's nice,' I say diplomatically, but what else can I say? And then Jack tells me everything I need to know.

'Yep, he doesn't see much of them.' Silence follows. 'He's a rubbish dad, really, but it could be worse, I suppose,' Jack says, blithely.

'Oh. How's that then?' I manage, quickly followed by, 'I'm sorry, Jack.' I feel like I made a bad choice, but then I wouldn't have Jack if it weren't for Liam, so I mustn't ever regret meeting Liam.

'Well, it would be a right disaster if I had a rubbish mum too!' and he laughs. And I laugh too as my heart swells.

I wish Jack were here, so I could get a proper gauge of how he really feels about all of this. But I have to trust that he's OK, that he's as laidback about the situation as he sounds. Jack has always been happy-go-lucky – he has a serious, caring side, too, though – and he tends to take things in his stride . . . like when his skateboard got stolen from outside the sweet shop in Market Briar. I felt so upset for him, and wanted to call the police or scour the streets for the culprit. But he just shrugged, and then promptly got himself a paper round to earn enough money to pay for a new one.

'Are you crying, Mum?'

'No! Don't be silly.' I find a tissue and dab my eyes, before taking a deep breath.

'What's that noise then?' Jack chuckles. 'Awww, don't go soft on me, Mummy,' he adds, teasing me. He used to call me Mummy at school, in the playground, in front of the other children, when I was training to be a teacher and trying to be professional with my very scary teacher face on, and it always made us laugh as we cycled home together.

'So, Jack, seeing as you *did all right*, as you say . . . when are you coming home?' There's a short silence. 'I miss you,' I say, going out on a limb – I've never been this direct with him before, figuring I shouldn't put pressure on him. The last thing I want is to make him feel obliged. No, I've always had it in mind that the best relationship a parent can have with their grown-up child is one where they actually want to spend time with their mum, and not visit them out of some sense of duty.

'I miss you too,' he replies right away, 'but I'll be back before you know it. It's just the summer holidays.'

'I know. Ignore me; I'm just being silly. Half term will come around soon enough,' I say, changing tack.

'Yeah, and I can always shoot down for a weekend . . . or we could go and visit Gran, get some winter sun, like we used to.'

'Yes, that would be lovely. You know, the village show is on soon.'

'Oh, is it? What date?'

'The eleventh of July, so not long now.'

'Ahh, I'll be in Cape Town by then. Shame, as the

village show is always a good day. Oh well, next time for sure, Mum.'

'Yes, I hope so! And, oh, before I forget, can you give Taylor a call please?'

'Taylor?' he says, tentatively.

'I didn't know you two were friends . . .' I quickly add.

'Err, we're not really. We had a laugh together last time I was home, that's all. No biggy.'

'I don't think she sees it like that, Jack. She seems quite upset that you haven't been in touch, or returned her messages,' I say, wondering what 'had a laugh together' means exactly.

'Don't know why. Look, I'd better go,' he then says, changing the subject again, like he has all the other times we've spoken.

'No you don't,' I say, quickly. 'Tell me what's going on please, Jack. Has she got a crush on you? And you're not into her, is that it? Because if so, then you need to tell her. It's not fair to let her guess this for herself, Jack.'

'I'll call her,' he says, somewhat reluctantly. 'I don't want her hassling you . . .' And I'm sure he tuts, which is very unlike him.

'Jack, it's not like that. She wasn't hassling me, she's a lovely girl, she . . .' I stop talking, conscious that he's never going to want to call Taylor now, if he thinks she's got his mum on his case about it.

'I said I'll call. Just leave it Mum, please . . .'

'Fine, OK.' I decide not to push it further.

'Yes,' he softens. 'I will. Promise. And I'll call you, and Gran too, before I go to South Africa . . . anyway, it's ages away yet, so I'll probably call you loads before then anyway,' he laughs. I get the feeling he's trying to make light of the Taylor situation, which has just the opposite effect and makes my curiosity increase.

'You better had,' I laugh too, pretending to chastise him, and grateful that the conversation has moved on to a lighter footing now.

'South Africa is going to be so awesome,' he says, getting back to the main focus in his life right now, and who can blame him? I guess it is a very exciting prospect for an eighteen-year-old with his whole future ahead of him.

'And you'll have a brilliant time. Are you sure it's OK for you to go with Stevie? Maybe I should call his dad and have a chat to him?' I can't help myself.

'Muuuuuum, no you won't. I am a big boy now.' *Yes I know.* 'It'll be fine, stop worrying.'

We say our goodbyes, and I put the phone down. It's only when I get into the kitchen to pour myself a much-needed glass of elderflower fizz that I realise I don't even know Stevie's dad's name! Or address, or any of his contact details, for that matter. I grab a pencil from my school bag and walk over to the magnetic memo pad that hangs on the fridge, and write: FIND OUT STEVIE'S DAD'S NAME, ADDRESS, EMAIL, PHONE NUMBER. SKYPE. EVERYTHING. DON'T FORGET!!!!!!

I underline the reminder three times before pouring myself a large glass of elderflower wine, scooping Blue up for a cuddle and wandering out into the garden to sit on my tree stump in the sun.

Fifteen

Eleven o'clock, and I'm sitting at the kitchen table, having just finished typing out the notes for this week's school newsletter, when there's a knock on the front door. Dan is here, right on cue. Punctual. Well, that's nice. A good start. And I'm still determined not to let him rankle me this time. Yes, I'm determined to keep an open mind and try to remember what Jessie said – bluster! Perhaps, and I'm all for giving people the benefit of the doubt . . . so long as they aren't rude or dismissing my lovely little village, Tindledale, as dull.

After closing the laptop, I walk down the hallway, pausing briefly to check my hair, and teeth (I cooked a cheese and spinach frittata for breakfast, with some eggs that Vicky from next door gave me over the garden fence, straight from her hen house), before pulling open the door. But Dan isn't here! How strange. I definitely heard a knock. I go to the end of the garden path and look down the lane, left then right, but there's no sign of him. Oh well, I must have been hearing things. Yes, that's probably it; the radio was on, *The Archers*, and I've made this mistake before, especially when my mind has been focused elsewhere. I remember one time, listening to a scene in the cowshed, I honestly thought one of Pete's herd had escaped again and was in my back garden – it's happened before, a large black and white Friesian broke through from the field and it took Pete, plus five of his farmer friends, to coax the cow back. She was far more interested in tucking into my vegetable patch – nearly cleaning me out of runner beans.

I wander back through into the kitchen.

And nearly have a heart attack. I actually gasp and clutch my chest like the heroines do in those old black and white movies.

There's a man standing by the Rayburn with a giant bunch of gloriously scented red, purple, pink and white freesias in his arms. I step backwards and bend down, instinctively reaching for Blue, who hops over my foot before scampering off to the cool spot on the tiles next to his food bowl, seemingly unfazed by this very large intruder.

'The top half of your stable door was open, so when

you didn't answer at the front, I . . .' Dan Wright pops his head out from around the side of the flowers with a cheery grin on his face. 'Don't worry, I made sure the rabbit didn't escape,' he adds, nodding at Blue.

'Oh, um, right! And thank you,' I manage, wishing my cheeks weren't still flushed from the shock.

'I didn't scare you, did I?' And Dan takes a step forward, sounding genuinely concerned.

'Err, um . . . no. Of course not!' I start, trying to sound fearless and in control, like it's an everyday occurrence to bump into a man bearing flowers in my kitchen – I don't want him thinking I'm some kind of wimp. But this is before I realise that my voice sounds shaky, thereby totally giving me away, so I quickly figure it best to come clean. 'Yes! Jesus! You gave me a fright,' I smile, but he doesn't reciprocate, so the smile freezes on my face. Silence follows. It throws me and I react. 'Why didn't you wait like everyone else does? Do you have a habit of breaking into people's homes?' And no sooner are the words out of my mouth than I'm cringing. Scary teacher telling him off again. I must stop it! Dan won't want to help with the village show if I carry on like this. Let alone open his restaurant here and really put Tindledale on the map. I inhale sharply and let out a long breath, snatching a few seconds to compose myself and start again.

I grin apologetically, and a little sheepishly, as he hands me the flowers.

'For you! And, for the record, no, I don't have a habit of breaking into people's homes; but this is the countryside, I reckoned it would be OK, you know . . . rural life, relaxed, laidback, where everyone seems much more easy-going . . . well, almost everyone . . .' He shrugs, locking his dark eyes on to mine, and I can't tell if he's having a dig at me. 'People mill in and out of the B&B all day long – just wander in the back door bearing various homemade food items for Lawrence and his guests. It's very cosy and bygone in a *Darling Buds of May* way. And your bike is outside. I saw you'd left it in the High Street, so I borrowed it to ride down here on.'

'Um. Right. Well . . . err, thank you,' I say, feeling taken aback, but smile as an image of him squashed on to my bike with a bouquet of flowers under his arm pops into my head.

'Kitty pointed it out, she was doing her window display when I walked past, so we had a chinwag about her food truck and I said I was on my way to see you, sooo . . . Anyway, the bike is here and I've even lifted the seat back up for you – had to adjust it to stop my knees from crunching under the handlebars every time I turned the pedals.' He shakes his head and grins.

'Well, you are pretty tall, to be fair,' I smile. He's a good head-and-shoulders taller than me.

'True.' Dan shrugs easily. 'You know, that would never happen where I live – a bike left unchained next to a bus stop?' He takes a sharp intake of breath. 'It would last roughly five seconds before it got lifted and, come to think of it, someone coming in the back door? Nah!' He waves a dismissive hand in the air. 'I'd have the bat out in the blink of an eye.'

'The bat?' I repeat, and promptly cringe as I remember what he accused me of last time. Dan opens his mouth, probably to point out once more my habit of parrot-like repetition, but then decides to stay silent, and smiles instead.

'Baseball bat. Can't be too careful where I'm from.' He nods.

'Maida Vale?'

'How do you know that?' His face immediately clouds in suspicion. Guarded, almost, like I'm one of his groupies and he's boxed into a corner – his eyes even dart towards the window, as if searching for a quick exit.

'Oh, I'm not sure, I think I read it somewhere, in a magazine maybe, ages ago . . .' I fib, not wanting him to know that I've watched him on YouTube very recently.

'Hmm, yes, that was a very long time ago.'

'So where do you live now then? It sounds very rough if you have to keep a baseball bat handy.' I crease my forehead as I wait for his reply.

'I don't really – my hipster beard is all the protection I need!' He laughs, raises an eyebrow and then drops his shoulders, seeming to relax. 'I live in Shoreditch.'

'Is that in London too?' and for some reason that I can't fathom, Dan seems to think this is the funniest thing ever. He does an enormous belly laugh, which makes his big, broad shoulders bob up and down like a cartoon character. 'Ahh, yes, that's right, I remember now – it's all skinny jeans and dirty burgers,' I quickly add, vaguely recalling a radio debate I listened to some time ago about urban living. Dan laughs even harder. 'What's so funny?' I shift the bouquet of flowers over on to my left hip and plant my free hand on the other.

'Nothing,' he splutters, attempting to recover, 'nothing at all. And yes, it is in London,' he adds, smiling nicely.

And I have to say that I really am very pleasantly surprised. He looks good – great, in fact. He's shaved the silly beard off; well, some of it. It's now an acceptable length and it suits him. He's wearing a smartish shirt, not the billowing sail-like thing he had on at the last village show meeting, and his hair is less unkempt and messy . . . more effortlessly ruffled. It seems like he's made an effort today, and that's nice. His aftershave is pretty delicious too; it's the same almond and oud as before, which must be his 'signature scent' and definitely a winner.

Hmm, perhaps Jessie has a point. Maybe Dan is 'taken' with me . . . But noooooo, I'm being daft. Of course he must have his pick of women fawning over him. He's a celebrity chef, famous, and all the school mums fancy him, not to mention the crowd in the audience on the YouTube clip – they couldn't get enough of him. He must be used to London women – women that dress like Jessie, in expensive clothes with jewelled scarfs and designer shoes, not homemade tea dresses and sweat-stained sun hats usually reserved for gardening only. I glance at the dress I'm wearing. My favourite – homemade by me last summer – it's a pretty yellow peony print cotton. It's so cool and comfortable in this hot weather, but now it seems a bit dowdy and provincial, especially with . . . oh no! Dan follows the direction of my glance. He looks at the ground too. I have two very fluffy faux-fur rabbits nestled around my feet. They were a gift from Lawrence last Christmas – to keep Blue company, he had said, and we had chortled together at the time, but now the bunny slippers don't seem very funny at all. 'Nice foot-wear!' Dan guffaws. An enormously expressive and demonstrative guffaw, not like the Shoreditch laugh that he just did – no, this is a different laugh, and I get that feeling again. It's not fear, it really isn't, or intimidation; it's like nothing I've ever felt before . . . uncomfortable almost, nervous perhaps, is the best way I can describe it, without analysing further. And it's certainly not a feeling that I'm used to.

'I'll change.' And after carefully placing the flowers on the counter, I go to scoot off down the hall to find my shoes, but Dan stops me. He grabs my arm. Not aggressively. Gently. And I stop moving and look back over my shoulder. His eyes are fixed on mine. Intense. I'm the first to look away.

'Don't change,' he says in a low voice, and the words hang in the air. A double-entendre of awkwardness. I can't be sure. But something I do know is that my cheeks are really hot now, flaming like a pair of plum tomatoes. Maybe I should go and stand inside my polytunnel, I reckon I'd look right at home in there lined up alongside the tomato plants. Oh God. 'Sorry, what I meant was, that, um . . . fuck,' Dan says quickly. 'Oops, shit . . . sorry.' He slaps his free hand over his mouth and pulls a face. 'I bet you never swear, being a teacher and all.' He looks at his other hand, still on my arm. 'What am I thinking?' And Dan suddenly drops my arm like it's a scalding red-hot poker. 'I should go,' and he takes several steps backwards towards the stable door.

'But, hang on!' I say, perplexed. Why the sudden U-turn? Just a few seconds ago he was being as nice as pie, but now it's as if he's panicking, having a change of heart. 'What about our Great Village Show, the juice bar, the restaurant? And . . . you can't go, we need you, I need . . .' I add, too fast, panicky, the words tumbling out then stopping abruptly. We're standing opposite each other now. Staring – or glaring, even. Neither of us really knows what to say next.

'Right! Yes. Juice bar. Your wine cellar.' Dan seems to pull himself together. His face changes. Relief? I can't be sure. He is all businesslike now. 'Right, where is it? Let's mix up some flavours and have some fun!' He seems to be back to his usual, confident, gregarious self now.

'Um, sure,' I say, feeling disorientated as I try to keep up with his changing demeanour. 'It's just here, next to the pantry.' I point to the stairs before lifting up the flowers. 'I'd best put these in water first; it would be a shame for them to wilt in this wonderful, warm weather.'

'Yeah, sure. Go ahead,' he instructs. 'They're only to . . . you know . . .' He shrugs and looks away.

'Well, they're lovely,' I say, and I think Jessie could have a point. Dan Wright does appear to be nervous – he's acting offhand now, like he's not bothered, or maybe he's giving me a glimpse of his much younger self, as a cover, perhaps? And I've seen the look on his face before. Jack, on his first day at university, behaved in exactly the same way: upbeat and in control, then casual and laidback, before indifference; but he wasn't fooling me. I knew he was nervous. And I have to say, seeing this side of Dan is actually quite refreshing. Far nicer than the persona he's portrayed when we've previously met. And I can't remember the last time a man bought me flowers . . . in fact, you know, I actually don't think I've ever had flowers bought for me – certainly not by Liam, and Will just wasn't that kind of guy; picking wild flowers from the hedgerow was more his style – so it makes a nice change, thoughtful too.

But then I let my cynical side get the better of me,

and I start to wonder what Dan is really up to, turning up with flowers, touching my arm; it's nice and flattering, but then I remember his 'country bumpkin' line, him pretending to hang himself with boredom over the prospect of living here in Tindledale. And what was that panicky look on his face just then all about? Hmm, I think I need to be careful.

Dan lifts up two carrier bags that he'd placed on the floor behind his legs. 'Oh, I brought lunch too!' he says casually, like it's the obvious thing to do. 'Well, it will be when I've cooked it. Don't mind, do you?' And he turns on his heel and lifts a giant chunk of clingfilm-covered Parmesan cheese up in the air, before dumping it on the counter and pulling a paper-wrapped package from the other bag. 'Crab carbonara,' he says, enthusiastically, opening the paper to show me a glorious whole pink crab. 'How do you fancy that? Fresh from Billingsgate – had my fish man deliver it this morning.' Dan cocks his head to one side before closing the paper, strolling over to my fridge and placing the crab inside, apparently making himself at home. He then unbuttons the cuffs of his shirt sleeves, as if limbering up to cook – like he really can't wait to get stuck in. Passionate. And it sure is very appealing. My pulse quickens. And I can't help staring as he loads the rest of the ingredients into my fridge.

Suddenly Dan pauses and whips a shrink-wrapped packet of hot dogs out of my fridge, as if pulling a rabbit from a hat.

'Do you actually eat this crap?' he demands to know, seemingly outraged. He pushes the packet towards me as if it's an exhibit in a murder trial.

'Err, no! They're for Jack, my son . . .' I quickly explain.

'*You feed this to a child?*' Dan roars, horrified, shaking his head in disbelief.

'Well, he's not a child exactly. And he's old enough to make his own mind up about what food he eats,' I say, jumping to Jack's defence. 'He's a student at Leeds University,' I add, proudly.

'*Really? You have a grown-up son?*' Dan says, incredulously. 'Blimey, were you a child when he was born?' and he laughs, his nice laugh this time, and I actually think he might be paying me a compliment, so I grin and pull a face.

Dan drops the hot dogs in the bin.

'But, hang on, you can't do that,' I splutter. 'Jack might turn up; I like to make sure I have his favourite foods in. Just in case . . .' I trail off.

'Trust me! You'll thank me for it in ten years' time

when his blood pressure isn't sky high from all the sodium they shove inside this processed junk,' Dan informs me in a matter-of-fact voice as he inspects – and then turfs out – a giant jar of mayonnaise.

'What's wrong with that?' I ask, going to retrieve the mayo. It was in the pantry and I only opened it last week to add to some tuna.

'It expired in April.'

'Oh.' Come to think of it, I did feel a little queasy after lunch on that day. 'Hmm, well . . . fair enough,' I shrug, making a mental note to check the contents of my fridge more frequently.

'Don't bother. You're much better off making your own. Dead simple. And my two boys love it!'

'Two boys?' I ask, curious to know more about him.

'Yes, Jacob and Charlie – twelve and thirteen. They live with their mum mostly, but come to me for week-ends . . . where the food is better, they tell me.' He laughs and I smile, liking that he's sharing this with me. 'Have you got any eggs?' he then asks, changing the subject and scanning the kitchen. 'Don't tell me you keep them in here!' and he sticks his disapproving face back into the fridge to search. I place the flowers on the table and then lift the lid of my chicken-shaped earthenware egg store, which I keep on the windowsill.

'Ta-dah! Freshly laid this morning,' I say proudly, thinking, ha! I bet he can't source food this fast for his restaurant in London.

'Great,' Dan nods, 'but get the chicken out of the sun.' And he lifts the earthenware pot and relocates it into the pantry. 'Perfect.' He turns to face me, planting his hands on his hips. 'So, are you up for lunch with me, or not?' And then he looks at his watch, as if, on second thoughts, he might have somewhere else more important to be.

'Um, well, seeing as you've asked me so nicely . . .' I start, and then stop when he purses his lips, tightens his jawline and a look of sheer exasperation covers his face.

'For crying out loud, woman. Why are you so –' he pauses as if searching for the most suitable word to describe me – 'infuriating!' he settles on.

'Me?' I exclaim. 'Err . . . take a look in the mirror, why don't you?' Did I really just say that? I sound ludicrous, like a silly schoolgirl. I instinctively look away. A loaded silence hangs in the air. And then, to my surprise, Dan holds up his palms.

'I don't need to!' he grins, sheepishly. 'Look, I know I can be an obnoxious bell-end. But I'm under a lot of pressure and I'm used to giving orders and answering to nobody but myself . . .' he states, and I stay silent, waiting for him to elaborate, but he doesn't. 'Will you please do me the honour of letting me cook for you? I'd really like to.' His eyes soften, making his whole demeanour seem so much lighter, less highly strung. His shoulders even realign themselves downwards by about two centimetres. The transformation is remarkable. And, of course, he's bound to be stressed. He's opening a new restaurant! Maybe that's why he's so volatile. Stress can have the most debilitating effect on a person. And he is a chef – a famous one off the telly, as Mary said – and the ones I've watched do seem to be permanently furious. Maybe it's a creative thing! Either way, I made a promise to myself . . . benefit of the doubt, and all that, so I take a breath and smile sweetly.

'Err, well, yes, that would be wonderful . . . if you're sure it's not too much trouble,' I start, now feeling very spoilt indeed. And it really is a treat, to have a celebrity chef cook for me, in my own kitchen.

'Trouble! Of course it isn't. Why would you think it's too much trouble?' he says, the thunderous look from our first meeting on the bridge making a rapid return. Oh dear. He really needs to learn to calm down. Never mind being concerned about my son's blood pressure, Dan really should be worried about his own.

'No reason,' I quickly say, my head spinning now. He's so volatile and I'm struggling to keep up.

'Yeah, well, we got off on the wrong foot, and Lawrence said freesias are your favourite,' Dan points to the flowers. 'And everyone loves my crab carbonara! They go mad for it in my restaurant.' He shoves his hands into his jeans pockets, looking suddenly despondent – he even rolls his eyes and pulls a face. How strange! And it makes me wonder if he's brought the flowers purely out of some misplaced sense of obligation. Hmm, maybe I was right to feel cynical after all. But then, Dan didn't need to go to the trouble of cooking lunch for me, sourcing fresh crab all the way from Billingsgate. And the flowers are gorgeous. I know Lucy doesn't open up her florist shop on a Sunday, as it's the only day she can spend with her new grand-daughter, so Dan really must have gone to a lot of trouble to get them.

'The flowers really are beautiful,' I say, picking them up and popping my nose into the bouquet to breathe in their divine scent, but wondering why Lawrence would tell Dan they're my favourite, when I'm sure we've never discussed flowers before. Oh well, it's very sweet . . . of both of them. 'Thank you.' I lay the flowers on the counter before ducking down to the cupboard under the sink to rummage for a vase, and then busy myself with unwrapping and arranging the freesias in an ascending height and colour coordinated order until I have them just so. Perfect.

I turn around to look at Dan. He's shaking his head and trying not to laugh.

'What?' I frown.

'Nothing!' he says, his face a picture of innocence now. 'You're just . . . so, err . . . precise. As well as infuriating!' he adds, cheekily. Instinctively, I open my mouth to retort, but Dan tilts his head to one side and raises a cheeky eyebrow, so I mumble 'sorry' instead.

'Don't be daft. It's nice. Charming. Endearing. And makes a change from the horrors I usually have hanging around me.' He pulls a pretend scared face.

'Oh!' I fiddle with my necklace. That was definitely a compliment. I reckon I'm starting to figure out Dan Wright. I smirk and poke out my tongue, and he laughs.

'Come on, let's get down to that cellar of yours!' And he actually grabs my hand and practically runs me across the kitchen and down the stairs, so fast it almost takes my breath away.

Downstairs, and the atmosphere hots up, literally. It's stifling here in the airless cellar and Dan's body, so close to mine in the confined space, is like a furnace right in front of me.

'Oops, um, sorry,' I say, bumping into his broad back as I step forward to find the cord for the light.

'Don't be,' Dan breathes, turning to face me. 'Here, let me help you,' he adds, and I realise that he's still holding my hand, which he gently lets go as he reaches an arm up and across me, feeling his way along the wall for the light switch, and treating me to a quick burst of his delicious signature scent. I feel my cheeks flush in the darkness.

'It's over here,' I say, stepping around him, my thigh tingling as it brushes the side of his leg and I very nearly gasp, but manage not to. Instead, I push a stray strand of hair from my face, which is now burning from the intensity of this very close encounter.

With the light on, we stand and stare at the assorted array of demijohns and bottles.

'Blimey, you sure do like making wine,' Dan grins, turning to look at me, folding his arms, and then, on quickly deciding against it, he puffs a long gust of cooling air up over his face before pulling his shirt out of his jeans. 'And it's hotter in this cellar than it is in my kitchen!' He fans the bottom of his shirt around, attempting to create a breeze for his hot body.

'Um . . . err, is it?' I manage, feeling flustered as I try not to stare on catching a glimpse of his very tanned and toned abdomen.

A short silence follows. I busy myself by bending down to retrieve a bottle of wine – more as a distraction than for any real purpose, but I can't just stand here and gawp at Dan's beautiful body, plus I can't work out if he really is oblivious, or not, of the physical effect he's having on me. I've never met anyone like him before. The men I've known in the past were far more obvious than Dan appears to be. They were more black and white – there was no real courtship with Will, he just came right out with it, that he wanted to sleep with me, and then Liam . . . well, we were young and he asked me out; in fact, I seem to recall that it was his friend who first told me Liam fancied me.

Dan stops fanning and coughs to clear his throat before stepping forward and crouching down next to the nearest wine rack, and the intimate moment vanishes, leaving me feeling confused and extremely flustered indeed. I'm usually rubbish at reading signals, but I know something just happened between us. What exactly? I'm not sure. Hmm, the feeling lingers . . .

Half an hour later, and after lots of bumping into each other and more intimate moments in the confined space, we've counted up twenty-seven bottles of elder-flower wine; nine bottles of sloe and blackberry gin, left over from last summer, which I hadn't even realised were still there; four bottles of a vibrant orange-coloured liquid that could be carrot and honey cordial, and a demijohn full of purple fluid with a cloudy white foam on top which, on tasting – Dan volunteered for the job, I didn't fancy it seeing the foam – he declared to be a magnificent beetroot wine that would just need skimming and straining. Oh, and we also have a case of mixed fruit cordials.

'Right. Well, we sure have enough for the juice bar!' Dan exclaims, carrying the last crate across the floor from the cellar door, before hauling it up on to the kitchen table, which is now completely covered with wooden crates and wine bottles. 'I'll start the lunch and have a think about a drinks menu – warm beetroot wine with a cinnamon stick perhaps,' he laughs, and I screw up my face. 'Whaat?' He does his nonchalant shrug. 'It could work!' Dan winks at me and pushes a hand through his hair, before striding across the kitchen to the fridge to gather all the ingredients together. 'Where's your wok?' he asks, flipping on the tap with his elbow like a pro – which of course he is – to wash his hands.

'Here.' I dive into a cupboard to retrieve it, and quickly hand it to him.

'Chopping board?'

'Yes chef,' I laugh, bringing my right hand up to the side of my head in an exaggerated salute. But before I can grab the wooden board and hand it to him right away, like a proper, efficient, fast-thinking kitchen assistant, Dan spots it next to the kettle, takes it, flips it over, and starts doing that super-fast slicing thing, making exceedingly quick work of a box-load of mushrooms.

'For the entrée . . . butternut squash velouté with sautéed cep and Parmesan crisp,' he explains, wiping his hands on a tea towel, which he then slings on to his shoulder for use throughout the whole culinary creative process, I assume.

'Ooh, I can't wait,' I say, wondering what velouté and cep are. I hope I like them.

'So, are you going to work this juice bar with me on show day?' Dan asks, casually.

'Um, sure, if I can . . . I'll most likely have my hands full with making sure everything else stays in order and runs to time, but I'm always happy to help out if I can,' I say, knowing there's already a list as long as my arm of school mums who've already volunteered for this particular task on show day – working with Dan. 'But won't you be busy with your food truck?' I ask.

'We could always combine the two – a food truck with an impressive wine list. In actual fact, that'll work better – we can flog the food and recommend the right wine or cordial accompaniment.' He stops chopping to ponder. 'And if it's a sell-out success, then we could make it a permanent thing, what do you say? Could work well for you if they do close down your school!' he grins and nudges me with his elbow.

'Err, um, yes . . . I guess so,' and I'm perplexed, yet again, by his bluntness. I guess he doesn't realise how much my school means to me. 'But what about your new restaurant?' I quickly recover. 'Surely you'll be very busy with that?'

Dan gives me a blank stare and puts down his knife. 'What new restaurant?'

'You know, the one you're opening in Tindledale. That's why you're here, aren't you?'

'No! What the hell gave you that idea?' And the thunderous look he does so well makes a very rapid return.

'Err . . .' I gulp, thinking: that'll teach me for speculating. And my heart sinks as I take in this news, wondering what it means for Tindledale then, and for my school. No exclusive Michelin-star restaurant to attract more people to the village to help boost the other local businesses. No celebrities helicoptering on to the village green. No media or TV channels doing special documentaries about Tindledale, the 'best place to live'. No 'putting us on the map' after all! I can feel my cheeks flushing again as I fiddle with my rabbit necklace, and I can hardly tell Dan that Lawrence and I have been, um . . . gossiping about him! And if Dan isn't here to open a new restaurant, then what's the real purpose of his visit? To Tindledale, the place he'd rather die than have to actually live in! 'Weell, I just assum—' But before I can answer properly, the back door bounces open, throwing me off kilter. I swivel my head to see who it is.

And gasp.

'*Muuum!* What are you doing here?'

Sixteen

'Playing gooseberry, by the looks of it!' Mum exclaims, in her usual extra-exasperated voice, eyeing up Dan as she swings off her pashmina and drops her handbag on to the window seat, before propping her purple-patterned wheelie suitcase against the table leg. 'Why didn't you tell me you had moved a boyfriend in, darling?'

Mum walks across the kitchen and engulfs Dan in a heady embrace, flinging her arms around his neck and pulling him in tight, her super-strong perfume permeating the air. And I'm aghast. Dan's face is a picture of surprise and intrigue.

'And quite the looker, aren't you?' Mum says, squeezing his cheek. 'Very Hugh Bonneville after a bacchanalian night out.'

I want to die.

Right here on my kitchen floor, clutching Blue for

comfort. Talking of which, where is he? Panicking, I near body-slam the back door shut, but Dan realises what I'm worried about and, quickly freeing himself from my mother's clutch, he grabs my hand to stop me from racing out into the garden.

'He's in his cage!' And Dan points to Blue, both little paws up near his mouth and merrily munching his way through a carrot. 'You put him away before we went down to the dungeon, sweetheart!' And then he twirls me into his body and plants a big, long, hard kiss on my lips, practically winding me. I gasp like a drowning person on reaching the surface when he eventually lets me go. Dan then leans backwards casually against the kitchen counter, with a very mischievous look on his face, and spreads his arms out wide.

'Whaaaat? What dungeon?' I stammer, my lips still smarting from his very passionate kiss, swivelling my head in his direction and then quickly back to Mum, who now has her mouth agape. Dan winks at me. And my whole body goes whoosh, and then sizzles like a lit firework, as I try to keep up with yet another swift, mercurial change in his behaviour. My stomach is actually swirling, but before I can get a proper grip on what just happened between Dan and me, Mum pipes up again.

'Oh, don't mind me. I'm very broadminded. Only last week, I went with my girlfriends to watch that *Fifty Shades* film. All that S&M stuff is very normcore nowadays!' And she plops her bottom down on my window seat before swinging one slender leg over the other and pulling out a carton of Lucky Strike, which she no doubt bought in bulk from Duty Free. Mum rips off the cellophane, takes out one packet and flips it open, before popping a cigarette in between her crimson-coated lips and adding, 'Now, be a dear and pass me those matches over there next to the gas hob!'

*

We're in the garden. Mum and I have just polished off Dan's perfect lunch, with me anxious and on edge all the way through as I tried desperately, but failed, to keep the conversation to general chitchat, and definitely with no more suggestive innuendo from Mum, who it turns out decided I was pining away without Jack, and offering to 'keep you company now that the weather has warmed up over here' as she no longer does damp, dark English winters any more, apparently. Right on cue, in the middle of this story, Jack then called to explain to me – luckily I had taken the home phone handset out into the garden – and wanting to check that Gran had arrived. He explained to her that I was OK about South Africa, as it turned out. He also told me that he had called Taylor, and that they were now 'cool', and that I could call Stevie's dad for a chat after all, and happily gave me his contact details.

So that's all fine, but then Mum spent the whole lunch telling Dan how marvellous it is that we are living together – of course, Dan did nothing to dispel this myth; instead, he played along, seeming to enjoy seeing me squirm with embarrassment. Even leaning in to me in a caring, comfortable, fun-boyfriend way, and saying, 'Don't be bashful, sweetheart,' when I tried to explain to Mum that she had got it all wrong, and that actually there was nothing going on between us, and Dan was merely here to help out with the village show. This all happened in between her regaling us with tales of how wonderful the weather is in Tenerife, and how I should seriously consider 'giving it a go' if my school ends up closing, to which Dan did a big guffaw on seeing my face, asking if he could come too. So Mum said of course he could and something about 'us lovebirds, and it being so romantic' . . . despite the S&M thing! I had zoned out by this point, resigned to being utterly humiliated, and having accepted that there was absolutely nothing I could do about it.

So now the three of us are drinking champagne – one of three bottles that Mum pulled from her wheelie suitcase after having already downed several large glasses of my elderflower fizz.

'Top up, darling?' Mum asks Dan, lifting the bottle of Piper whilst swiftly batting away a bee. 'Megan's home-brew is OK, but it's practically non-alcoholic. Time for the good stuff. *Salud!*' she giggles, ignoring Dan, who's shaking his head as he goes to put his hand over the top of his glass, but she just bats that away too and fills the glass anyway, until it's almost brimming over. 'Sooo, where did you learn to cook like that, Dan? You're very good – have you ever considered doing it professionally? I have a friend who owns a Spanish paella place in Playas De Las Americas and he's always on the look-out for decent chefs – they never stay, you see!' And after doing an extra-long draw on her cigarette and puffing it up into the beautiful, bright blue and *very clean* Tindledale sky, Mum actually leans forward and pats Dan's knee, as if she's bestowing some kind of special wisdom. 'No, they come for the summer and then scarper when the tips dry up during the winter months, so if you play your cards right I could put in a good word for you!'

And forget my earlier feelings of resignation, I now just want to die all over again. Instead, I clear the dishes from the table and beat a hasty retreat back inside.

'Ooh, Megan, bring me a blanket back with you, love, please, it's getting very chilly out here,' Mum calls after me, putting on her pretend fffffreeeezing voice. I glance at the barometer on the doorframe – hmm, seventy degrees Fahrenheit, so on a par with the Canary Islands then – hardly arctic, as she's making out. 'OK, but I'm going to the bathroom first,' I yell back in a grumpy voice. I take a deep breath and close my eyes momentarily, wondering if she's planning on staying for the whole summer. If so, I'm going to have to get used to being publicly humiliated. And in my head I'm already concocting ways of keeping Mum away from the rest of the villagers, my school, and our Great Village Show. Jesus, I can't let her anywhere near the judges – heaven knows what she might come out with. No, my mother is a flaming liability!

Feeling frustrated and quite ludicrous, I near sling the plates and cutlery into the dishwasher, before giving the door a hefty kick with my bunny-clad right foot. Then I disappear into the bathroom, just to give myself a moment of normality. I feel as if I've slipped into some sort of parallel universe. And I still need to work out exactly what happened when Dan kissed me. The sizzling sensation on my lips is still very, very much there and, dare I say it, I think I might want to experience that moment all over again. Damn it! And of all the people, it had to be him. Dan flaming Wright, who is actually OK some of the time, but for much of the rest of the time he's volatile, crass, maverick and a . . . oh, I don't know, a . . . *troglodyte*, I guess could fit – dictionary meaning is 'crude, savage person', according to one of the Year Six pupils, who'd written it in his English essay and then explained it to me when I tested his comprehension.

I pull the door to, lock it, and sit on the closed toilet seat, resting my head in my hands, wondering what would have happened today if Mum hadn't turned up. Why did Dan kiss me? Was it purely to play along with Mum's inference? Or to get a rise out of me? A reaction? Maybe that's just his sense of humour, he likes playing games, it's what he finds funny . . . taking the mickey out of people. I remember again the 'country bumpkin' comment, but that was a long time ago. I would have thought he'd have grown out of all that stuff by now. Oh, to be honest, I really don't know what to think, but something I do know is that I can't get Dan out of my head now. And what about what happened in the cellar? The humid air down there was charged, for sure. It's so mystifying, and I'm not sure I like feeling this way. Confused, and with no sense of control. I shake my head as if to clear the discombobulating thoughts from my mind, and can now hear Mum and Dan talking through the open window – my bathroom is on the ground floor off the kitchen, as it is in lots of these old cottages in Tindledale.

Mum is speaking. 'So how did you meet Megan?'

'It was here in the village – on the bridge in the garden at Lawrence's place—' Dan starts.

'Oh, were you living in the B&B?' Mum asks nosily, and I'm guessing Dan has nodded in reply, because she then adds, 'Never mind, darling, I know how hard it is for you youngsters to find an affordable place to live. That's why I bought this cottage for my Megan. But you don't have to worry about any of that now. And isn't Lawrence lovely? Did you know he was gay – although he hides it very well, don't you think?' and Mum actually lowers her voice when she says the word 'gay', and seemingly sees nothing wrong in assuming that Lawrence would have to set out to deliberately obscure his sexuality, like we are still living in the 1950s or something. Oh God. I press my head further into my hands. She really has no filter whatsoever, and doesn't even wait for Dan to reply. 'And with a heart of gold. Lawrence has been *very good* with my Megan,' she goes on in a voice that now makes me sound as if I'm some sort of half-wit who needs special care.

I stand up and reach across the bath to go to close the window, unable to listen to any more of her nonsense. But then I hesitate, arm in mid-air. I can hear Dan talking now.

'Yes, Lawrence is a great guy – in fact, if it wasn't for him, then I don't think I'd be here with Meg now . . .' And it sounds as if he's pleased, happy with this outcome. That's nice, but why then, earlier, did he seem to delight in seeing me squirm?

'Ooh, *really*?' And Mum makes a noise like the verbal equivalent of big, intrigued eyes – she never could resist hearing about other people's personal stuff.

'Yes, that's right. You see, Meg and I didn't get off on the right foot at first.'

'Well, you can't blame her, darling; it's been a very long time since my Megan had a man. She probably just needs a bit of practice.' *Oh please, somebody shoot me and get it over with.* 'In fact, there was a time when

I thought she might be –' and Mum lowers her voice again before mouthing – 'the other way . . .'

'The other way?' Dan clarifies, and I just know from the way he's said it that he's got an amused look on his brutish face. I bet he's thoroughly enjoying this; perhaps he isn't so nice after all. Hmm, but then he must be feeling humiliated and a bit embarrassed too, after having my mother offer him the chance of a job ladling giant mountains of paella around one of those massive metal tureens for tourists. She clearly has no idea who he is. Come to think of it, he was actually very modest in not pointing out this fact to Mum, while I failed, spectacularly, to get a word in edgeways during lunch as I tried several times to let her know.

'Oh no, but she certainly isn't the other way,' Mum hastily adds, sounding panicky now. 'Definitely not. Well, she can't be, can she? Not now she has you!' And at this precise moment my foot slips on the mat over the stripped wood floor, so I end up catapulting myself across the whole width of the bath. Help! I go to grab the window frame, but my hand knocks the handle instead, which in turn makes the window bounce backwards on the frame. Oh no! They're bound to have heard and will now know that I've been eavesdropping.

They'll assume I've slammed the window on purpose in a fit of temper or whatever. I very quietly prop the window back open as if to imply that it was an accident – no fits of temper in here, no eavesdropping at all, oh no! I'm a perfectly calm and rational human being when my mother is around. Hmmm!

There's a ringing in my ears; I must have banged my head . . . or is that the phone? I manage to reinstate myself into an upright position and I'm straightening my hair in the mirror when I can hear Mum talking.

'Laaaaaaawrence!' Ahh, it was the phone and Mum has taken the liberty of answering it. 'We were just talking about you!' *Mother! Jesus, the woman has no tact whatsoever.* 'Yes, hold on, he's right here.' There's a short silence. And Dan is talking now.

'Yep. Thanks Lawrence.' Another silence. 'OK, I'll do that right away.'

'What is it darling?' Mum asks Dan.

'I need to make an urgent call – I better go and ask Meg,' he says, sounding distracted.

'Oh, no need. Here,' and I assume Mum is handing the phone to Dan. I hesitate, and then curiosity gets the better of me and I sit back on the closed toilet seat. Besides, I'm not ready to face my mother again, just yet. 'Make the call, and don't mind me, it's time for my siesta in any case,' Mum chortles. 'I'll pop upstairs and find a blanket for myself, Meg is taking for ever – she must be doing a number two.' *Oh, for crying out loud!* 'Won't be a mo, darling. I'm looking forward to snoozing in the garden.' And she chuckles some more as I die a little more inside.

Mum comes indoors and I assume Dan is making his urgent call. I stand up, feeling ridiculous for still hiding like this, and I'm just about to open the bathroom door and go back into the garden when I hear Dan talking in a soft voice.

'Hey, no need to apologise, it's fine. I've missed you too.' My hand freezes on the door handle. Who is he talking to? One of his sons, perhaps? 'I'll be back very soon, babe.' No, it must be a woman, he wouldn't call one of his sons 'babe'! There's a pause. 'I can't wait to see you either, darling, and don't worry, we'll sort it all out . . . I've missed you as well.' Silence. 'Nothing important. Just working. Yes, I love you too, sweetheart. You're everything to me.'

I freeze, and stand motionless by the door, listening to the sound of my heart hammering inside my chest. My hands feel numb.

Babe.

Sweetheart.

Just working.

Nothing important.

I feel like such a fool. A fool for even considering that something happened between Dan and me down in the cellar. I clearly read it all wrong. And no wonder he hesitated and changed tack after his 'don't change' line. He's been playing me. Well, thank God I didn't make a fool of myself and respond to his flirtations, I was right to be wary, to be cynical. He clearly has a girlfriend. And now I have to face him and act as if nothing has changed. He may be brazen enough to carry on like that, but I'm definitely not.

I take a deep breath before splashing some cold water on to my face, willing my hands to stop shaking, but I feel so humiliated, and I wonder if his girlfriend knows that he's been here, in my home, sourcing ingredients to cook lunch for me, and bringing me flowers, flirting and kissing me passionately on the lips, which I must now assume was clearly just for show – to embarrass me in front of my mother. Talking of which, where is she?

I eventually manage to get it together, and quickly head upstairs to grab a blanket for Mum (they'll know I was listening if I go outside without one), then make my way back out into the garden. I needn't have worried about facing Dan, as he's gone. There's no sign of him anywhere. I look around, like a character doing a comedy double take. No, definitely no Dan. Just my mother is here and she's snoring gently in a deckchair, a champagne bottle in one hand, my favourite patchwork blanket clasped in the other and her mouth hanging open.

I push the blanket around her shoulders and slip the bottle from her hand, before flopping into a deckchair too and finishing the last of the bubbles.

'*Salud*, indeed, Mother!' I tilt the top of the bottle in her direction. 'And, for the record, Dan looks nothing like Hugh Bonneville.'

Seventeen

The following morning, when I come downstairs, there's no point in even attempting to get any sense from Mum – to find out why Dan left without even saying goodbye to me. She's still fast asleep; there was a brief interlude last night where I managed to walk her in from the garden and on to the sofa in the lounge, but there was no way I was going to manage to steer her up the stairs to the spare bedroom, she was far too wobbly. So, after tucking a blanket around her, I rolled her on to her side (I read an article once about drunk people inhaling their own vomit and dying, so I worry about it), and propped some cushions under her before leaving her to it.

I finish my breakfast – boiled eggs with Marmite soldiers – and, after making my packed lunch, I tiptoe past the pulled-to lounge door on my way out to school, pausing briefly to check that Mum is actually still breathing. She stirs as I open the door.

'Why didn't you wake me, darling?' she asks, pulling herself upright, the imprint of my hand-stitched appliqué owl cushion embedded on the side of her face. 'And why am I huddled up like an old woman?' she then complains, tossing the blanket away in disgust.

'Because, Mother . . . you were drunk!' I tell her, picking the blanket up and folding it away on to the armchair.

'Oh, I do wish you wouldn't exaggerate, darling. I only had a few drops of champagne.'

'And completely showed me up in front of Dan.'

'Did I?' she asks, incredulously. 'Gosh, I'm very sorry if that's true.'

'It is. Why else do you think he left so abruptly?' I ask, thinking I really should get going – I want to get to school in plenty of time to make sure today's activities are properly organised. Pete is bringing a couple of his calves down for the children to feed and pet, which is bound to impress the inspectors. And Sybs is due in this afternoon to do some more crafting work with the children on their secret project.

'Did he?' Mum asks, looking vague.

'Yes. Do you mean to tell me you were *so* plastered

that you can't remember?' I admonish, sounding like Mrs Pocket ticking off a child. Mum huffs and crosses her arms. I take a big, deep breath and stare at a flower in the middle of the floral wallpaper on my feature wall – I really should replace it soon; it's looking a bit dated now. Mind you, if my school closes down and I'm out of a job, then I'll have all the time in the world very soon to make home improvements. And then something strikes me. 'Mum, how long are you planning on staying?' I brace myself, waiting for her answer.

'Ooh, I'm not sure yet, Megan. Why? Are you trying to get rid of me already?'

'No, of course not,' I half-fib, folding my arms across my chest and hating how I always seem to regress back to a sulky teenager whenever Mum's around for any length of time. I'm a grown woman, not the nineteen-year-old girl I was when she scarpered off to Spain, telling me it would be 'an exciting adventure' when I first balked at the idea of being left on my own with the responsibility of a house to run. I soon got used to it, of course, I had to; and then being a lone parent with a baby wasn't easy either, but I coped. And she's right when she says that Lawrence has been good with me, although I wouldn't have phrased it quite like that – he's been a wonderfully kind friend over the years. And he was here, which is more than I can say for her.

I inhale sharply, feeling mean and ungrateful, as it's thanks to Mum that I have this lovely little cottage, not forgetting the glorious holidays Jack and I have enjoyed with her. I just wish sometimes, in a way, that I could be a bit more like her perhaps. Gregarious and outgoing. I always feel inadequate around her, prudish and prim. Yes, if I was different, less of a home bird, more adventurous, I could join Jack in South Africa for the summer. Mind you, I'm not sure he'd want me muscling in on his adventure, but it's a possibility. But really I like normality: routine, familiarity, my home, my garden – I find comfort in the certainty of knowing the snowdrops, daffodils and geraniums will appear along my front path in early spring, followed by the glorious pink peony blooms on the bush beside my washing line in April. I like things to stay the same, the way they always are. It makes me feel safe and secure and actually very happy.

'Jolly good. We are going to have so much fun,' Mum says, sounding very chipper as she cuts into my thoughts, and I smile, relenting. Perhaps it won't be so bad having her around. She means well, and she can be quite good company – if she steers clear of the bubbles, that is.

'So you have no idea why Dan left then?' I try again.

'I'm sorry, darling, I'm not sure. My memory isn't what it used to be . . .' Mum does her tinkly laugh.

'Hmm, so nothing to do with you being sozzled then?' And I give her my best scary teacher face before shaking my head and smiling.

'Oh Megan, don't give me that look – he'll be back . . . and in the meantime we can enjoy some girly time together. How about we paint on some face packs and watch a rom-com? There's a box of churros in my case – from the patisserie near my apartment that you like. We could heat up some chocolate to make a dip. Come on, it'll be such fun,' she beams, hopping across the room to pat her hair back into place in the mirror.

'I have to go to work,' I say, feeling a little exasperated now. And why hasn't she got the hangover from hell? By rights, she should be feeling very fragile this morning. If I had drunk as much as she did yesterday, then I'm sure I'd be hiding underneath my duvet right now, refusing to move.

'Of course! Silly me,' Mum chirps. 'Well, I'll just have to manage on my own then . . .' And she near leaps back on to the sofa and reaches for the TV remote control. 'Would you be a dear and pop the kettle on before you leave?'

Ten minutes later, and having begrudgingly popped the kettle on, I'm cycling past the allotments near my school when I spot Jessie over in the far corner, wearing jeans, a T-shirt and pink polka-dot wellies. She's bent over pulling cabbages from a patch – for the food bank, I assume – and the triplets are chatting and giggling away as they form a little production line, passing the cabbages along to each other before loading them into a selection of wooden crates on the ground, next to a van with the words 'Sam Robinson, Landscape Gardener' inscribed down the side. Ahh, that's nice that he's helping her out.

'Hi Jess,' I yell, ding-a-linging my bell, but she mustn't be able to hear me, and carries on with the cabbages. I glance at my watch and see that it's just after eight – far earlier than I had realised – so I swing my legs off the bike and rest it against the fence, figuring I have plenty of time to stop for a chat – the inspectors don't usually tend to turn up until at least nine o'clock.

I'm making my way down the tiny gravel path that snakes in between the centre of the allotments, flanked either side by the most gloriously golden buttercups, some of them nearly knee high, when a man appears from the doorway of the potting shed. It's Sam. And for some reason, I instinctively stop moving. Jessie is walking towards him. Beaming, he hands her a mug. She takes it from him and then he says something that makes her laugh, before gently lifting a stray strand of hair away from her face. And the way Sam does this, so intimately, makes me turn away. I feel like an intruder, interrupting a tender moment, as if I'm spying, so I go to walk back to my bike. I've almost reached the fence when I hear my name being yelled by one of the children.

'Miss Siiiiiinger. Look, Mummy, it's Miss Singer,' the voice says, excitedly. I immediately swivel on my heel, and turn to face the allotments. Jessie is standing now, facing me, but where's Sam? He's disappeared, back inside the potting shed, I guess. Well, he didn't need to go on my account. If he makes Jessie smile, then that's good enough for me – it's about time she had some happiness in her life.

Millie is running towards me, laughing and clutching a bunch of dandelions. I walk towards her and, when we meet, she flings her little arms around my legs to give me a huge hug. I stroke the top of her head before crouching down to talk to her at eye level.

'What a wonderful greeting. Thank you, Millie.' She grins and pushes the dandelions towards me.

'These are for Blue, I picked them all myself,' she tells me, her sapphire eyes twinkly in the early morning sun, and I'm dazzled by the incredible contrast from that day I first saw her in Kitty's café. Even since Millie played in my garden, her hair seems blonder, her skin brighter – and now she has a warm honey-coloured tan from being outside in the sun, too – but there's something else as well . . . happiness! She's happy and relaxed. Not withdrawn and indifferent like she was when she first came here. Obviously, her daddy being away is having an enormously positive effect on her.

I take the dandelions from her and she slips her hand into mine as we walk on further along the path together.

'Meg, so lovely to see you,' Jessie says, glowing as she walks towards us, pulling off her gardening gloves with her teeth and slinging them under her arm to give me a hug. 'It's my turn to harvest the crop for the food bank – Mrs Pocket has drawn up a rota, so we,' she inadvertently gestures towards the potting shed, before pausing to correct herself, 'um, I thought I'd make an early start before the weather gets too hot.'

'That's nice. Lovely to see you too – how is it going?' I ask, gently hugging her back, pleased when she doesn't flinch. I glance over at the crates and see that they're brimming with a veritable rainbow of colourful, freshly picked home-grown produce – cabbages, kale, carrots, potatoes, sweetcorn, butternut squash, plums, parsnips, apples, pears, and plenty of punnets of strawberries – such a wonderful variety.

'Good, really good,' she nods, grinning as she steps back to see my face as she asks, 'Sooooo, how did it go yesterday?'

'Um, err . . . yes, it was OK thanks,' I say tentatively. 'Dan cooked lunch!' I add, making big eyes.

'Ooh, lucky lady. I bet it was amazing.'

'It was. The food, I mean, it was truly delicious . . .' I nod, awkwardly, not really sure of what else to say to her – that he kissed me? And I liked it. But he might have just been messing around. And he has a girlfriend?

'Aaaaaand?' she asks, giving me a quizzical look. But there's a short silence as we're distracted by the children playing tag, darting in and out between us, all laughing and attempting to squidge each other with juicy, ripe, half-bitten cherries from the orchards surrounding the allotments. 'Come on now,' Jessie laughs, half-heartedly chastising the children. 'That's enough – the fruit and vegetables aren't for playing with. It's precious produce that we need to crate up, so let's get on with it. Chop chop!' she claps her hands together. 'Go and pick up the cherries, please, and put them in the punnets over there.' Jessie shakes her head and rolls her eyes, and I'm struck by the contrast in her appearance too. She's glowing, happy and vibrant, and it suits her how she has her hair now – wound up into a loose, messy bun, and not a trace of make-up – fresh faced, a classic English rose complexion with a smattering of freckles across her cheeks, joining on the bridge of her nose. I glance at her hands, and the nail polish is gone too. And, wait a minute! So are her rings – her platinum diamond engagement rock and matching wedding ring. She spots me looking and shrugs apprehensively.

'Oh, I, um, always take them off before coming to the allotments – just in case the mud ruins the diamonds,' she explains, before slipping her gloves back on. I smile, but feel dismayed when a dart of disappointment for her flicks through me.

'Ahh, I see. I thought for a moment there, that you had . . .' I grin and pause, not wanting to overstep the mark – not keen to interfere in her marriage, even if her husband is abusive, philandering and controlling. I've been over that scene outside Kitty's café so many times in my head, where Mr Cavendish had lost his key, and now see it in such a different way – Jessie was fearful and feeling intimidated out there on the High Street when he tapped his cheek and demanded she kiss it. With the benefit of hindsight I see it, and should have said something, if only to ask if she was OK. I would love to be able to turn back time and have the opportunity to give the charming Mr Cavendish a piece of my mind. Although what if he had later taken it out on Jessie? Hmm, and I feel torn again now, it isn't my place to tell Jessie what to do; she needs to come to the realisation herself. Jessie nods for me to continue, '. . . um, had a think about everything,' I settle on, seeing as Millie is now handing me more dandelions.

'I'm starting to,' she says cryptically, and I know exactly what she means so I nod and touch her shoulder in support. 'Sooo, tell me, how was the rest of your date with Dan? Anything else happen apart from lunch?' she asks brightly, changing the subject and giving me a spill-the-beans inquisitive look.

'It wasn't really a date,' I correct, and then explain, 'my mother turned up for a surprise visit, just as Dan started cooking.' I stare at the dandelions.

'Oh dear,' Jessie tries not to laugh.

'Indeed. And luckily he had brought plenty of ingredients with him as it was then three for lunch instead of two,' I shake my head. 'And then he had vanished by the time I came back after popping to the bathroom. Pfffffft! Just like that,' I say, smiling wryly as I wave a palm in the air.

'Well, that's unfortunate. Didn't he say goodbye?' Jessie creases her forehead.

'No! He just disappeared. Lawrence called to talk to him and then I overheard him on the phone, to his girlfriend, and then he was gone . . .'

'Hmm, that sounds a bit strange . . . His girlfriend? I saw the way he looked at you in the pub garden.' Jessie shakes her head. 'I'm surprised, are you sure?'

'Yes, quite sure,' I say quietly.

'Have you spoken to Lawrence? Maybe he can shed some light on why Dan would just disappear, without even saying goodbye . . .'

'I haven't yet. But that's a very good idea – maybe I'll call him later. I'm wondering now if I offended Dan somehow,' I mutter, deep in thought, as I let my mind flick through the sequence of events yesterday.

'Why would you think that?'

'Um, I'm not sure.'

'Then you must try to stop worrying, or you'll end up convincing yourself that you did something wrong. Call Lawrence. I bet there's a simple explanation. I'm sure he wouldn't just have upped and left without good reason. It's rude, if nothing else.' She pauses, and I can't help thinking that maybe he did do just that. He *can* be rude! And I know he's impulsive – I saw that on the bridge when he tossed his phone into the water. Who does that? But then Dan Wright isn't like anyone else I've ever met; it's as if the rules don't apply to him. Maybe my mother had already nodded off and he got bored of waiting for me to return, or – and then it dawns on me – he heard the window slam shut and realised I was eavesdropping like some silly schoolgirl, preferring that pastime to actually sitting in the garden being sociable. No wonder he left! He most likely thinks I'm ridiculous. Especially next to the women he's used to, the London women with their designer clothes and pretty scarfs with diamanté detailing. His actual girl-friend! And he did say that I was infuriating. And with Mum going on the way she did. Who can blame him?

'Maybe later, after school, I'll see what Lawrence has to say,' I venture.

'Yes do,' Jessie grins.

The children are busy now, over by the produce boxes, so I decide to go for it.

'And talking of men disappearing, why is Sam hiding in the potting shed?' I ask, leaning into Jessie and lowering my voice. She hesitates, opens her mouth, closes it, and then hurriedly asks, 'Do you have a few minutes?'

I check my watch and nod, and she dashes over to

the shed. Moments later, and she's back. 'Sam will keep an eye on the children,' Jessie adds, before linking her arm through the crook of my elbow and gently steering me away.

We walk a few steps until she's certain the triplets are out of earshot and then swiftly tells me everything.

'Oh Jessie, what are you going to do? That's the most romantic story I've ever heard,' I whisper, briefly placing my free hand over my heart, after she's finished explaining how she's known Sam since they were babies – their mothers were best friends. Sam and Jessie grew up together in the same village and were then childhood sweethearts. Her first kiss. Her first love. They were inseparable until Sam went off to agricultural college, followed by a year's volunteering in Africa, cultivating the land so a new school could be built. Meanwhile, Jessie met Sebastian at an awards dinner in London – something to do with one of the farming magazines that she used to write for. He pursued her, relentlessly, and she found it flattering. He wowed her with gifts and trips to the ballet, opera, art galleries and the very best restaurants . . . all the things she had never experienced, having grown up in a little village, where she later felt so lonely and isolated without her mum, and desperately missing Sam after they had drifted apart.

'Sebastian really did sweep me off my feet,' Jessie explains. 'He met me at a vulnerable time, and it's very distracting and quite intoxicating being whisked off to Paris for the weekend, or riding in a gondola along the Venice waterways, watching the sunset from the deck of a yacht in the Caribbean – that was my birthday treat. Mind you, the warning signs were there even then, when he created a scene one evening, insisting I go back to the room and change, as the dress I had chosen to wear for dinner wasn't suitable. I had foolishly thought he was just looking out for me, the naïve, unworldly country girl, who didn't have a clue about high society nuances; that he was helping me, enlightening me. And then . . . well, when I found out I was expecting the triplets . . . that was kind of it! We got married right away,' she finishes quickly and quietly.

'It's OK,' I say, softly, seeing her body stiffen.

'But it's not OK, is it?' Jessie stops walking and turns towards me. 'Not really! I can't have Sam in my life. I'm married. It's wrong. Very wrong.' I turn sideways to see her face; her eyes are glistening with tears.

'It's going to be all right,' I say firmly. 'We'll figure it out – I'll help you, however I can.'

'But we've only just met – what must you think of me?'

'Don't be silly. We're friends, isn't that what friends do? Help each other out. They don't judge and, besides, if you don't mind me saying so . . . from what you've told me, and from what I've witnessed myself of your marriage, it doesn't seem to be in . . .' I pause, '. . . um, great shape,' I look at the ground.

We start walking back to the children, who are now having the times of their lives, weaving in and out of the buttercups, trying to catch Sam who is pretending to be a horse, or is it a gorilla? I can't be sure as he's doing a silly mixture of galloping, followed by swinging his arms from side to side down in front of his body. Either way, the triplets are loving it, shrieking and shouting, 'Go faster, horsey, faster!'

Smiling, I glance again at Jessie, and see that silent tears are trickling down her cheeks. I sweep an arm around her shoulders and gently pull her into me.

'And how does Sam fit in now?' I ask carefully, not wanting her to feel that I'm making any kind of assumption or judgement, as it's pretty obvious there's something between them. Jessie lets out a long sigh, as if she's relieved to finally be able to share her burden.

'You are going to think I'm dreadful,' she starts, apprehensively.

'Try me, I'm here to listen,' I say lightly.

'Thank you,' she gives me a watery smile. 'Sam and I are friends. Sebastian knows about him, but he doesn't know that we're back in touch. He . . . I haven't told him yet . . . but I will, I have to. Sam is staying here in Tindledale. He wanted to be close by; he doesn't want us to drift apart again.' Jessie's voice wobbles before fading, and I'm shocked, not from what she's telling me, but that nobody noticed another newcomer here in the village. I wonder where he's living? And then a thought pops into my head, a potentially very dangerous thought, but surely not . . . Sam can't actually be at the farmhouse while Sebastian is away? But Jessie swiftly allays my fears by adding, 'Sam's renting the studio flat above the bookshop in the High Street – he managed to secure a big contract landscaping the grounds at the Blackwood Farm Estate.' I let out a small inward sigh of relief.

'And are you just friends?'

'Yes.' Silence follows. Jessie takes a deep breath. 'Sorry . . . no, no we aren't . . . . It's more than that, but not what you might think, we aren't having a proper full-blown affair, I couldn't do that. Even if Sebastian has a habit of doing so.'

'Hey, you don't have to apologise or explain to me . . . or even tell me anything at all for that matter, unless you want to. If it helps, then I'm here, but you must do whatever you feel comfortable with.'

'Thank you. I'm so pleased you're my friend. And I'd like to tell you, I think I need to, as keeping this all to myself is near on driving me mad. When Sam and I were first back in touch – he found me on social media and was living in London too – he sent a message to let me know that his dad had passed away and that his mum had been asking after me. Anyway, we met up in London and chatted about the good times, the fun . . . and he, well, I feel alive when I'm with him . . . He makes me feel how I used to feel, before . . .' She stops talking. 'It was later, a month or so after the funeral, actually, when I went home to see Dad, and I bumped into Sam again. He was back in the village visiting his family too, and although I had thought that moving here, away from London and the distraction of Sam being there, would mean an end to it, he persuaded me to have a drink with him, for old times' sake, and well . . . it was a difficult time, I felt so low and isolated and I had just found out about another one of Sebastian's . . . indiscretions. Dad was looking after the children for the night and well, I . . . stayed with Sam for the whole evening. It happened, and I've felt ashamed ever since. And now he's here, saying he loves me and needs to be close to me and I can't get him out of my head, even though it's wrong. I think I'm still in love with him, but I can't be, I just can't . . .'

And Jessie starts crying all over again. I put both arms around her and give her a big hug, catching Sam's eye over Jessie's shoulder. He's standing by his truck with a very forlorn look on his face, his shoulders dropped as if he has the weight of the world on them, and then he seems to pull himself together and rounds the children up, sitting them in a little row on the back of the truck before doing some magic tricks to keep them entertained. Or perhaps it's to protect them from seeing their mummy feeling so sad.

Jessie pulls away and turns too.

'He's so good with the triplets, and they adore him,' she says, and I urge her to find a way out of this intolerable situation.

'Oh Jessie, please, you can't carry on like this,' I whisper, 'it's no good for any of you . . .'

Eighteen

S ix o'clock, and the inspectors have left the school.
I'm in my office having just finished off tomorrow's
lesson plans for Year Five – I'm helping out as their
class teacher had to dash to the emergency dentist
in Market Briar with a broken tooth after selecting
an extra chewy toffee from the tin in the staffroom –
when I decide to call Lawrence.

He answers right away.

'It's Meg, how are you?' I push a stack of exercise
books away from the corner of my desk so I can rest
my back – I must have jarred it, as it's been aching ever
since I slipped on the mat in the bathroom.

'Exhausted,' Lawrence starts. 'I've been mopping and
sweeping and putting up trellis tables all day long in
the village hall ready for show day. You're doing an
inspection on Thursday evening as part of the village's
final dress rehearsal, remember?'

'Am I?' I say, leaping up and turning around to quickly flick over the page in my open desk diary. Ahh, yes! It's right here, after school. I tap the page and sit back down to rest my back.

'Don't tell me you had forgotten . . . Surely not, you volunteered at the last committee meeting, in an extra-zealous moment when you were hoofing it through the agenda, keeping us all on track. You suggested the three committees come together to make sure the village square and all of the surrounding lanes, fields, station car park, Scout hut, farm buildings, Country Club, allotments, shops and anywhere else within a mile radius of Tindledale is properly organised, tidy, decorated and ready to dazzle the judges on show day,' he laughs. 'But I know how busy you are, so if it's too much . . .'

'No! I'll be there, Lawrence. I can't wait to see what you've done. And the village hall is an integral part of the show; you know we get scored specifically on the presentation of it.'

'And quite rightly, too: the hall is at the heart of all great villages,' he says brightly.

'It sure is. Which reminds me, the parish council have supplied the plug-in heaters, yes?' I ask, remembering that 'arctic' comment last time from the judges.

'They sure have. Eight shiny new heaters, dotted

around the hall, and mounted on the walls too,' he says impressively. 'Just in case our inclement British weather decides to turn the thermostat down on show day.'

'Great.' I make a mental note to cross 'heaters for hall' off my village show to-do list.

'So how is it all going at the school?' he asks. 'The other heart of our great village.'

'Hmm, well, we're none the wiser really – I wish the inspectors would hurry up and make a decision, I just want to know now.'

'Of course you do,' Lawrence sighs.

'Exactly. But we've been told the results of the viability assessment won't be shared before the new academic year starts in September – so that's after the village show, and after the end of term,' I say, and he tuts. 'Yes, and when this was questioned at the governors' meeting, we were told it still gives us plenty of time to "manage the outcome of the inspectors' findings". So, in other words, we have all summer to worry and speculate about it, and then a year to prepare for closure if that's what they decide,' I sigh and cross my legs, and then quickly uncross them when my back twinges.

'Oh dear, that's a long time. It must be such a worry.'

'It is. I've been trying to stay positive, but it's hard sometimes . . . But apart from showing how wonderful the school is and how mad the council would be to close us down, there really isn't very much more I can do . . .'

'Hang in there,' Lawrence says kindly, making me smile; he's always been so supportive. 'We'll have to make sure the inspectors see Tindledale in the Great Village Show spread in the Sunday supplement magazine.'

'Very true! And do you still think we have a chance of making the top ten?' I ask tentatively.

'Absolutely. Meg, we must polish our performance and aim high, and not let last time's spectacular failure mar our confidence,' he says, sounding very actorly all of a sudden, as if he's cheering on a troupe of thespians before a big performance, which I suppose show day is – Tindledale's chance in the spotlight.

'Yes, you're right, Lawrence. I mustn't be all doom and gloom; it's still all to play for . . .'

'Yes, absolutely. Let's try to stay positive . . . I think you'll be very pleased with the way the hall looks. Sybs, Hettie and the rest of the creative committee have done a splendid job in decorating the place, having kept the overall Traditional Tindledale theme of the show in mind, with boughs of hops and pretty wild flowers decorating the tables, coupled with a selection of vintage artefacts. You know, they've even restored the Tindledale WI's tea urn, the original one from the 1920s, or whenever it was they were first inaugurated.'

'Great. It sounds as if you've all done a fantastic job, and I can't wait to see it,' I say, feeling excited and hopeful now for a successful village show this year. There's definitely a buzz around the place, and the inspectors have already commented on how marvellous the school hall looks with the memorabilia wall and the mini-museum. They've even agreed to come along on show day to see the children in action – I mentioned the secret project and they are as intrigued as I am.

'And I'm about to head back to the village hall now for a final dress rehearsal – the Tindledale Players have decided on a *Midsummer Night's Dream* theme for their carnival float.'

'Wonderful, and very artistic – will they be reciting lines from the play as their truck goes by?'

'I doubt it. At the last meeting they were all still bickering over who was going to get to dress up as Titania, queen of the fairies,' he puffs, 'not to mention the dramas we've had with our truck driver.'

'But I thought the farmers were more than happy to get involved with their flat-bed lorries?' I ask, making another mental note to talk to Pete – he's in charge of the local farmers' group, so maybe he can sort out whatever the problem is.

'Yes, they are. But it seems our truck driver, George, the hop farmer, is enjoying a dalliance with two of the Tindledale Players, so now both women are refusing to participate in the carnival and ride on his flat-bed float unless the other steps down, so it's currently a stalemate . . . Anyway, enough of all that, how are you?'

'Um, yes, fine, but curious to know what happened to Dan yesterday?' I ask, a little apprehensively.

'I was going to ask you exactly the same thing,' he says. 'What on earth did you do to him?' Lawrence laughs, and my heart sinks. Dan must have said something to him.

'Nothing, I don't think,' I say slowly, feeling my way. 'What makes you think that?'

'Just teasing. Sorry Meg, it was a joke, that's all. I imagine it's something to do with his London restaurant . . .'

'Oh, why is that then?'

'Because he's gone!'

'Gone! But I don't understand,' I say, trying to hide the wobble from my voice. He can't just go! My mind is whirling. 'Is he coming back?' I mentally cross my fingers, hardly able to listen to the answer.

'I've no idea. There was a phone call, a woman – all gushy and urgent sounding – probably his manager,' Lawrence sniffs, seemingly knowledgeable about such things.

'Pia?' I ask, wondering if that's the woman Dan was talking to, telling her he loved her, but then that doesn't make sense – and certainly not the impression he gave me. He said she scared him.

'Yes, that was never her name. How do you know?'

'Dan mentioned her,' I say quickly, wanting to cut to the chase to find out what's going on. 'And did you know that he wasn't even here to open a new restaurant?'

'How do you know that?'

'He told me so.'

'Right. Well, that's a shame,' Lawrence says, sounding disappointed. 'Maybe that's why he left in such a hurry, if it's fallen through or whatever and he's annoyed about it.'

'Maybe,' I say, wondering why he didn't just say so . . . and why he denied it when I asked him. It doesn't add up.

'Anyway, so Pia called and said she needed to talk

to Dan immediately so could I please pass on a message and make sure he called her back; and then rattled on about how on earth do we actually function out here in the sticks, and in this day and age, without even basic mobile coverage.' He pauses.

'*Rude*,' we both say in unison.

'He threw his phone away, so that's hardly Tindledale's fault,' I then jump in protectively.

'Well, quite. But she wasn't listening to any of that. And then she hung up, leaving me to relay the message to him.'

'Wow!' I say, wondering whether to be impressed or petrified.

'So I called your house phone and a woman answered,' Lawrence tells me.

'My mother arrived yesterday.'

'Oh dear.' Lawrence knows Mum, or to be more precise, he knows what she's like. 'Ahh, yes, I thought I recognised the voice, but I wasn't sure as she was slurring slightly so I didn't like to ask. Is she OK? Not ill or anything?'

'If you mean, was my mother slurring because she's had a stroke or something, then no, there's no excuse. She was tipsy on champagne in the middle of the afternoon.'

'Ahh, well, jolly good, that's the best kind of tipsy, if you ask me,' Lawrence laughs again. 'So, to cut a long story short, I passed on the message to Dan and then he appeared back here a short while later. Soon after which, a car arrived, he got in, with a face like thunder – even more so than his usual thunderous look, if that's possible, and he was gone.'

'Oh. So now what?' I ask, flatly, and feeling ever so slightly panicky.

'Your guess is as good as mine.'

'But he can't just disappear, Lawrence. Our Great Village Show is only a week away! What about the food trucks, the juice bar? Is any of that still happening? Not to mention my kitchen table, which is about to collapse under the sheer weight of all the wine we had set aside for show day . . . He had promised to sort out a proper drinks list, to pair all the wines and cordials with the most appropriate item on the street food menu.' I inhale sharply and rack my brains to come up with a workable solution with less than a week's notice. 'And what about Kitty, and the Tindledale bakery, Sonny and Cher in the Duck & Puddle – we are all relying on Dan and his food trucks.'

'Sorry Meg, I just don't know. Let's just hope he gets in touch, and soon.'

'I don't want to bank on it. No, we can't leave it to the last minute. We need properly organised refreshments for all the visitors, dotted around the whole village as planned. The street food that Dan planned was supposed to set us apart from all the other village shows, and with a celebrity chef to boot; it was going to be a proper kudos thing. The school mums have even said that they know of people from Market Briar and beyond who are coming to the show just to try to catch a glimpse of Dan.' I make a note on my diary page to call an emergency meeting with all the caterers in the village, so we can come up with a back-up plan: we have to. I underline it five times. I feel so let down, what on earth is Dan thinking? I knew he couldn't be trusted; I should have gone with my first impression of him. Rude. A maverick. And he hates village life; he more or less said so in that YouTube clip. I bet it was all just for show, to impress us at the meeting: offering to supply food trucks and cover the cost, it's a very extravagant gesture – his PR people in action again, and most likely told him to do it, just as they wanted to orchestrate his visit to my school. I take a massive breath and stand up, desperate to calm down and get a grip. And I was right; Tindledale can certainly do without the likes of Dan Wright. I tuck the phone into the crook of my neck and push up my sleeves – a symbolic gesture making me feel in control. I'm determined to put on a Great Village Show, no matter what it takes.

'But, I do have some other news,' Lawrence says, punctuating my thoughts. 'Something that might cheer you up, and could very well still help to put Tindledale on the map. And ensure our place in the Sunday supplement magazine.'

'Oh, go on,' I say slowly.

'I've arranged for Fern to visit us on show day!'

'Fern?'

'Yes, Meg, you know . . . the lovely Fern Britton – do keep up,' he laughs. 'She stayed here with me at the B&B that time, when she was filming in Market Briar.'

'Oh yes! Of course, I remember now. Wow! She's famous, off the telly as Mary would say . . .'

'Yes, that's right,' Lawrence agrees, and I feel brighter already. 'And she loved her stay in Tindledale, so with her allotment TV programme, I thought she'd be perfect to pop along to our Great Village Show . . . The local radio station are sending someone along too, and a TV reporter, so one way or another, Tindledale is going to get some great media coverage on show day,' Lawrence rallies.

'Indeed,' I say, greatly buoyed by the news of Fern coming to our Great Village Show and trying to keep my disappointment about Dan at bay. 'So how did you manage to swing it?'

'Well, we kept in touch and I thought there was no harm in asking; as luck would have it, Fern is free on that day and is delighted to help out . . .' There's a short silence. 'Oh, Meg, I'm so sorry, I'm going to have to go, a guest needs me.'

'OK, lovely to chat. See you later.'

We end the call, and I hang up, basking in the news of Fern Britton being here on show day, but then the feeling soon subsides and I suddenly feel deflated all over again. I sink back into my desk chair. For some unfathomable reason, my eyes are all filmy and my back is constricting – a full-on tight spasm. I breathe deeply and lean forward in my chair, but I still feel . . . crushed! So disappointed. Dan has gone. So much for his 'don't ever change' comment. And what kind of a fool am I, for thinking it was possibly something more than it was, after his long, hard, passionate kiss? And actually wanting him to do it again! I must be mad. Was it really all just a big joke to him, after all? And, on top of all these feelings, and just to compound things further, I'm convinced of it, I'm truly shocked at my reaction to the news of his sudden departure. Especially as I have no idea if I will ever get to see him again . . . and to think that I thought I didn't even like him. A rude, mercurial maverick, a troglodyte, and I still thought all these things about him just a few minutes ago – in fact, I still do right now! He is all of these things, and now I can add unreliable to his battery of unattractive traits.

So why then do I feel so upset? It doesn't make any sense. Clearly, I'm going mad, because in spite of all of this, I think it's fair to say that I may well actually like Dan Wright very much indeed. But I don't want to like him, I really don't. He has a girlfriend – I would never do that. So why would I feel attracted to someone like him? It goes against everything that I think is important, and besides, I'm not even looking to meet a man, I'm fine as I am. Not that Dan is interested in me, that much is obvious, because a man that is interested in a woman doesn't just up and leave without any warning, without so much as a pleasant cheerio and a wave goodbye. And not only did Dan leave my house, he's left Tindledale too . . . he's got as far away as he can from me. But none of this matters anyway, or makes any difference; my feelings are irrelevant, because there's nothing I can do about any of them. Dan has gone.

I've missed my chance, if there was even a chance of anything happening between us. Not that I even know if I wanted something to happen, and certainly not when he has a girlfriend. Oh God, it's so confusing. But either way, I'll never know, because it's too late now . . .

Nineteen

The village hall looks every inch as good as Lawrence told me it did. Better in fact, as the civic committee has had an enormous laminated map of Tindledale made with numbered marker points, showing where each of the attractions are going to be located on show day. It's mounted on the wall outside, nice and central to the village, and is the perfect place for our guests, plus the villagers of course, to find their way around. It's like the kind of maps that zoos and theme parks have at their entrances; I remember from last year when we took the nursery and KS1 children to the petting zoo near the seaside.

'So what do you reckon?' Lawrence asks, appearing behind me with a broad grin on his face.

'The hall looks amazing, and I especially love this map,' I say.

'Me too, isn't it genius? Rumour has it that it was

the general's idea, and he personally funded it, too, when the parish council balked at the price of having it custom made.'

'Really? Gosh, that's very generous of him,' I say, impressed, and thinking how it just goes to show that first impressions can be so misleading. The general has certainly come up trumps for Tindledale – firstly with the OBE medal and display cabinet in my school, and now this! And then I spot the snag – the food trucks and juice bar are still here on the map. I tap the board discreetly, on the red number eleven – Cher's venison burger bar, located in the newly tidied station car park. Jessie was there all day yesterday, weeding and clearing, now that the dilapidated old caravan has finally been towed away.

'What are we going to do?' I whisper, looking back over my shoulder at Lawrence. It didn't go down well when I told all the caterers at the emergency meeting last night in the Duck & Puddle that Dan has left Tindledale so it seems we are going to have to make do without the food trucks. And Lawrence hasn't heard anything more from him, other than another call from Pia to settle Dan's bill. Lawrence didn't have a chance to ask anything further, as Pia was very brusque – barely drawing breath, he told me, as she read out the long card number and security digits before practically slamming the phone down.

I swallow hard to quash the feelings of disappointment and sadness rising up inside me. I've not slept very well the last few nights, and I'm not sure if it's Mum's snoring that's making me feel so unsettled – yes, I can hear her whistling peaks and troughs from the spare bedroom, even with my bedroom door closed. Or maybe it's because my back is still hurting, or perhaps knowing that Jack is flying to Cape Town today . . . But the truth is, it's none of those things really. When I've woken up, it's with only one person in my head. Dan. I just can't help it; he has got under my skin in a way no man has in years. I keep wondering what he's up to. Where is he? And, more importantly, why did he leave? And then I get angry all over again that he's gone, leaving us with this dilemma and potentially ruining our chances of making the top ten villages list, and leaving me feeling . . . well, bereft. And I know that I have no right to be, not when he's already with another woman. And I'm certainly not going to try to contact him, definitely not. No, I've had my fair share of men just upping and leaving – Liam did it, and then Will, and it's not like anything really happened between Dan and me . . .

'It'll be all right,' Lawrence says, putting his arm around my shoulders. 'Cher is doing a big barbecue in the pub garden now, in addition to having a trellis table with a pergola cover in the station car park – she's calling in extra bar staff to help out and act as "runners" between the two locations. Kitty has the café, of course, to serve up her delicious cakes and cream teas, so isn't overly anxious about not having a food truck too, and apparently the bakery is bringing out its old delivery van. It has a serving hatch so they can sell artisan bread to the hipsters down from London.' We both smile.

'Perfect. It won't be as slick as Dan's candy-striped, awning-clad chrome food trucks, but it'll do, and just goes to prove that Tindledale really can do without the likes of Dan flaming Wright.' I sound defiant, and try to look defiant, but inside I feel flat and sombre – I have to try and pick myself up for everyone's sake.

'Exactly. And I'll help you transport your crates up to the hall, so you can still have a juice bar – it'll just be a trellis table with plastic cups, but never mind. Now, let's not worry about it for a moment longer. We have a Great Village Show to put on!' And Lawrence turns on his heel and heads off towards two women, who I assume are the ones warring over George, the hop farmer, as they're both standing with their arms folded across their chests, looking daggers at each other. Oh dear, Lawrence sure has his work cut out with those two – I remember them from my school, always bickering and complaining about the other one to whoever was on playground duty. Some things never change.

'Hi Meg.' It's Sybs. 'Have you seen this?' She hands me a colourful pamphlet from a pile in her bag, which I take after giving Basil a quick stroke.

'Thanks.' I open it up. 'Wow! Very impressive.' It's a mini-concertinaed version of the map so visitors can carry it around the village with them. It even has a little section of vouchers – 10 per cent off when you buy any home-grown produce in the main marquee, 15 per cent off the cost of a ride on a heavy horse-drawn vintage plough; buy one get one free on face painting, next to a picture of my Reception class children with leopard and zebra faces (ahh, so that's what Mary was up to with the camera at the teddy bears' picnic that day). There's a free day-pass to the Country Club, half-price piano lessons with Pam (Dr Ben's secretary) when you book a course of ten, so there is quite a good selection of offers, and there's even a free wash and blow dry for your dog when you book them in for the nail-clipping service at the

Paws Pet Parlour – which reminds me, I must catch up with Taylor soon to see how she is after Jack called her. I fold the pamphlet back up, thinking how professional it looks, and certainly a step up from last year's village show fiasco.

'And see there.' Sybs turns the pamphlet over and points to a picture on the back.

'The commemorative stone!' I say, impressed.

'That's right,' she grins.

'Is it here? In place?' I swivel my head towards the direction of the village square, but can't see of course, as it's around the corner, opposite Ruby's vintage dress shop and the bus shelter.

'Yep, it sure is. And Hettie is over the moon. Marigold's husband, Lord Lucan, too.'

'Ooh, I can't wait to see it,' I say, lifting my wicker shopping basket on to my arm – it's crammed with all kinds of paraphernalia that I thought might come in handy this evening – staple gun, glue, pens, markers, fluoro cardboard signs, tissues (in the run-up to the last village show there were lots of tears as some villagers got overwrought by the enormity of the preparations) and plenty of packets of biscuits to pop on to the plates next to the numerous tea urns dotted around the place, to keep all the organisers sustained.

'Come on, I'll walk over with you,' Sybs says, slipping her arm through mine and clicking with her tongue to give Basil his cue to come along too.

Twenty

Back home, and I've just changed into my nightie and dressing gown and scooped Blue up for a cuddle on the sofa after sorting Mum out with a hot bath – for some reason, she 'forgot' to bring any of her 'pampering stuff' as she calls it (she had packed it all into a separate vanity case, which she subsequently left in the boot of her car at Tenerife South airport), so she's now soaking herself in my extra creamy bluebell foam bubble bath, which I treated myself to in the little farm shop after doing the bluebell walk through the Tindledale woods – when there's a knock on the door. Feeling very disgruntled, I pop Blue down on the armchair and slip on my bunny slippers before pulling the lounge door to and making my way to answer it. I'm just about to open the front door, when there's another knock, much louder this time, and very insistent, so I go to pull open the door, with a suitable rebuke already prepared: *honestly, it's almost ten o'clock, and very bad manners to be hammering on my door at this time of night.* But before I have a chance to actually say anything, Mr Cavendish barges past me and storms into my house with a murderous look on his face.

'Err, excuse me!' I start, racing down the hallway after him. He's standing in the kitchen now, pacing around with his hands on his hips. 'You can't just barge in here. What do you want?' I ask, stepping towards him, and wondering what on earth is going on. He's clearly furious, but why is he here? He's supposed to be in Zurich. And if he's here, then what about Jessie? And the children? Do they know that he's here in Tindledale? At my house. Should I call Jessie and find out what is going on? But why isn't he at home, in the farmhouse? And then a horrible, sickening feeling runs through me and I instinctively move away from him by taking a few steps backwards. I need to call Jessie. I need to go to her and make sure she's OK. The children, I must make sure they're safe, and why didn't I talk to Becky? I never did mention my concerns after Millie told me about the iron burn incident. And what if it's now too late? What if he's hurt Jessie again? Oh God.

'A word with you,' he spits, angry eyes flicking around the kitchen like a feral animal on high alert.

'I think you need to calm down first.' I hold up my palms in a peaceful way, going straight into teacher mode, but then rapidly realise that this might antagonise him further, so I change tack. 'I don't know what the problem is, but if I can help in any wa—'

'Help? Is that what you call it? I think you've done enough of that already. Filling my wife's head with your nonsense. We were perfectly happy before you came on the scene . . .' he bellows into my face, stepping closer towards me, and instinct tells me he's done this before – warned people off. Jessie did say that any friends she has made in the past have tended to drift away after meeting her husband, and now I can see why. I bet he goes around intimidating them, scaring them off so he can keep Jessie all to himself, controlled and lonely, unloved and uncared for. Well, he's got another think coming if he reckons for one second he's going to frighten me away.

'Err,' I open my mouth, but he flings up a hand with such ferocity, it startles me and I immediately stop talking.

'Don't interrupt me. I haven't finished.' Silence follows as he glares at me, but I manage to hold eye contact, unflinching.

'Actually, that's where you're wrong,' I shout, still

holding my nerve. 'You don't scare me. You're a bully! Now get out of my house. You're not welcome here, and you certainly weren't invited, so I'd like you to leave. Right now!' And I stand aside so he can go out the same way he came in here, but he doesn't move. Instead he looks me up and down before giving me a sneering look. I take a deep breath and will myself to stop shaking. Adrenalin is surging through me so fast, and I can hear my own blood pumping inside my head. But I'm not backing down. No way. Jessie is my friend and that isn't changing any time soon, just because he doesn't like it.

'Enjoy yourself, did you?' Mr Cavendish sneers. 'Giving my wife a crash course in being assertive. Women's rights, or whatever rubbish it is you people spew? What are you, some kind of burn-your-bra freak? That's if you even need to wear a bra . . .' And he drops his eyes to my modest chest. I instinctively fold my arms and glare back at him.

RUDE. VERY, VERY RUDE!

I draw a long breath in.

'Look, Jessie and I are friends—'

'Oh yes, I know that,' he interrupts again. 'She told me all about you – how caring and kind you are, and how right you were when you said that she needed time to think about her life. Listen, my wife has everything she ever needs, and do you know why? Because I *give* it to her. That's right, me, her loving and loyal husband.'

Well, I know that isn't true!

He stabs at his chest with a pointy index finger and I actually think he might be deranged. Deluded. Psychotic, even. 'You're nobody to her, so stay away . . .' he finishes, panting slightly as he comes to the end of his diatribe.

I change tack. 'You need to go. You're clearly very upset.'

'So long as you understand. You keep away from my wife. You stop trying to change her. She doesn't need friends like you. That's why we moved here, to get away from all the other busybodies getting inside her head.'

'I want you to go,' I try again, feeling quite scared now. Abusive and threatening is one thing, but the way he's behaving is something different.

'I'm going nowhere until you swear to keep away . . .' And he actually pulls out one of my dining chairs and drops down on to it with a weird, sort of sneering, manic smile on his face. Jesus. I spot the hands-free phone on the kitchen table. I can call Mark at the police house, but Mr Cavendish sees it too and jumps up. He smashes the phone across the room, causing it to shatter against the side of the Rayburn, and then goes to grab my arm, but the chair topples slightly, catching his foot, so he stumbles instead. My heart near leaps into my throat, and what's that buzzing noise inside my head? I can't breathe. My throat has closed and my chest feels as if a concrete slab has been dropped on it.

Suddenly, I see something in my peripheral vision. A movement.

The bathroom door.

'*GET OUT!*'

It's Mum.

And, I don't believe it. She has a pink bath towel twirled around her head, and is sopping wet, with bubbles all over her naked body, only just covering her modesty.

Mr Cavendish doesn't move. His jaw drops open. Mine too. And before he can respond, Mum swings the white wicker laundry basket lid up in front of her like a shield, which she then uses to body-slam the charming Mr Cavendish.

'Go on! You heard her. *GET OUT!*' Mum screams with such ferocity – I've never heard the like of it from her before, and it's utterly terrifying.

She's bashing the wicker lid into Mr Cavendish's side

now, over and over and over, all the while shrieking at him to leave. And, oh my God, she's now dropped the makeshift shield and has grabbed a glass demijohn from the kitchen table. Mr Cavendish looks petrified as he tries to bring his fists up to protect himself. But Mum is on a roll; she's like a Ninja, a super-hero or something, as she hurls the demijohn up high in the air with both hands before aiming it at Mr Cavendish's head.

'*NOOOOOOO!*' I scream, flinging my hands out as if to stop her. 'Not his head, Mum! You'll kill him,' I plead, with a sudden image flashing inside my head of her shuffling into a prison visiting room to see me when she's serving a life sentence for his murder. 'He's not worth it,' I pant, slapping my hands on to the back of his pinstripe shirt and shoving him as hard as I can.

'Get off me,' he yells, wrenching himself free. 'The pair of you are fucking crazy. Jesus, I've a good mind to call the police and have you both arrested for assault!' And he's in such a hurry to escape that he gets disorientated and runs into the bathroom and promptly slips, just like I did on the bathroom mat, but instead of catapulting forward across the bath, he goes backwards and ends up in a heap on the floor, so I do the first thing that comes into my head and run across the kitchen and, after quickly kicking his outstretched arm out of the way, I fling the bathroom door shut and then immediately drag the armchair from over by the Rayburn and wedge it firmly under the handle so the charming Mr Cavendish is secured inside.

'Ha! That's my girl. Well done Megan,' Mum puffs, placing both hands on her hips. I instinctively turn away as the suds have started to melt now and there are some things a daughter should never need to see. A sparkly vajazzle is definitely one of them.

'Mum, run up to the police house and get Mark – here, put this on,' and I rip off my dressing gown and sling it in her direction before loading wine crates on to the armchair, just in case the charming Mr Cavendish tries to push the door open. Hopefully, with the added weight, he'll be going nowhere until Mark gets here.

'I'm not leaving you alone with him,' Mum protests, with a furious look on her face. 'I'll call 999.'

'You can't. He smashed the phone,' I quickly tell her. 'Go on, I'll be fine. He's going nowhere – and there's no way he'll fit through the tiny bathroom window,' I state, loading another crate on to the pile already stacked up on the armchair. 'Hurry. I need to make sure Jessie is OK. God knows what state she's in, what he might have done to her before he came looking for me.'

'Jessie?'

'Yes, Mum. His *wife*,' I tell her, feeling frantic now.

'Poor woman!' Mum promptly shoves her feet into a pair of my gardening clogs by the back door, and is off, running down the side of my cottage on to the lane and up into the village. The police house is only a five-minute walk away, so if she runs all the way, she'll be there in no time.

*

Just moments later, or so it seems, and my tiny cottage is crammed with people in police uniform taking Mr Cavendish away. Gabe and Vicky are here too; they heard all the commotion and saw Mum tearing down the lane in a dressing gown, so thought it best to come round and check on me to see if everything was OK. I borrowed their phone to ring Jessie, and she's fine, shaken up after the terrible argument that erupted when Sebastian turned up out of the blue, but she's OK – Sam is with her now, and I'm going down to the farmhouse to see her shortly, just as soon as everyone has left.

'Honestly, I'm fine, thanks,' I say, gratefully accepting the blanket from Vicky.

'Are you sure?' she asks, and I nod.

'How about I make you both a nice cup of tea?' Gabe offers, glancing at Mum, who thankfully has kept my dressing gown well and truly on, and with the belt tied securely around her waist.

'I think we could do with something a bit stronger!' And she grabs a bottle of carrot wine from the table, pulls the cork out and takes an enormous glug before collapsing in the window seat with a very harried look on her face. 'And to think I came to Tindledale with my heart set on spending some nice, quiet, quality time with my daughter! How wrong was I? Things sure have moved on around here – in my day it was all cows and sheep and strawberries and fields. Lots of fields.' She rolls her eyes before glugging another mouthful of wine. 'Honestly, nowadays, if it isn't lunatics breaking into people's homes, then it's S&M dungeons in your cottage basement.' She points to the steps next to my pantry door and Gabe and Vicky exchange horrified looks as I shrivel a little inside. An image pops into my head of the *Tindledale Herald* headlines – *Local teacher with S&M fetish – even has own dungeon!* It could happen! If Mum keeps on like this.

*

It's nearly midnight when Mark and I get to Jessie's farmhouse. There's a light glowing from the kitchen window and I can see Jessie sitting at the pine table with her head in her hands. Sam comes to the door right away, on seeing me.

'Meg, thank you for coming, and I'm so sorry for everything. Are you OK?' he says, concern etched all over his face.

'Sam, I'm fine, honestly, it probably sounded a lot worse than it was.' Sam looks at Mark, who nods and asks him, 'Is there somewhere where we can talk?' Mark turns to me. 'Meg, maybe you could see if Jessie is OK?'

'Sure, and I'll make us some tea,' I smile, before making my way to the kitchen.

I put the kettle on and then sit next to Jessie. She doesn't move. I edge closer and put an arm around her. We sit silently for a few minutes until she subsides into me and sobs for a good few minutes. Eventually, and all cried out, she leans back in her chair.

'Oh Meg, I am so, so sorry,' she says, her voice trembling. 'And I will totally understand if you want nothing more to do with me . . .'

'Hey,' I lift her chin and look into her eyes, 'why on earth would you say that?'

'Because I'm a mess!' She looks away. 'And I've brought trouble to your door.'

'No you haven't. Sebastian did. You didn't make him come to my house. It's not your fault. He's a grown man who makes his own decisions. You are not to blame. Do you hear me?' I say firmly, and Jessie nods.

'But I should have left him ages ago, I can see that now . . . and I should never have told him that you agreed with me, in that I needed time to think; but he was so angry, furious when I suggested we needed time apart and I felt helpless, hopeless, in that moment. I felt so desperate. It was as if I needed to somehow show him that I wasn't the only one who thought so, to somehow give credibility to what I was saying. Sebastian never listened properly to me, he never took me seriously, but then why would he? I'm feeble. I'm pathetic. I'm a terrible person. You know, I didn't even have the courage to tell him it was over. No, I shouldn't have mentioned you at all . . . I should never have dragged you into my shambolic life.' She sniffs before reaching for a tissue from a box on the table.

Silence follows.

'That's a lot of "shoulds",' I smile gently. 'How about you go easy on yourself for a change? Stop telling yourself off. It's going to be fine. I promise you. You'll see, and you are not feeble or pathetic or terrible. Now, I'm going to check on the children and then I'm going to make you a nice cup of tea,' I tell her, patting her shoulder as I go.

'Meg, I really am terrible,' Jessie says quietly, and I stop moving. I turn back to see her face is ashen as she stands up.

'What is it?' I ask softly, touching her arm. She looks petrified. A short silence follows. She closes her eyes and then takes a deep breath, before telling me.

'I'm pregnant!' she sobs. 'And Sam is the father.'

'Oh.' A short silence follows. 'Does he know?' I ask softly, conscious that Mark and Sam are in the next room. I close the kitchen door just to be sure they can't hear us. Jessie shakes her head. 'Oh Jessie, why haven't you told him?' I ask gently, remembering how she didn't touch her Pimm's at the meeting that time, or my elderflower fizz in the garden – it makes sense now.

'I don't know. I, just, I . . . I guess I was in denial for a while, and then I got scared. Scared of what Sebastian would do, what he still might do. He'll take the triplets away from me.'

'He can't do that,' I quickly say.

'But he said so – when he found out that Sam had been in touch, and that I went to the funeral, he told

327

me that if I saw him again, then he'd make sure I . . .' Jessie drops her head into her hands. 'Meg, I don't know if I can go through with this pregnancy. I can't risk losing the children that I already have, I just can't do that.'

'That's not going to happen,' I say, going to her and putting my arms around her again.

Twenty
One

Show day. And the weather is glorious. A cloudless blue sky and the already warm sun is dazzling and hazing over the fields beyond the stream at the end of my garden. It's only early, but I've come down here to sit on my tree stump beside the magnolia bush and enjoy a mug of tea before the day really gets under way.

Drawing in a big lungful of the fresh-mown-grass aroma, I wave over at Gabe, who is cutting his lawn one last time in the hope of winning a rosette today as part of the Garden In Bloom section of the village show. I sigh quietly. It's lovely that everyone is so excited about the whole day, but I just can't seem to summon any real enthusiasm. I know I should feel driven and motivated to save my school, but somehow, ever since I met Dan, and then he left so abruptly, things seem to have changed.

Vicky appears at the top of the path waving a phone in the air. She dashes towards Gabe and urges him to switch off the lawnmower at once.

'Meg,' she calls out. 'Meg, you need to come right away.' I jump up and tip the last of my tea out on to the grass before running over to her.

'Is everything OK?' I ask, over the fence.

'Yes, yes, quickly. Cher from the Duck & Puddle is on the phone, says she needs to talk to you. It's urgent. She's been calling your house phone and . . .' Vicky hurriedly hands me the phone which I press to my ear.

'Hello, Meg?' Cher pants, as if she's been running too.

'Yes, what's the matter? Is everything OK?' I ask, twiddling my silver rabbit on the chain, and thinking I'm not sure I can handle very much more drama. I'm still reeling from Mr Cavendish's outrageous behaviour and subsequent arrest. That's right, Mark called me yesterday to see how I was and to update me on the situation – Mr Cavendish is now banned from coming within a five-mile radius of Tindledale. Hurrah! And Jessie is thrilled with this news too, as it turns out that her husband has a pregnant mistress in Zurich, whom he lives with when he's there . . .

and to think that he had the cheek to castigate her for the indiscretion with Sam.

'Yes, and no!' Cher says. 'Sorry, Meg, can you hold on for a second?' There's a muffled noise while I wait for her to come back on the line, interrupted by an intermittent beeping noise and a man yelling, 'Keep going, that's right, back it up mate, back it up. STOP!' and then Cher is back. 'Gosh, it's all happening here. Meg, I think you need to come down here to the station car park before it's completely gridlocked and I lose my mobile signal again – I managed to get one bar by waggling my phone around in the air near the little ticket Portakabin. I think they must have a Wi-Fi hub, or whatever they're called, in there,' she explains in a rushed voice.

'What's happened?' I ask, trying to keep calm and glancing down at my pyjama bottoms, I was planning on having a relaxing bath to help soothe my back before putting on my navy and white polka-dot sundress and new, floaty, chiffon scarf. I treated myself to it online especially for show day – it has little rabbits on with diamanté studs all over it.

'Um, six food trucks! That's what happening right now. An enormous transporter turned up and is offloading them as we speak. All paid for, apparently, and the driver is refusing to take them away. What shall we do?'

'Keep them there!' I quickly say. 'I'm on my way.' And I hand the phone back to Vicky.

'Everything all right?' Vicky asks.

'It sure is,' I beam. Suddenly I am filled with a rush of energy and my heart is pounding fit to burst. So Dan didn't let us down after all. But now I'm totally confused as well. What does it mean? Maybe Tindledale isn't so dull to him, after all – why else would he supply the food trucks, and out of his own pocket too? But then what about his girlfriend?

But I don't have time to work it all out – I have got to get to the station, and fast. Yes, we came up with a make-do solution for the catering today, but this is so much better! We are now going to have proper retro chrome food trucks with pink-striped awnings dotted around the village. Tindledale is going to look magnificent, and this will really give us the edge when the judges arrive later. 'Right. Let's get down there,' I tell them, before going to leave.

'Why don't you go and get ready, and then I can give you a lift, if you like?' Vicky offers calmly. 'It's a long way down to the station. It'll give me something to do while Gabe perfects his garden.' She gives Gabe an affectionate pat on the arm.

'That would be a huge help. Thank you, and then I can whizz back later and pick up my bike,' I grin.

'No need, we can just strap it to the back of the car – the cycle rack is already in place,' Gabe offers, and I give him a quick hug before bombing back inside and taking the stairs two at a time up to my bedroom.

Having showered, dressed and blow-dried my hair in record time, I'm just about to grab my Cath Kidston basket – having already packed it with everything I could possibly think of that might come in handy today – when Mum appears in a puff of bluebell-scented air. She's fully clothed, thankfully, with a face full of make-up and hair that is all swingy and much more carefully blow-dried than mine.

'Darling, I had to use the last of that bubble bath, hope you don't mind,' she says casually, spritzing her wrists with my new 'signature scent' (I treated myself to that too), after swinging her pashmina around her shoulders.

'Um, oh, right,' I mutter, and I take the perfume bottle from her clasped hand and hide it under the scarf in my basket, for *me* to use later.

'Let's go shopping on the weekend.' Mum claps her hands together. 'We could go up to London and make a proper day of it! New clothes. My treat!' she says, glowing, before adding, 'Whatever you want. And you could do with a pair of pretty heels to really show off your lovely tanned legs, if you don't mind me saying so!' And I spot her sneaking a look at my Joules navy festival wellies, which may not be her style, but they match my dress and are far more practical for cycling around the village in, and I imagine I'm going to need to cover a lot of ground in a short space of time today to keep an eye on everything. Suddenly I feel really enthusiastic about the day again. I really want to make sure Tindledale is in that top ten list in the Sunday supplement magazine. 'Come on, what do you say?'

'Muuuuuum!' I exclaim, sounding just like Jack. 'My clothes and footwear are fine. Anyway, I need to go. I don't have time for this. Here,' I press a bundle of show day pamphlets into her arms. 'You can be in charge of giving those out.'

'Sure. You know me, Megan, always happy to help out!' she quips, before pursing her lips.

Sighing and shaking my head, I close the front door behind us and we make our way down the path to

Vicky's car – a cute convertible classic Beetle in cherry red.

'Oooh, she's a beauty,' Mum trills, eyeing up the car. 'But I'd better get my headscarf or my hair will be ruined,' and she goes to dart back inside.

'No time! Sorry Mum,' I swiftly say, packing her into the back passenger seat before closing the door and jumping into the front with my basket on my lap.

We're whizzing along the lanes, with Vicky carefully slowing down as we take a bend – you never know what livestock could appear at any given moment: deer, horses, chickens, peacocks, pheasants, rabbits, rams. There was even a pair of ginger-haired llamas in the middle of this lane last year; they had escaped from the fields on the other side of the valley. We are just about to pull into the station car park when something catches my eye.

'STOP!' I bellow.

'What is it?' Mum shrieks straight into my left ear, looking horrified as I swivel my head to bat her away from me. Vicky does an emergency brake, bringing the car to a sudden standstill.

'I don't believe it,' I shout, getting out of the car and running to the hedgerow that runs the length of the field next to the station where the new houses are going to be built. I plant my hands on my hips and shake my head. Vicky and Mum are standing right behind me now. 'Look at this!' I lift a hand from my hip to point to a placard.

DON'T GO TO TOWN ON OUR LOVELY
LITTLE VILLAGE
No to new houses!

The words are written in big, bold, ugly black letters on a garish, fluoro orange background. It looks horrendous and hardly conducive to the 'community spirit' element of today's Great Village Show.

'This is definitely not what we want visitors to see as soon as they arrive for our village show – it's not very friendly or welcoming, is it?' I shake my head.

'Certainly not. Here!' Mum flings her pashmina in my face.

'What are you doing?' I say, sweeping myself free from the silky cloth, which I then roll up into a ball to hurl over my shoulder. It lands on the back seat of Vicky's car.

'Getting rid of this! What does it look like?' Mum states, picking her way across the grass, with her five-inch heels sinking mercilessly as she grabs hold of an old fence post to steady herself.

'But we can't do that,' I say, half-heartedly, really wanting to rip the sign down, but thinking: what if someone from the parish council has put it there? Or what if one of the school inspectors drives past at this precise moment and sees me, the acting head teacher, involved in an act of blatant vandalism? I'm sure that wouldn't go down very well in their report.

'Yes we can.' It's Vicky who takes action, and she's bent down now, with her hands around the pole, trying to ease it free from the mud, but it's no use, it's not budging. I glance at my watch. It's almost nine o'clock, and people are going to be arriving soon.

'OK. Step aside,' I say, like I'm some kind of heavyweight wrestler going in to the ring as I wade in and wrench the placard free. I have to give it three good tugs before it comes loose.

'That's my girl. Now get it in the back of the car,' Mum shouts, right into my ear again, as Vicky and I drag the sign away. With the placard sticking conspicuously up out of the car from the back seat, Vicky puts her foot down and speeds us off to the car park, where Sonny and Cher take one look at the ugly orange sign before swiftly tossing it face down under the ground sheet inside the marquee.

'We can deal with that later,' Sonny says, wiping his hands on his black and white chequered chef trousers. 'First we need to organise these.' He points to the six super-shiny food trucks. 'And then I need to get back to the pub.'

'One of them can stay here,' Cher says, having already loaded her trays of venison burgers into the little fridge unit in the nearest one.

'And we'll shift the rest wherever they need to go!' Pete calls out from the window of his flat-bed truck, as he swerves up beside us into the station car park, with the engine still chugging and seven or eight farm boys on the back who all jump off and instantly start sorting out the keys and the paperwork with the delivery guy.

'I called Pete too!' Cher grins, lifting a giant catering bottle of ketchup into her truck.

After we've checked all the locations on one of the pamphlets, the farm boys pile into the food trucks and off they go, convoy style, up the steep lane back towards the village.

'Hop in,' Pete says to me. 'You're needed in the village hall! Sybs said something about a giant marrow!'

'Oh God, no, not again! And the show hasn't even really started yet.'

*

A few hours later, and with all potential disasters averted, I've dispatched Mum to listen to the brass band on the village green. She has already done a stint in my juice-bar truck, completely ignoring all instructions, as per the temporary events licence, to not start serving any of the wine until after eleven o'clock. 'But darling, it must be gone eleven somewhere in the world. Where does it specifically say that it has to be here in Tindledale?' she had said, and my mind had been boggled by her skewed logic.

Now Molly has volunteered to take charge of the truck, so that I can walk along the High Street to do a final check of the window displays. Fern will be here very soon with the TV camera and reporter, so I want everything to look perfect – Lawrence is bringing her to the village square at three o'clock to do an official ribbon-cutting ceremony around the commemorative stone, and I've already spotted a couple of judges wandering around the village with their clipboards – having finished handing out rosettes in the village hall to the best entries in the various produce categories, and with not one single cross word over a marrow. I had a quiet word with the two offenders from last time, telling them jokingly that they'd better behave this year or I'd give them each a half-hour detention, and they both laughed somewhat sheepishly but then seemed determined to set a good example to the actual school children in the village hall who, incidentally, were behaving impeccably.

Lots of the children were winning prizes, too – taking rosettes for the best-decorated hen's egg, the prettiest pot of three dahlias, making a dragon's nest from straw and glue. A boy in Year Six even won the Tindledale Trophy for his watercolour painting depicting a montage of hot-air balloons. Talking of which, there's a red and white stripy one hovering overhead right now. Shielding my eyes from the bright sun, I take a proper look up. WOW! It's truly spectacular, and I can't wait to have a go. I make a mental note to head to the field where they're taking off from, just as soon as I've seen the mini-carnival go by.

The whole village looks amazing – pristine, like something out of a film. Every single lawn and lamppost is tidy, with hanging baskets bulging with red, purple, pink, yellow and white flowers. Even Molly's bush has had a trim, which will no doubt go down well with the WI woman and her husband on his motorised scooter. There's a lovely, vibrant buzz in the village too; there are lots of people I don't recognise, so they must be visitors, or potential newcomers intending to move here, with any luck. I smile at a family walking towards me, each of them eating with a fork from a plastic bowl.

'Mmm, that smells delicious,' I say, as they go to walk past.

'It's from the restaurant,' one of the boys says, pointing to the end of the High Street.

'Restaurant?' I turn my head, wondering what he's talking about.

'Down the end and turn right,' the dad says, 'but be fast as these takeaway dishes are going like hot cakes,' he laughs, lifting his bowl up as if to salute me.

Seconds later, and I'm standing outside the double-fronted shop overlooking the green. It's no longer a newly plastered shell with bubble-wrap-covered chairs piled up high in the middle. No, it's been transformed into a palace! Outside there are several round pretty painted wooden tables, each with a gorgeous gold and white parasol above. And inside is like an Aladdin's cave – a rich red carpet with sumptuous purple and gold wallpaper and several crystal chandeliers hanging from the ceiling. It's amazing and magical. And makes me hold my breath as I step inside.

A woman with shiny long black hair swept up into an elegant chignon, wearing a turquoise sari with several gold bangles on her arm, which jangle as she comes walking towards me, appears right away.

'Hi, would you like a menu?' she smiles, offering me a large square of cream and gold embossed card.

'Oh, um, no . . . thank you. I was just passing, maybe later,' I grin, thinking Jack is going to love this place too – now he can have a vindaloo whenever he wants one, without having to traipse all the way over to Market Briar. 'Yes, definitely later. Your restaurant looks amazing, and the food . . .' I spy a waiter pushing a trolley with a colourful collection of dishes on, 'I can't wait to try it all.' I laugh, wondering whether I have enough time to squeeze in a curry. I'd love to sit outside and watch the world go by across the village green, but then I look at my watch and see that the carnival is due to start in fifteen minutes, so probably not.

'Perhaps you'd like one of our takeaway menus – we'll be doing deliveries soon as well, to the houses in and around the village. Do you live in Tindledale?' the woman asks politely.

'Yes, yes I do. I'm the acting head teacher at the village school,' I tell her. 'I'm Meg.' And I offer her my hand, which she shakes enthusiastically, placing her other hand over the top of mine and giving it a hearty squeeze, making me warm to her right away.

'Ooh, it's so lovely to meet you. I'm Yasmin, and . . .' she pauses to beckon a man over, 'this is my husband Ash, and, oh, where are the children?' she asks him, before calling out a list of names. Five seconds later, four girls and one boy appear. I want to clap my hands together in glee – they're all primary-school age. 'Say hello to Meg, she's going to be your new head teacher,' Yasmin tells them.

'Um, actually, I'm only the acting head teacher and well, I should probably tell you that the school might be about to . . .' But nobody's really listening and the children are eagerly doing as they're told, chatting and laughing as they step forward one at a time to shake my hand. I'm very impressed by their manners as I keep it in mind to make sure the inspectors know about the *five* new children here in Tindledale. I wonder if it would be very inappropriate to tell them today when I spot them wandering around the show? Just so I can be sure they include this wonderful fact in their report.

*

Later, and the mini-carnival is well under way, and the crowds have all gathered on the pavement to watch the floats go by. Brownies, Cubs, Scouts and Guides, all waving and looking smart in their uniforms, majorettes twirling their batons and doing gymnastic moves along to the marching band that's playing right at the front of the procession. Behind them is the Tindledale Players' float, and I'm thrilled to see that Lawrence has managed to bring an end to the bickering, as the two girls are flitting around the enchanted forest in their fairy costumes, like they're the best of friends now. Lawrence, walking alongside the float, spots me, and ducks through the crowd to join me.

'There you are! I've been looking all over for you,' he says over the music, 'where have you been?'

'I'll tell you later,' I beam, thinking he's going to be delighted when he hears about Tindledale's new restaurant – he can team up with Yasmin and Ash to offer Indian cookery weekends instead!

'OK, but you mustn't move from here,' he says, and we turn together to watch the rest of the carnival go by.

The various local charities travel past next – the Cats Protection float has somebody dressed up in a furry cat onesie; they must be roasting as the sun is beating down on us now. It's scorching! But right on cue, the Country Club float arrives. They have real grass on the back of their truck and a paddling pool from which five life-guards, all looking very impressive in red swimming trunks, are filling giant water guns and spraying the crowd. We all cheer as they go by.

And then I gasp.

On dear, and I think I'm about to cry too.

Proper tears. I turn to look at Lawrence.

'Did you know about this?' I clasp my hands up under my chin.

'I might have had an inkling,' he says, an amused smile dancing on his lips.

I turn back to the carnival and see a group of my school children walking past now, with Sybs, Dr Ben, Becky and Mary helping them to hold up three giant handmade banners made from thick black velvet material with gold edging looped around wooden poles. There are even gold tassels hanging resplendently from the top of each banner, twirling in the warm breeze. I wave and clap and then clutch Lawrence's hand as the first banner says '*Tindledale*', the second says '*Village*', and the last one has '*School. Established 1841*' on it in gold lettering, cut from brocade and stitched on by hand. The secret project! I can't believe it. This is wonderful. And must have taken ages. And Sybs and the children can't possibly have made the banners all by themselves – surely there wouldn't have been enough time.

'What do you think?' A group of school mums have gathered around me.

'It's amazing!' I say, quickly brushing away a tear that has managed to escape and trickle down my cheek.

'We knew you would think so.'

'Did you all help out?' I beam, scanning their faces.

'Sure did! We're not going down without a fight. Talking of which, look over there,' one of the women nudges me gently in the arm, and then points across the street. Two of the inspectors are standing on the pavement and it's hard to tell for sure as there are so many people gathered in the crowd, but they seem to be smiling as they watch the Tindledale Village School banners go by. And yes, one of them is clapping now, along with the rest of the crowd. Hurrah! This surely has to be a good sign . . .

The carnival over, I quickly cycle over to the juice bar to see how Molly is getting on.

'Sold out!' she says, on seeing me.

'Really?'

'Yep, just flogged the last of the "snips". Granny Elizabeth's parsnip wine sure went down a treat – they couldn't get enough of it. Your elderflower fizz too, especially with the cucumber twist over ice – I made it just as you said,' she laughs.

'That's amazing,' I say, leaning my bike against a tree before stepping inside the truck.

'Sure is. And I've handed over all the proceeds to the parish council treasurer. She came by a few minutes ago, so if you want to potter on down to the fields with me, I think the ploughing competition is about to start soon.' Molly unties her apron and rolls it up under her arm.

'That would be lovely. I thought I might try a trip in one of the hot-air balloons,' I grin.

'Hmm, well, rather you than me – not sure I trust being in a basket all that way up in the air.' She shakes her head.

'And thanks for helping out this afternoon,' I say, gesturing around the truck, wondering if Mum will give me a hand later to get all these empty wooden crates back to the cottage.

'Ahh, no problem – least I could do. None of us wanted you to miss the kids in the carnival,' Molly chuckles, whipping a cotton hanky from her pocket to wipe her face. 'Blimey, it's a hot one today . . .' She puffs, pushing the hanky back away.

'It sure is,' I smile. 'So you knew about the banners too?' I ask, clearing away the last of the plastic cups into one of the empty crates.

'Of course,' Molly says, resting her hands on her ample hips. 'We all did, the whole village pitched in . . . well, all the crafters at least – they've been stitching, *and bitching*,' she tilts her head and rolls her eyes, 'about the school having to close, for ages now. Sooo, it was the least we could do.'

'Hopefully it won't come to that,' I quickly interject, seriously hoping that we've done enough to show the inspectors what a terrible mistake the council would be making, especially as we now have an additional five children, not to mention the families that are going to live in the new houses.

'Hear hear. Not if we can help it. Anyway, we've been stitching the banners down at Hettie's House of Haberdashery – we had to do something to show our support. That school of yours has been good to all of us, and our children. It'd be a crying shame if they close it down.'

'Indeed.'

After locking up the food truck and making sure the keys are safely stowed in my basket, Molly retrieves her bike from behind the truck, and we swing our legs over our saddles and start cycling alongside each other along the lanes, chatting as we relish the breeze on our faces and the welcome shade from the many willow trees that run the length of the Blackwood Farm Estate.

We reach the fields on the estate, and Molly heads off to find Cooper to watch the ploughing competition with their four sons. I spot Jessie with Sam and the triplets, and stop cycling to give them a cheery wave – they all wave back with big, happy grins on their faces, the children running and skipping around with enormous pink puffs of candyfloss on sticks clutched in their hands, clearly having the time of their lives. Ahh, I'm so pleased that things have turned out well for Jessie and the children, that they seem to have found their happy-ever-after.

I've just cycled on past the marquee where the dog show is going to take place, when Taylor spots me and waves me over to the fence.

'Hi Meg, thank you so much for talking to Jack,' she beams.

'Oh, you've spoken to him?' I ask tentatively.

'Yep, loads of times, on Skype. And he's promised to call me from South Africa too,' she beams, brushing her hair away from her face.

'He has?' I ask, resisting the urge to raise an eyebrow. Well, there's a turn-up for the books.

She glances back over her shoulder to see her mum, Amber, beckoning for her to hurry up. 'Oops, better go,' and she reaches over the top of the fence to kiss my cheek. 'I need to help get the dogs ready for the show.' And she dashes off, leaving me with a big smile on my face as I cycle on to the next field where the hot-air balloons are – I'm so pleased she seems brighter now.

And the smile freezes on my face.

I stop cycling and stand motionless with my feet on the ground either side of my bike. I don't believe it!

What's *he* doing here?

It's Dan. Dan flaming Wright. Bold as brass, striding around with his hands in his jeans pockets and his trademark thunderous scowl set firmly in place. There's a spindly woman running behind him, trying to catch up, swearing and muttering as she tries to stay upright on the grass in the highest and spikiest stiletto shoes I think I've ever seen, while struggling to balance a pile of files with an iPad perched on top. I spy a group of farm boys sniggering and nudging each other as she totters past.

'Dan! Dan, please! They're obviously not here. Come on. Let's get back to London,' the woman yells after him, nearly bumping into the general, who immediately steps aside and apologises in a very old school, chivalrous way.

'I'm not going back. How many times do I have to tell you, Pia?' he says, stalking off into the distance. Ahh, so this is his manager, the scary Pia. Well, she doesn't look very scary to me. And who is Dan searching for?

'Maybe I can help?' I fling my bike down on the grass and step in front of Pia, who looks me up and down before saying, 'No you can't. Not unless your name is . . .' She pauses to shove the files under one arm, before wrestling to free a finger with which to tap the screen of her iPad . . . 'Lawrence or Meg?' Pia stops moving and suddenly Dan turns around. He pushes a hand through his hair and walks quickly back to join us with a massive grin on his face.

'See! I told you she would be here,' he says, his eyes flashing as he looks at me. 'I can take it from here,' he tells Pia. 'You can go back to London.' And he rummages around in his pocket. 'Here, take my car.' He drops a bunch of keys on top of Pia's iPad.

'But Dan! Wait. What about your schedule? We need to get back!' Pia protests.

'How many times must I tell you? I'm not coming back.' Dan shakes his head.

'But—' Pia starts, and then instantly stops talking when Dan holds out his hand to me.

I open my mouth.

What is he doing?

'What do you say?' Dan asks, his thunderous face softening.

'Um, what do you mean?'

'You and me taking a trip up there?' And he points to a basket attached to a sunshine yellow and white striped hot-air balloon. 'I think we need to talk.'

'Do we?' I ask, stalling for time as I race through all

the possible things we might have to say to each other, starting with me asking, 'Why did you leave without saying goodbye?' or, 'What about your girlfriend?' or 'Why are you permanently furious?' or how about, 'Why did you even come to Tindledale if it wasn't to open a restaurant?' Dan studies me for a moment before taking my basket from my arm and dumping it on the grass. 'Hey, what are you doing? You can't do that?' I yell, going to pick it up, but he kicks it away, out of reach, before swinging one arm around my body and hoisting me up and over his shoulder, fireman style. 'Stop it! Put me down at once, you idiot,' I yell, beating my left fist on his back while desperately attempting to keep my dress from riding up over my bottom and exposing my knickers to everyone in the field with my other hand. I can hear the farm boys clapping and cheering. Oh God. I'm mortified. And I sure as hell hope that none of the inspectors are watching me making a show of myself. And, uh-oh! Oh no! I spy the reporter from the *Tindledale Herald* near the edge of the field with a pen poised eagerly over a notepad.

I can see the headline already: *Local acting head teacher romps in field with celebrity chef on show day . . .* Cringe!

'For crying out loud, woman!' Dan bellows, before marching us over to the basket. 'Now, get in there and tell me, *honestly*, that we don't need to talk. That you don't like me. Even just a little bit?' he says, with a particularly cocky and arrogant smile on his face.

'Like you? You must be joking,' I protest, doing my scary teacher face as Dan gently lowers me over the side of the basket before hurdling over himself.

'Take us up,' he commands, in his uniquely rude way, to the pilot – a fifty-something man who, on instantly recognising Dan Wright, celebrity chef and culinary bad boy, immediately does as he's told, giving the signal for the guys on the ground to release the basket from the holding strings.

'Say *please*!' I can't resist telling Dan, as the balloon starts to rise and my tummy flips.

'*Please*!' Dan pouts over his shoulder to the pilot, before grabbing both of my hands and drawing them in close to his chest. 'Now, will you please drop the scary teacher act and just tell me . . . admit it!'

'Admit what?' I say, trying not to look into his raging eyes.

'You know what! That you like me?' And he stares intently, and I can't be sure, as it's brief, but a flicker of something darts across his face. Doubt, maybe?

Uncertainty? Is he nervous again? I can't be sure. 'There's something there, isn't there?'

'Stop it!' I say, determined not to get caught out again. I pull my hands free and take a step back.

'What's the matter?' he asks, moving towards me.

'Look, Dan, I don't know what I feel, to be honest. But you can't just turn up here after leaving me, and Tindledale, with no idea about what was happening with the juice bar, the food trucks – you didn't even say goodbye! And what about your girlfriend? The woman you rang from my house? The woman who means everything to you? The woman you love! What does she think about you turning up here again out of the blue demanding to know if I like you?'

I turn to look away, drawing in the intoxicating view, the people and fields and trees below us, growing smaller and smaller as our balloon drifts up into the air, giving way to a picture-perfect cloudless blue sky. I can't bear to look back at him, but suddenly I feel his arm on my shoulder. He turns me around towards him, and is grinning like some kind of crazy looper.

'What?' I ask him, crossly. 'What is it now?'

'You really are the most infuriating person I have ever met!'

'Meeeee?' I retort, unable to believe his flaming

brazenness. '*You are*, more like!' I go to move away from him, but Dan pulls me closer.

'My sister,' he smiles. 'My gorgeous, sad, useless-in-love sister, Anna, who had just had yet another bust-up with her equally useless boyfriend. That's who I was talking to. And I'm really sorry that I left in such a hurry, I truly am, but Anna needed me; she can get very low, and, well . . .' He stops talking and looks away.

'Oh,' I mumble, feeling like an utter idiot. A short silence follows. 'I'm sorry, I got carried away, I guess, and, um . . .' I pause. 'Is Anna OK?' I quickly ask.

'Yes, she's fine now.' Dan looks into my eyes. 'Thank you. You do understand, don't you? I'm all she has, since our parents went; there's nobody else to keep an eye on her,' he explains quietly, and I nod before reaching a hand out to touch his, as suddenly he seems weary, like he has the weight of the world on his shoulders.

We're heading south now towards Tindledale, to the High Street, I can see the village square with the commemorative stone, and is that Fern? Yes it is! Wow, she's laughing and chatting to Lawrence and a group of people with clipboards. One even has a camera; maybe she's giving an interview to the village show judges! I sure hope so, as that will really boost our chances of a top ten place. I can see the war memorial now and I spot the tiny flicker of a candle in the lantern that Kitty lights for Ed on special occasions – yes, of course, I remember, it's his birthday! And I gasp. It's so emotive – the whole village scene is spectacular, magical and special. We float on down the hill until we reach Hettie's House of Haberdashery, where Hettie, Sybs and Dr Ben are standing outside on the path waving up at us – I give them a big wave back as we travel on. I can see the duck pond on the village green now, and the bandstand that's been erected especially for show day, the white marquees and all the people sitting in their stripy deckchairs. I wonder if Mum is still there, getting sozzled on Pimm's, no doubt. And I can't help smiling, as she may be an acquired taste, my mother, but I've actually enjoyed having her around. I feel my spirits lifting as we fly higher again, relishing enjoying the fruits of all our hard work from this unique viewpoint. I can't stop smiling, suddenly feeling all the weight of expectation and worry lifting from my shoulders. We're drifting over the Duck & Puddle pub now and I can see people in the garden, children and dogs darting around, having fun in the sun on the grass.

Dan coughs dramatically to get my attention.

'Are you going to answer me?' he asks, giving my hands a gentle squeeze.

'Um, sorry?' I lean in so he can hear me over the sudden whooshing noise of the gas as it's released up into the balloon to keep us afloat.

But Dan doesn't ask me again; instead, he lifts my chin and presses his mouth on to mine, hard on my lips, which immediately sting from the sheer force of his kiss. And whoosh! The same feeling comes over me as I had that time in the kitchen. I'm sizzling like a just-lit touchpaper, my body feels as if it's on fire, and my stomach is swirling – flipping, in fact – over and over so much that it makes me feel dizzy. The air. The sky all around me. The gentle warm breeze in my hair as we float on over my beloved Tindledale.

I can feel my body relaxing now, releasing, letting go as I melt into Dan's embrace, his lips softening, kissing me tenderly too, and I kiss him back before drawing my hands free from his and flinging them around his neck. I can't help myself. In this moment, I feel happy and light. I haven't felt this way in such a long time – if ever, in fact – and I don't want the feeling to end.

Eventually, we break apart. Dan's forehead is resting on mine, and then he moves his mouth up to kiss the bridge of my nose. We both laugh, unsure really of what to say, until Dan gently turns me around. Standing behind me, he places his arms around my back to rest his hands on the edge of the basket in front of me, and we just stand, together, silently embracing the view all around us, the fields dotted with sheep and buttercups and cows and hedgerows and farms and flowers. Now we're floating above my school; my great village school with the clock tower on the gabled roof, the tiny patch of tarmac for a playground. I quickly close my eyes and do a silent prayer, a wish, asking for it please to stay open. I even cross my fingers.

'It'll be fine. You'll see,' Dan whispers in my ear, as though reading my thoughts.

'I hope so,' I say, turning my face sideways up to his, but it's no use, he's so tall and my head barely reaches his shoulder, so I have to turn around properly to face him. He lifts a stray lock of hair away from my eyes.

'Tell me,' he asks again, before quickly adding a very polite, 'please?'

And I hesitate, but only momentarily because I can't deny it any longer, damn it! Dan flaming Wright is very attractive indeed – in a brutish, maverick, and quite frankly *rude* way. But a man with the audacity to sweep a woman off her feet, literally, before dumping her into a giant basket and kissing her hard on the lips up high in the air has to be worth a shot. And maybe Lawrence was right; perhaps it is time for me to broaden my horizons.

I look up and into Dan's eyes.

I smile and tell him.

'Yes!'

And maybe Tindledale *can* do with the likes of Dan Wright, after all . . .

Epilogue

One year later . . .

Summertime, and the air is laden with the heavenly sweet aroma from the candyfloss stand on the far side of the village green. Carousel music drifts towards us as we reach the merry-go-round, and I just know that today is going to be a glorious day. A marquee takes pride of place in the centre, dazzling against the blue and white scudding sky, with Sybs' polka-dot bunting stretching all the way over to the Duck & Puddle pub sign, which is swaying gently on its hinges in the warm breeze.

'Hello Miss Singer.' It's Lily, on top of Mark's shoulders, one hand gripping her left ankle, the other slipped around a woman's hand.

'Hi Lily, Mark,' I nod, smiling at the woman, who smiles back as I reach up to give Lily's hand a tweak.

'Meg, this is—' Mark starts, going to introduce me to the woman, but Lily, looking as if she's about to burst with excitement, tells me instead.

'Her name is Belle, just like the princess. And Daddy *really likes* her. He told me. *And* I saw them kissing,' she giggles, before dipping her face down to do a squelchy kiss on the top of Mark's bald head, and we all laugh.

'Nice to meet you, Belle, I'm Meg.' We shake hands.

'I've heard so much about you,' Belle says. Maybe we could meet up for a coffee some time – I'm a speech therapist.' She beams openly.

'Ooh, yes, we must. That would be lovely,' I say, wondering if she might be up for doing some sessions with Archie Armstrong now that I'm no longer able to.

'And I hear congratulations are in order,' Belle says.

'Thank you,' I reply, feeling thrilled that it's now official.

I've officially been confirmed as the new head teacher at Tindledale Village School, which has won a reprieve. The inspectors said they were very impressed by my dedication to the school and the wider community, and also with our varied curriculum and nurturing environment. Not to mention another Outstanding

Ofsted rating, and the influx of new pupils, ten from the new houses down by the station, eight transfers from St Cuthbert's, Ash and Yasmin's five children and Jessie's triplets, of course. The new baby will be coming soon, too. Talking of which, Jessie's divorce eventually came through and she now lives in a cottage in the village with Sam, blissfully happy spending time with her new family, while cultivating honey from the hives in their garden, and then writing about it for her new column in the *Home Farmer* magazine. Plus we have a few new families that moved here from London – Tindledale made it into the top ten in the national village show competition, which meant we were included in the Sunday supplement spread, complete with a lovely picture of the commemorative stone that now has Highly Commended inscribed on it, too. And then, shortly after that, Vicky and Gabe popped round to my cottage one evening to share the most wonderful news – they had been approved to adopt two sisters, and brought them home to Tindledale in time for Christmas – they've just started at my village school too.

After saying goodbye, I walk on over to the marquee to deliver my gifts – three framed cross-stitch samplers with definitely no spelling errors on this time – one for each of the new babies. That's why we're all here on the village green, in fact, to celebrate the triple christenings of Florence and Henrietta (or Hettie as she's fondly known, named after Hettie senior who owns the haberdashery shop), born to Sybs and Dr Ben. The twins arrived last month, and then Billy, who was born a fortnight ago to Cher and Sonny. Sonny is, rumour has it, planning on proposing to Cher today. I can't wait to see that. If it's half as romantic as Dr Ben's proposal to Sybs in the snow at Christmas time, a year to the day after their first kiss, followed by their spring wedding a few months ago on the village green, then it'll be truly magical.

'Thanks so much, Meg,' Sybs leans in to give me a hug after taking the presents from me. 'Ooh, Lawrence was looking for you earlier,' she says. 'He said to ask if you can pop over to the village square,' she glances at her watch, 'um, five minutes ago.' She laughs. 'Quick, you'd better hurry.'

'Oh, OK, thanks,' I say, thinking it a bit odd. I wonder why he's there and not here on the green at the party with everyone else.

After walking from the village green to the square, I instantly see why. Lawrence is beaming as he leans against the bus stop, because standing inside the bus shelter, with a rucksack over his shoulder, and holding Taylor's hand, is Jack.

My heart soars.

'What are you doing here?' I yell, instantly running to Jack to pull him in for a massive cuddle. 'Oh Jack, why didn't you tell me you were coming home for the summer? Or you, Taylor? You never said a word,' I breathe, breaking away from Jack to grin at them both. 'What a wonderful surprise. I'm so happy to see you. Here, let me look at you properly,' I say, flipping open his jacket.

'Muuuuuum! Stop it, I'm fine,' he says, batting my hand away and laughing.

'Are you sure? You look like you've lost weight,' I say, not having seen him since Christmas – he took Taylor camping at half-term. They're boyfriend and girlfriend now, after a bumpy start, because Jack wasn't sure if he wanted to be in a long-distance relationship having just started at uni, and then he confided in me that Taylor had a pregnancy scare, that's why she was so keen to talk to him last summer, fearing that he'd 'loved her and left her' as it were. Anyway, they're happily together now and it seems to be working out well for them both.

'Yes Mum!' Jack insists. 'I'm fine. But I sure could do with one of Dan's outstandingly good burgers,' he grins, linking his arm through mine as we all make our way back over to the village green where Dan is doing the food for the christening party.

After our hot-air balloon ride, Dan and I spent plenty of time together getting to know each other better. He explained that he had never come to Tindledale intending to open a new restaurant – he'd come here for some much-needed R&R. He was suffering from a severe case of restaurant burn-out, or 'paparazzi bullshit', as he so eloquently put it.

'That's why I felt permanently angry,' he told me the evening after the hot-air balloon ride. We were sitting on the sofa in my cottage, sipping elderflower wine. He had his arm round my shoulders, his right ankle resting on his left knee (he is a bit of a 'spreader', it has to be admitted), and was stroking my hair. 'I hated how I got caught up in the celebrity of it all, forced to be deliberately provocative.'

'Like in that old YouTube interview?' I ask him.

'Yes, exactly,' he nods quietly, ruefully. 'Pia always wanted me to cultivate the bad-boy image because she said that's what the public wanted. But it's my fault, too – I was so caught up in dealing with the pressures of the restaurant that I didn't really fight her on the PR front. I was too weak; just went along with what she said, not really thinking it through.'

I squeeze his knee. It's hard to imagine Dan as 'weak'.

He goes on. 'Then, as my career took off, I just found it increasingly difficult to free myself from that persona. It was like playing a part, you know?'

I nod. 'Like me with my scary teacher act,' I smile.

'Well that one never fooled me for a moment,' he laughs. Then he looks thoughtful again. 'I was just a small boy who loved cooking with his granny in the country. I'd forgotten that for a while,' he says sadly. 'And I'd almost given up hope of finding myself again. But then I came back to Tindledale.' He takes another sip of his wine.

'I so enjoyed the anonymity, being a normal person away from the cameras, with no fuss, having a quiet, gentle life. I loved tossing my phone into the stream that time!'

'I just couldn't believe you'd done that – I had you down as a madman,' I laugh.

'I felt a bit like one . . . But it was a welcome relief, and then when your mum had no idea who I was, offering to help me become a paella chef, I couldn't help myself from going along with it.'

We laugh again, both amused at the memory. 'God, I was mortified when she said that,' I tell him. 'But it seemed even worse to tell her who you really were.'

'Absolutely,' Dan had grinned. We still laugh about it now.

One year on, everything is different. He's calmed down a lot: the fresh, Tindledale air has done him the world of good, and he has been known on occasion to be very relaxed and smiley. Maybe that's because he's doing what he loves, cooking food for people to enjoy eating without worrying about what the restaurant critics write about him, or if his Michelin stars will get taken away.

Yes, Dan sold his three-Michelin-starred restaurant, The Fatted Calf, and set himself up with a food truck. Now he travels around the villages in it, serving delicious street food alongside my home-brewed wines and cordials. Pia has gone; all the image-making and press conferences and planted stories and TV interviews are part of his old life. The life he wanted to leave behind to start afresh in Tindledale.

Dan and I are blissfully happy, and my tiny cottage has never been so busy, with me being a part-time stepmum to Dan's two boys. Jacob and Charlie are a handful, but I wouldn't have it any other way. They are boisterous and noisy and perfectly wonderful; they make my tiny cottage feel just like home.

We reach the food truck and, after hugging it out

like they always do, Dan urges Jack to try his new dish, a minted lamb (locally sourced, of course) burger with a beetroot and tzatziki relish on a sourdough bun and hand-cut fries with a truffle oil drizzle.

'You'll love it,' Dan tells Jack enthusiastically as he hands him a plate. 'Now get stuck in.' Jack wastes no time in doing just that. Dan gives Taylor and Lawrence a burger too, before they all wander over to the marquee, leaving us alone.

Dan turns to me. And after wiping his hands on a tea towel, he says, 'Come here!' in a very bossy and filthy voice. 'You scary teacher you,' before pulling me in close for a kiss, pressing his lips on mine and taking my breath away, just like he always does. When I manage to surface, I gasp and lift one eyebrow.

'Err, aren't you forgetting something?' I smile, tilting my head to one side.

'*Please*,' he says, fixing his thunderous eyes on to mine, and I laugh before moving in for another breath-taking kiss from the rudest man I ever had the wonderful fortune to meet.

The Great

Village

Recipes

Meg's
Marvellously Fizzy Elderflower 'Champagne'

Ingredients

For 4.5 litres (one gallon) you will need:

Five or six heads of elderflower

Two lemons

750 g (1 ½ lb) sugar

Two tablespoons of vinegar
(preferably cider vinegar)

Enough plastic fizzy drinks bottles to hold the elderflower champagne. Plastic bottles are better than glass because you can give them a squeeze to see how much pressure has built up, and if you forget them for a few days they won't explode – the crimp at the bottom will pop out instead, and the noise of the bottle falling over will alert you.

Note that there is no added yeast in this recipe. The flowers are not scalded or sterilised, which leaves the wild yeasts naturally present on the blooms to do the fermentation for you.

Method

- Pick nice young flower heads, where the flowers have not yet started to drop petals or turn brown. You'll get pollen on you, but don't worry – it doesn't stain. Use the flowers promptly or the aroma will change and become unpleasant.

- Put 4.5 litres (1 gallon) of water in a large lidded saucepan.

- Add the elderflower heads (having shaken any bugs off them first) and two sliced lemons. Put the lid on, and leave it for 24 to 36 hours.

- Strain the liquid through a clean cloth. A sieve will do fine if you don't mind a few petals or tiny bugs in the drink, and it won't alter the taste one bit.

- Add 750 g (1 ½ lb) of sugar and two tablespoons of cider vinegar, and stir until all the sugar has dissolved.

- Pour into plastic bottles. Put the tops on to keep fruit flies out, but don't screw them on tight yet – just stand the bottles in a corner and keep an eye on them. After a few days they will start to make tiny bubbles as the wild yeasts get to work on the sugar.

- After one or two weeks the bubbles will gradually slow down. When they look like they have pretty much stopped, screw the lids down and put the bottles somewhere fairly cool.

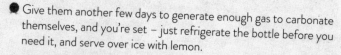

- Give them another few days to generate enough gas to carbonate themselves, and you're set – just refrigerate the bottle before you need it, and serve over ice with lemon.

- The elderflower champagne is still 'live' and continuing to ferment, so the longer it is stored the more alcoholic (and drier) it will become. Keep a note of how long it takes to be perfect for your taste, and bear that in mind for following years: by three months old it will be too dry for most tastes, but unless you make large quantities it's unlikely to last that long.

- The trick with this method is to keep checking the pressure in the bottles, particularly for the first few weeks. Just give each bottle a good squeeze – if you can't squeeze the sides in at all, then the pressure is getting too high. When this happens, very gently loosen the cap until you hear gas releasing, and wait until the noise dies down (be careful of the froth) before tightening up again.

If fermentation won't start, wild yeast gives the best results for elderflower champagne, but it isn't 100 per cent reliable. If fermentation doesn't start within ten days (tiny bubbles at stage 6), then add a tiny pinch of yeast to each bottle. Leave to stand for five minutes, then give it a gentle shake to disperse the yeast. There's no need to use fancy yeast because we're not trying to produce a high-alcohol drink: bread yeast is fine, as is general-purpose beer or wine yeast.

If you 'rescue' a batch in this way, it will tend to end up too dry unless you intervene. Taste a little from time to time and, when it's just right, screw the lids down and move it to the fridge. Enjoy poured over ice with a twist of cucumber, preferably lounging in a stripy deckchair!

Kitty's
Traditional Tindledale Huffkin Buns

Ingredients

480 g (1 lb) plain white flour

8 g (½ tablespoon) fine salt

7 g (¼ oz) easy-bake dried yeast

8 g (½ tablespoon) sugar

150 ml (¼ pint) lukewarm milk

150 ml (¼ pint) lukewarm water
(or more)

30 g (2 oz) lard

Method

● Put all the ingredients except the lard in a mixing bowl and mix to a dryish dough.

● Turn out on to the worktop (if you are not using an electric mixer) and knead until smooth – you may need a little more water.

● Cut the lard into small pieces and dot a few over the surface of the dough. Fold it and knead, then repeat until you have incorporated all the fat.

● Put the dough in a bowl; cover with cling film and leave to rise for 1½ hours or until doubled in size.

● Take the dough out of the bowl and divide it into three pieces weighing about 280 g each.

● Shape each into a flat oval loaf and use your thumb to press a hole in the centre.

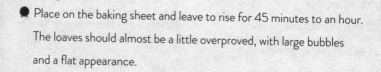

- Place on the baking sheet and leave to rise for 45 minutes to an hour. The loaves should almost be a little overproved, with large bubbles and a flat appearance.

- Preheat the oven to 220°C/425°F/Gas mark 7, then bake the huffkin buns for 20 minutes or until they feel approximately ⅓ lighter in weight.

- Take out of the oven and wrap them in a cloth so the crust stays soft.

- Pour a filling of your choice into the hole on top and enjoy!

Dan's Food Truck
Hearty Handmade Scotch Eggs

Ingredients

4 large free-range eggs

275g/10oz sausage meat

1 tsp fresh thyme leaves

1 tbsp chopped fresh parsley

1 spring onion, very finely chopped

Salt and freshly ground black pepper

125g/4oz plain flour seasoned with salt and freshly ground black pepper

1 free-range egg, beaten

125g/4oz breadcrumbs

Vegetable oil for deep frying

Method

- Place the eggs, still in their shells, in a pan of cold salted water.

- Place over a high heat and bring to the boil, then reduce the heat to simmer for exactly nine minutes.

- Drain and cool the eggs under cold running water, then peel.

- Mix the sausage meat with the thyme, parsley and spring onion in a bowl and season well with salt and freshly ground black pepper.

- Divide the sausage meat mixture into four and flatten each out on a clean surface into ovals about 12.5cm/5in long and 7.5cm/3in at its widest point.

- Place the seasoned flour onto a plate, then dredge each boiled egg in the flour.

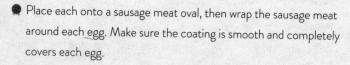 Place each onto a sausage meat oval, then wrap the sausage meat around each egg. Make sure the coating is smooth and completely covers each egg.

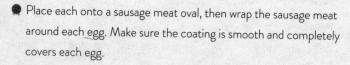 Dip each sausage meat-coated egg in the beaten egg, rolling to coat completely, then dip and roll into the breadcrumbs to completely cover.

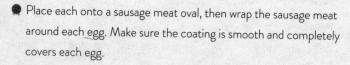 Heat the oil in a deep heavy-bottomed pan, until a breadcrumb sizzles and turns brown when dropped into it. (CAUTION: hot oil can be dangerous. Do not leave unattended.)

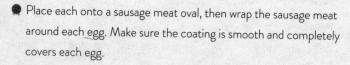 Carefully place each scotch egg into the hot oil and deep-fry for 8-10 minutes, until golden and crisp and the sausage meat is completely cooked.

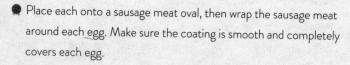 Carefully remove from the oil with a slotted spoon and drain on kitchen paper.

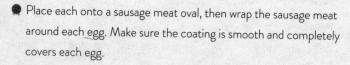 Serve cool.

Dan's Food Truck
Delicious Lamb Burgers with a Tzatziki Relish

Ingredients

25g bulgur wheat

500g extra-lean lamb mince

1 tsp ground cumin

1 tsp ground coriander

1 tsp smoked paprika

1 garlic clove, very finely crushed (optional)

Oil, for brushing

Large burger buns, sliced tomato and red onion, to serve

For the tzatziki

5cm piece cucumber, deseeded and coarsely grated

200g pot thick Greek yogurt

2 tbsp chopped mint, plus a handful of leaves to serve

Method

Tip the bulgur into a pan, cover with water and boil for 10 mins. Drain really well in a sieve, pressing out any excess water.

To make the tzatziki, squeeze and discard the juice from the cucumber, then mix into the yogurt with the chopped mint and a little salt.

Work the bulgur into the lamb with the spices, garlic (if using) and seasoning, then shape into 4 burgers. Brush with a little oil and fry or barbecue for about 5 mins each side until cooked all the way through.

Serve in the buns (toasted if you like) with the tzatziki, tomatoes, onion and a few mint leaves.

Catch up with more great reads from Alexandra Brown in the Carrington's series, which are all available to buy in paperback and ebook now!

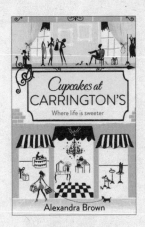

'Adorable, comical and magical
. . . a festive delight'
Closer